YOU

From the way our first day, in which we had
become friends if not lovers, had ended,
I believed that we would go on together.
Indeed, when you walked away from the
dock — I guess you didn't know you were
supposed to help with the Tender Loving Care
of the boat — I didn't have the feeling that
you were going away mad. For you paused,
looking back, to say, 'You never did tell me
your name.' 'Russell,' I said. 'Russell Walford.'

Also in Arrow by Anonymous

YOU

BY ANONYMOUS

ARROW BOOKS

Arrow Books Limited
62-65 Chandos Place, London WC2N 4NW

An imprint of Century Hutchinson Limited

London Melbourne Sydney Auckland
Johannesburg and agencies throughout
the world

First published in Great Britain 1982
Published by arrangement with Bantam Books

Reprinted 1984, 1985 and 1986

© Bantam Books, Inc. 1975

Printed and bound in Great Britain by
Anchor Brendon Limited, Tiptree, Essex

ISBN 0 09 930000 1

DEDICATION:

For HER, an encore

AUTHOR'S PREFACE

The ultimate simplicity is a man and a woman in love. As with the famous first book of this series HER, so YOU is written in *the earthy language of love . . . the best and truest tongue in the world.*

YOU depicts the straight and simple path walked immemorially by lovers. The millions of readers of these books now have in hand YOU, a love story that, I feel, embodies both the simplicities and profundities of a man and a woman together. I want the ardent reader to recollect in the reading his/her own first love, her/his middle love, his/her last love. Again, as I said in the Author's Preface to HER: *It has been my intention to arouse my reader, not by the scenes and events of the book but by his own particular remembrance. I want him to recollect in tranquility those great times when, clasped by a woman's arms and legs, a voice has breathed into his ear, "Fuck me. Oh God, fuck me." I want the woman reader to recollect in tranquility those times she has been compelled to utter those words. I want them both to remember how beautiful and true was the language of their passion . . . to know, all over again, that at such times a man is never more a man, a woman never more a woman, and that they are joined into a meaning infinitely greater than the sum of their parts, for their coupling is an equation of love.*

Anonymous

Anonymous gives you Leslie Dollar. Anonymous gives you Russell Walford. Anonymous gives you . . . YOU.

Anonymous

THE FIRST LETTER
to
her

I suppose this letter to you is meant to be magic; at least, the only reason for writing it that I can admit to myself is to shape within me the memories that until now I have been so deeply afraid to live with. Certainly I cannot hope to alter those lives that we have lived together. I cannot—and I don't believe I would want to, even if I could—alter your own memories into something other than they already are.

So it is purely magic . . . with which I can conjure you up as you were, me as I was, and how the two of us were together. For the truth is—and here I must tell you a whole truth, where you have known only a half truth before—you were not only the first woman I ever laid, you were also the last. Does that surprise you? Not that you were the first, for you already knew that, but that there has been no one after you? I hope it will give you something to think about, as I have so often thought, these latter days in which I was making up my mind—though I didn't know the decision was building inside me until I sat down to begin—to write this letter.

There is a magic in words. The poets have always known that with words they can build a reality more real than real, show truth in words when the truth is obscured by deeds. This kind of magic I now seek, in order to create me and you all over again, moment by moment of all our time and, in this evocation of what you and I were, hope that we shall be truer than when we lived amid all the uncertainties and ambiguities of love and lust. Let us not this time, my love, go blindly from the day of beginning to the moment of end; let us, instead, shape it clearly in words and at last, even if too late, see it whole.

Now that I must deal plainly in plain words, I must make myself tell the secret I have not told anyone until now ... you, least of all. All these years, my love, you have been symbolized to me by one small packet of words, a phrase that has been my secret definition of you, in which I cherished you, always naming you so in my deepest, most secret, thoughts and feelings. Always and forever, from the beginning to the end, you have been *the girl with the golden cunt*.

Silly? I will grant that it is silly. Romantic? No. For it was planted in my mind not with a romantic rush of revelation, but rather in a grubby, derogatory fashion, and by another man. I should have been ashamed. But I was not, nor am I now, that this magic caption caught my imagination at the moment of hearing and has remained there all this time.

YOU

Otherwise, perhaps, we would not have shared all these things, both good and bad, that we have shared. I must be truthful about this part of it, also; the bad times when I have wished, more than anything in the world, that I had never loved you, had never found a sweet first home for my rampant manhood in your golden cunt, but instead had gone forever empty through world and time. Yes. It has been that bad. And it has been that good.

This is the way it began, that summer I was seventeen, and you were sixteen, and the world was as young as we were.

The family—and I—had just got down to our summer place. Bill and I were down at the dock, getting my boat ready to go into the water. There's always much to do to bring a sailboat into trim after a winter's lay-up and we were so anxious to begin the summer's sailing that we were laboring like dogs to finish the work and begin the fun. A perfect day for sailing, the Gulf Coast sky high and blue, a steady southwest wind laying a sparkling ripple on the bright water. A day for sailors.

Except for the sailing, I had never cared much for those many summers of my boyhood in the old waterfront house that had once belonged to my grandfather and which, Father kept assuring me, would one day belong to me. It was pre–Civil War, the small rooms cramped with old wicker furniture and humidity-molded books and ancient magazines. Even in Pass Robin, with all the beautiful Gulf Coast sunshine, the house seemed dark, even gloomy—and Dad always invited a steady stream of houseguests. But of course it was out of the question that the family should ever go anywhere else for the summer.

That was the way it had always been; the way it always would be.

So I spent most of my time on the boat with Bill. I did like that. Bill was the only Pass Robin native I had ever made friends with. That had come about because his father, a carpenter, had done some work on the house one summer and had brought Bill along several times. Bill, when he was eleven and I was ten, had taught me to sail in a tiny catboat, old and slow and leaky; the next summer, father had given me my first boat and from then on it had been me and Bill and the boat. Until this summer that I was seventeen.

The funny thing was, I had never really liked Bill. He was simply the fellow I went sailing with. From the time in September when we left Pass Robin until the day in June when we returned, I gave him not a single thought. Bill, a year older than I, was stocky and thick, strong bodied and tireless. He had blunt workman's hands—he would be a carpenter like his father—and his light brown hair was bleached white by the Gulf Coast sun. There was a meaty thickness to his mouth, a lumpy nose, and heavy brows on which the hair was bleached bone white. His eyes were a faded blue.

I was suddenly taller than he, this summer, because I had shot up to a long-legged height that astonished even my folks. I think it disconcerted Bill to discover that I had outgrown him. I never knew what Bill thought about me, any more than he knew what I thought about him. We did not feel about, think about, talk about, such things as friendship. To Bill, I am quite sure, I was simply the summer visitor, the son of parents famous and wealthy in a way he could only dimly understand. To me, Bill was a native of

Pass Robin, the old town that had been both a fishing village and a staid, quiet resort town since before the Civil War. He was simply the guy I sailed with. I was simply the guy he sailed with. Until that first day of the summer when we were working to get the boat rigged; and you came walking by.

Maybe you don't remember—I'm sure you don't. But I have never forgotten the first time I saw you. No—that's not quite the truth. I had surely seen you before, in those summers now past, for in Pass Robin everyone saw everybody sooner or later. But you were a child and I was a child; and though I had seen you, I had not seen you. Not until today.

You were wearing a yellow dress. Just a simple thing, the sort of dress a Pass Robin girl would wear in the summertime. For all I knew, you had ordered it from the Sears Roebuck catalog, or your mother had bought the material and made it for you on her sewing machine. No matter—the dress was beautiful, because you were beautiful.

At the moment of your passing, we were taking a breather, sitting on top of the cabin to drink a bottle of beer. The first time I had shared a beer with Bill; last summer he had still claimed I was too young, though he was himself only seventeen. I was splicing a line while we rested, a job I've always liked. But when I saw you, my hands stopped their movement.

Yellow dress. Yes. It flowed over your body like gold, showing the shape of your thighs, and that is where I looked first. Then at your lovely breasts, small then, you were sixteen, remember, but so shapely under the thin flow of gold cloth that my heart ached for the pure beauty.

Yellow dress. Red hair. Yes. Even under the Gulf

Coast sun, your hair showed dark glints, for it was never bright red but dark and heavy, brushed to your shoulders in a gleaming fall, thick and dark-glinted and curled under at the ends.

Then I looked at your face; and my heart turned over. It was your mouth mostly. You were not close enough for me to know that your eyes were green. So my eyes dwelled on your mouth, the full, rich curve of lower lip, the thinner line of upper, so prim in contrast yet with its own promise too, so much subtler than the lower ripeness.

Then, as ever, you walked like an Indian, in a smooth gliding that indulged nothing of the ostentatious ripple of a woman who knows when men's eyes are devouring her. I truly think you did not know; you were unconscious of us and, so, completely unconscious of your revealed beauty. You simply *were*, in your entirety; you neither knew nor cared that boys and grown men, even old men, lusted after you with greedy eyes and minds. You were inside yourself, dwelling in your own secret land, self-contained and self-possessed—and so utterly, completely, overwhelmingly lovely.

I looked at Bill. He was looking at you, too.

You continued walking along the dirt path that bordered the docks, placing your feet firmly and precisely one before the other in an Indian line. In your face showed only an inward brooding upon your secret thoughts and I conceived of myself as gazing upon you from a hidden vantage because you did not look at us. I could only believe ardently that you were thinking about the next time you would make love.

Yes. You had this in you, then and always. Any

man gazing upon you could only harbor the conviction that your mind was dwelling on the rose-colored idea of your vagina with a penis in it, plunged deep and full. No matter what penis—any penis. My penis. Used ruthlessly, all its passionate hardness existing only to satisfy those intensely selfish desires of your body.

I know now, in the reality of my experience of you, of other women, that such thoughts were far from your mind. It was only my imagination, fevered by what must be the sole focus and meaning of your beauty. Even an experienced woman seldom makes for herself such direct and directed fantasies as does a man.

When I spoke to Bill, it was in a low, strained voice. "Who's that?"

His reply was almost a whisper, though he tried to make the words casual. "That? That's the girl with the golden cunt."

Not said with beauty, with love, my dear, but grossly, even nastily, from the mouth of a boy whom I had never really liked though we had been sailing together now for seven years. But even though every decent cell of my body rejected this lewd tastelessness, the words fastened themselves into my imagination so that ever since, through all the great turmoils and greater passion we have shared, you have ever been in my most secret being the one and only girl with the golden cunt.

You had passed by now. I looked at you walking away. You were so beautiful from the front, I expected to discover a flaw in this rearward view. But such was not the case. Your hips did not entice attention; you simply walked as a young, healthy girl walks. Your rear was lovely in its ripe, demure fashion, the yellow dress shaping through the straight stillness of your lower back and draping from the flat curve of your buttocks. There was also an outward flow of flesh, your hips curved widely to receive fully the weight of a man. You were made for lovemaking, for bearing the consequences of lovemaking. And you did not know it, you did not even glance over your shoulder as you went away.

I had to clear my throat. "I guess you've been in it, then."

He made a short laugh. "Who hasn't?" He laughed again, more successfully this time. "Want to tear off a little piece, buddy? All you got to do is ask." He snickered again. "Ask and it shall be given. Just like it says in the Good Book."

There was a sick queasiness in my stomach. I didn't want it to be so. I wished fervently to believe that he was lying, bragging in his lying. Yet I had to believe it, because all on a summer day I wanted you so desperately I would have seconded a dozen men inside that lovely body. Even as in the same moment I was sickened by the vivid imagining of Bill's gross maleness sprawled on your body, pounding away at your damp, hot flesh, spouting his seed into your abandoned need.

I picked up the bottle of beer, drank from it. It was a mistake; it came foaming up faster than it went down, so that I had to clamber to the side of the boat and spit it out. With it came the nasty taste of bile, bitter and strong, and I clung there, my stomach churning.

"What's the matter?" Bill said.

I straightened, wiped my face. "A fly must have got in it," I said. "Or else I swallowed wrong. God!"

YOU

Slowly, I returned to my place, picked up the line I
had been splicing, and with tedious perfectionism began to work. Bill finished his beer with a flourish,
tossed the empty bottle to the embankment. He was
still looking in the direction you had disappeared.

I hesitated. But, in spite of myself, I had to ask.
"Why do ... why do you call her that?"

He grinned. "The hair between her legs is red,
too," he said. "Prettiest sight you ever seen, fellow."
He spit into the water, wiped his hand across his
mouth. "You can have your natural blonds. Give me a
redhead every time."

I saw it, so vividly that you might as well have
paused and lifted your dress to show me the described
garden of earthy delights ... even though I had not
had a woman, I had never laid my hand on a mount.
Not that I wasn't ready and waiting—after all, I was
seventeen, and full of prime. However, with all my
summers spent in Pass Robin with my parents, with
the rest of the year taken up by prep school, there
hadn't been all that many opportunities. Of course, I'd
listened to the older fellows talk about their great
conquests among the willing girls of Poughkeepsie. I
had been to Poughkeepsie once or twice myself,
breaking honor to sneak away from school. But
willing girls had been unaccountably scarce during
my desperate forays.

"But who is she?" I said, forcing the continuation
of conversation about you through the tightened muscles of my throat, even as I could not constrain myself from saying them.

"She's a Dollard," Bill said. He spat into the water
again. "Know that big old yellow house down there
on the point? She belongs to that bunch. Her daddy's

11

a commercial fisherman . . . when he's anything at all."

That wasn't anything to sneer about. Roughly half the village of Pass Robin made their living from commercial fishing. It was the only reason for Pass Robin to exist; that, and the summer families who owned the old summer homes and the new little fishing cabins that were beginning to spring up like mushrooms in those days just after World War II.

"But what's her first name?"

Bill studied me then, grinning. "I believe you are anxious for a little taste of that," he said. "Well, you'd better make damn sure to use a rubber. She's already had the clap twice, from what I hear."

I was angrier still. But I couldn't show it, not yet. I was stubborn, too. "Tell me her first name."

His voice became mocking. "Think I'll let you find it out for yourself. Hell, you don't need to know her name, anyway. All you got to do is holler 'Hey you,' and shake your whangdoodle at her. She'll come to taw." He looked anxious. "You do have a whangdoodle about your person, don't you?"

I was in no mood for raillery. I stood up. "If we intend to try her today, we'd better get to work. Let's run up the sails and see what kind of shape they're in."

That's the story, my love, and so now, perhaps, after all this long time, you will understand our bad beginning. I should have told you these ugly things long ago, but somehow I never could. You see, it hurt me so deeply to hear this fellow Bill dirty your beauty with his idle tongue. Yet I could not keep from listening. Something in me wanted to hear and to believe, because I had to be convinced that it was possible for me to lay you, too. Such utter loveliness was unapproachable by the boy I was then; seventeen years old, too tall this year for my own strength, gangly and awkward and untried.

I had never been a successful fellow, at school or at home. Mother and Father were kind and loving in their way but I was—at least I thought myself to be—a by-blow in their life together. Mother used the entire summer in Pass Robin to prepare for her annual fall show in New York; from early morning until the light failed, she was painting. Father was ever, winter and summer, in hot pursuit of those ideas and philosophies that had brought him so much fame and so little money, so that our accustomed sojourn in Pass Robin was practically an intellectual seminar. Not only did he give much of his time to writing letters—those brilliant letters, exchanged with all the brilliant people that inhabited his world, which have now been published and are such an integral element in the history of American thought and philosophy—but each summer he would draw up a list of people he wanted to talk with that year and invite them sequentially, sometimes two and three at a time, to spend a week with us. Those bungalow-porch sessions were so prized they were practically a command performance.

So I was accustomed to feeling rather left out of things. True, they had given birth to me and in due time they expected a certain fame and accomplishment on my part also. On the day-to-day basis, however, they granted me little time and less thought. Somehow, they expected me to grow into achievement of my own accord, simply because I was their son. So, ready for all that seventeen years brings one to the brink of, I came and went in their house like a shadow. They truly did not care whether I spent my time sailing a boat or screwing a goat.

I must also say, in all honesty, that day in and day out my parents were unfailingly kind and loving. But the gentleness of parental love is not enough for a boy of that age. I felt smothered, I was like a weed trying to grow in the deep shade of two great oaks. So stately and established, so secure in their reputations and in their friends, they had not the faintest conception of the needs and insecurities and turmoils of a boy on the edge of manhood.

What could I hope to do they had not already accomplished? How could I expect to earn the respect and prestige they accorded so graciously to their contemporaries? I didn't even have the incentive of future economic need; my father, as conservative in practical matters as he was daring and experimental in contemplation, would leave to me an estate larger than that which he had inherited. No. No room for me, except that space I could shape for myself. And I did not even know how to begin.

Though I did not yet realize that the anger, the shame, of what he had said about you had bitten so deeply into my soul, the first sail of the summer was the last time I ever went out with Bill. The preparations finished, we took her out, going about the necessary tasks with mutual goodwill and long-established cooperation. But before we were well underway we had got into a major fight. As in summers past, Bill assumed that he was captain and I was crew. But this time I challenged him, asserting my right to captain my own boat . . . challenged, and challenged again, and in my anger and shame would not surrender my claim until Bill, a short-tempered fellow at best, knocked me over the side.

I didn't want to fight him. My reluctance was not simply a matter of strength or courage; all those summers, going back to when he had taught me the art and craft of sailing, had given Bill the Indian sign on me. But when he came about to fish me out, expecting to find me properly subdued, I came aboard fighting, though I knew I couldn't win. To my later satisfaction, I did get in two solid licks before he put me over again with a roundhouse right. This time he let me swim around until I was tired out. Then, hands on hips, he stood before me as I huddled wet and miserable and exhausted on the gunwale. "What the hell's the matter with you, anyway, old buddy?"

I looked up at him with my one good eye—the other had been closed by his roundhouse right—and said sullenly, "It's my boat, Bill. It's time you found that out. Let's go in." Without another word, we tacked for the shore.

Not the reason, of course, and I knew it, even if Bill didn't. Still, the guilt of hidden jealousy and anger did not suffice to alter my determination. Bill, finished with the last task, leaped off the bow and turned to wave one hand. "See you tomorrow, old buddy."

I had remained in the cockpit, waiting until he was off my boat before I spoke the words. "No, Bill," I said quietly. "I don't think so."

He had the right to be surprised, I suppose. Taking my anger as a fuse for his own temper, he had blacked my eye. But it had been without lasting animosity, as far as he was concerned. Tomorrow we would sail, and the next day; we would take our full summer of sailing together and where it counted he would be captain and I would be crew, for he had always held dominance in our association.

He whirled around to look at me. I watched his face, seeing the strong, competent, unintelligent boy who would become a strong, competent, unintelligent man. He would marry, and on his wife he would beget children in his image. He would become a carpenter, as his father was a carpenter.

I had to recognize, however unwillingly, the pain showing itself so nakedly in his ugly face. His eyes were bewildered by the change in his old sailing buddy. Crude though he was, careless of himself and of others, caught in his need to prove himself a man among the men of Pass Robin, so that he had bragged about his deeds of conquest—I had to believe that he had lied, I had to believe that he had told the truth—with all this, some deeper part of himself had cherished our partnership and he did not understand why, here and now, it had to end.

He couldn't admit this. Least of all to himself. So he lifted his hand, saying, "Well, buddy, if that's how you feel about it," and walked away.

At the dinner table, my father inquired casually about the black eye and I had to say that I didn't think Bill and I would do any more sailing together, stating that I couldn't stand him any more, in fact I loathed his guts. Father, in his calmest, most dispassionate tone, remonstrated with my hatred. But even at the table, with my parents and that week's houseguest, a genius of a mathematician who had the habit of marking up the white tablecloth over coffee with esoteric equations—even there I was thinking about you, I could feel the hard-on rigid and hungry between my legs.

16

Escaping to my room, I got into bed naked, wanting to feel the sheets cool and sensuous against my sensitized skin. No moon, so the night was as dark outside as the room was dark inside. I needed the darkness, against which to shape my vision of you. Staring at the ceiling, slowly I made you naked, gloating minutely on your breasts, on the sloping loveliness of your thighs, the warm mystery of golden red hair. Then, holding you vividly and concretely in my mind's eye, I gripped my penis.

Slowly, lovingly, I made the fantasy while my hand slipped tenderly on my quivering tool. Carefully, because I didn't want to lose it too quickly, I put the yellow dress on you, walked you down the path toward where I waited on the boat. *Hi,* I said, *Want to go sailing?* You paused. You looked at me. I did not know, then, that your eyes were green. So I could not put a color to them. But they were lovely and warm and glowing and you said, *Yes, But only if you'll fuck me. I've got to get fucked today.*

I held the vision in stasis, dwelling on it, while my cupped hand slipped faster. Not too fast. But faster. I wanted to look at you as you spoke those marvelous complaisant words, know as real and hard as my erection that I could enter into your golden flesh. *Sure,* I said then, with a fine carelessness. *Sure I'll fuck you. If that's what you want.*

I let it ebb then, bringing you aboard, working the boat out of the slip and getting the sail up with tedious attention to detail, catching the perfect breeze that floated us gently toward the three little islands so far out in the gulf they were only dusty clouds marring the horizon. Our desert islands of an afternoon's romance. When, conscientious sailor, I could turn my attention to you again, you had taken off the yellow dress and were half sitting, half lying in the bow, your arms braced back to show me your lovely, naked breasts.

Come here, I called, and you came willingly, leaning over to put your mouth on my mouth. I nearly lost it when you kissed me with such fiery thoroughness, for I put up my free hand and took the weight of your drooping breast into my hot palm. Gritting my teeth, I made myself come down out of the taut arch of loin; I couldn't let the dream of the girl with the golden cunt be over yet.

You'll have to take off your clothes, too, you whispered. *I won't fuck anybody with clothes on.*

I have to steer the boat, I said.

I'll take the tiller, you said. So I gave the tiller into your competent hand and, as I slowly removed my shirt and the salt-stained dungarees, I could feel your eyes on me. You were impatient, you yearned for the first glimpse of my gift.

Your eyes widened, your lips parted, when you saw the splendid animal between my thighs. *Oh yes,* you said. *Yes!* And then you smiled and closed your eyes in rapt anticipation, and it made me proud.

My hand was scarcely moving now; the teasing of my moist palm over the tender head sent ripples of sensation through my every fiber. This must be what sex felt like. I had never really liked to jack off, finding it only a hasty, self-guilty makeshift. But this, now, was different—and the difference was you. Glowing all over, both mind and body engulfed in the imagined sensation of your flesh, I was caught up into a slow writhe of ecstasy.

But still I did not allow completion. We sailed

toward the middle island yonder, you beside me now, pressing your naked body against my naked body, your hand resting on my muscular thigh, not passionately but with a tender cherishing. Then there intervened the work of getting the sail down, coasting up on the shelving beach, and taking out the anchor to fasten firmly into the sand. I gave myself plenty of fantasy time for these necessities of prolonged reality.

You stood waiting at the edge of the growth. But when I hurried to take you in my arms, you went on, disappearing into the bushes. I hastened, fearful you would tease me beyond endurance. But teasing was not in you, you were generously ready, lying with knees up on the pile of soft sand in a tiny clearing among the sea oats. You looked up at my naked stand and your knees fell irresistibly apart. You said, *Fuck me, darling. Please fuck me now. Please.*

With that moment I had to finish, for my imagination, in its ignorance of female flesh, could not conjure up an intimate view of your private parts, nor the sensation of entering. My hand was flying now, my breath panting hotly in the darkness, as I began to come into orgasm, feeling it come and come and keep on coming, boiling richly over my fist.

I did not get up and go to the bathroom. No, I could not yield it; turning on my side, I curled in on myself, putting my wet hand under my balls, holding them, cherishing the sticky warmth of pubic hairs wetted by my come. I pulled the covers over my head, letting my nostrils fill with the sea-bottom smell, and I knew myself rank and ripe with seed. Turned in upon my mighty lust, residual though it was, I went immediately into sleep . . . a slumber comforted by the knowledge that I would wait for you tomorrow, the next day, I would wait as long as time needed. Then somehow I would speak to you and you would answer, saying, as in the fantasy, all the right things and I would have all the right replies. And so I would make love to you in reality as I had just made love to you in imagination. And the world would be as whole, as beautiful, as complete, as you.

I had been at the dock since before breakfast, and it was past noon when you came. Not for a minute had I dared to leave my post of vantage. I had endured the first eternity of suspense by dint of working on the boat but, too soon, it was as sparkling and ready as I. By then I was hungry and disgusted—but, withal, still determined.

When I saw finally the flash of yellow dress that heralded your advent, it triggered through my heart the terrifying knowledge that in this next minute I would have to make you pause long enough to take notice of my need. I began to tremble. My throat was dry, my stomach had rolled over, I realized I had never known how to speak casually and enticingly to any girl—much less you, the girl with the golden cunt. You'd surely laugh at me, you would toss your haughty head and turn away.

You were near; it was time for me to speak. I opened my mouth. Nothing came out. You didn't look at me. You were walking in your still way, turned in upon yourself. I remember distinctly the sadness of your face; not an immediate, direct sadness, but residual and long lasting. Now that I think about it—though I have not the slightest inkling of the meaning of this truth—I have never known a woman truly beautiful who did not show an enduring sadness as an essential ingredient of her impact. Perhaps it is the deeply ingrained realization that the curse of such beauty is never to be known for herself alone, the cast of mind, the depth of feeling, the needs of the heart. The flesh is all, when it is such lovely flesh.

At that beginning of ourselves, certainly the flesh was all. But I can say this now, my only love: the flesh was the beginning, and the ending, and much else in between. But surely I penetrated beyond flesh into yourself, as you penetrated into me; and though you may wish to deny many of the truths I will write before this letter is finished, this one truth cannot be denied.

You were past me now as I clung strangled and aching to the safety of the boat. Only a few seconds remaining before you would be irrevocably gone. My voice came strangely to my ear, a hoarse croak. "Hi."

You turned. You regarded me. "Hello," you said.

For the first time I had heard your voice. But there was no time in which to marvel at the textures and meanings with which you endowed that single word. I could feel myself beginning to blush; a tingling ran like electric shock through my body. But I had to keep it going.

I was grinning horribly. I know, for I can see myself as I was then: lanky, awkward, ugly, grinning, as I bent forward speaking so urgently that I might have been begging you to run away to the South Seas. As, in a certain way of truth, I was.

"Want to go sailing?"

Still the ghastly croak, reinforced by the rictus of a ghastly smile I couldn't seem to take off my face. It's a wonder you didn't laugh at me. But you didn't laugh. You didn't smile, either, as you returned toward me, three steps, then paused again.

"Sailing?" Your tone was dubious, but poised somehow on the edge of possibility.

"Sure," I said, taking frantic refuge in a careless (I thought) wave of one hand, a casual (I thought) inflection of a perfectly ordinary invitation. "I need some crew, and Bill's not here today. You know old Bill, don't you? I go sailing with him all the time. But he's not here now."

I stopped the inane run of words, watching your face, waiting for the name and memory of Bill to register. I expected to capture in your eyes an acknowledgment. But you only said, "I've never been sailing. I don't know anything about it."

I was surprised into naturalness. "You mean you've lived here all your life and never been on a boat?"

"Not on a sailboat." You were no longer looking at me, but at the boat. You moved closer, to the edge of the dirt path, and when your eyes returned to me, I discovered their greenness. Overwhelmed, I had to look away.

"It's a fine day for sailing," I said. "Be a shame to miss it just because there's nobody to crew." Actually, the small boat could be handled perfectly well by one person. But I counted on you not knowing that.

"But I wouldn't be any help."

"I'll teach you," I said. I was beginning to feel confidence now; somehow we had veered onto the track of last night's fantasy and you were beginning to make the right responses. "Come on, hop aboard and let's take off."

Your eyes lingered on me. They were somehow puzzled, yet thoughtfully sure of themselves. "I can't do that." You spoke the denial, I felt, with a faint regret. How many times, I wonder now, had you stood on the point, where you and all the rest of the Dollards lived, to watch the fleet of white-sailed boats, so rich and careless, going out for fun and recreation instead of for the necessity of earning a seacoast living? It must have been the reason for your temptation toward adventure; certainly there could not have been much enticement in my awkward appearance and approach.

"Why not?" I said, reinforcing my bold challenge by telling myself gloatingly that I knew I could lay you now, you understood perfectly well that's what we were talking about, not sailing at all. And you wanted it, oh yes, I could sense it in you. You actually *wanted* to go "sailing" with me today. "What else have you got to do?"

A shadow showed in your green eyes. "Nothing much. Walk down to the drugstore. Have a Coke. Check the mail. Walk home again."

"You can do that any time." Bolder by the minute. "But only right now can you decide to go sailing."

A difference entered into the manner of your seeing. Believing I understood the difference, a trembling started in me all over again.

"You're Bill's summer friend," you said, as though you had only now placed me.

"Sure," I said. "Me and old Bill, we've been sailing together for years."

You turned, looking up the steep shelving of land toward the summer house. "Is that where you live?"

"Yes."

"I've seen you. Your family comes every summer."

"Ever since I can remember," I said. "I've seen you, too. But I don't know your name." You were a child then, I thought to myself. I was a child. But not any more, neither one of us.

Your eyes, as you regarded me again, were still dark in their greenness. There was a pent waiting in your face, as though you were listening for an answer somewhere deep inside yourself where all the answers came from. I thought I knew what the question had been, too. I felt myself trembling on the edge of a victory I wouldn't know how to exploit.

"Is it fun, sailing?"

"It's hard work," I said truthfully. "But more fun than just about anything." Anything, I meant, except that other thing you and I would do together before your foot touched mainland again. "I can teach you to crew in no time. Why, before you know it, you'll be running it all by yourself."

That's the only way I can understand it. It must have been all those white sails sporting in the gulf all your life; the happy people, the summer people, living so close to where you lived in that big old run-down yellow house but with lives so different from your life, rich with comings and goings, trains and northern places, when you had never once been away from Pass Robin.

I saw the final, yielding hesitation. I saw you glance the way you had come, toward home; I saw you look ahead toward downtown Pass Robin where you had meant to go. Then you held out your hand for me to help you aboard. For an awkward moment, I only stared. Then, with an effort, I took your hand, touching you for the first time. I can still remember the damp smudge of sweat in your palm, how the dampened contact tingled all the way to my shoulder.

Still holding your hand, though you were safely aboard now, I said, "What's your name, anyway?"

Your eyes changed again, I saw the hesitation, how you averted your face. "My name is Leslie."

I did not understand. But I understand now, my love, as I also know that you were as innocent, as frightened, as I. It was the first time you had spoken aloud your secret name, giving it to a stranger as a label for yourself. You were, then, Leslie to me, as you have always been, and always will be. And eventually you became in truth and in fact the Leslie you yearned to be. So I will not enter into this letter the ugly name that really labeled you at the time of our meeting.

I was grateful for your ignorance of sailboats. It allowed me to make an everyday thing of your coming aboard. Immediately I began instructing you in the nomenclature of the boat as I hoisted sail and moved away from the dock. Perched on the coaming, you listened with absorbed attention, for from the first minute you loved sailing. When she heeled over, taking the breeze full, and the sun-sparkling water began to slice along the hull, creating those sounds only a sailboat can make, the creak of tackle and slap of canvas, the hiss of the living hull moving through living water, you gasped, clutching at saftey with both hands. But almost immediately you relaxed into the complex sensations and, turning your face into the wind, breathing deeply, you were happy in that sudden way of happiness I did not know about then.

"Like it?" I called.

"Love it," you called back. For the first time, I heard laughter in your voice. Then you said, looking back at me, "You do this every day, don't you?"

"Just about every day the weather holds good. Come here. I want you to feel the tiller."

I continued the lesson. But, as I explained and demonstrated, an oppression was growing in me. You had not, you see, acted your part in reality as you had acted it in last night's erotic vision. You had, yourself, brought the consideration of sexual intercourse frankly into the foreground. But now, in this reality, you seemed totally absorbed in the pleasures of sailing, leaving the next move up to me. When I didn't have the faintest idea how to go about it. *Just ask,* Bill had said. *Ask and it shall be given.* So simple. But exactly how *did* you ask a girl to make love?

But, I told myself with determination, if Bill can have you, I can, too. That's what we believed, the boys of my generation; if a girl would give it to one fellow, she'd give it to anybody. Bill had assured me that you did do it. *Who hasn't?* he had said with that evil snicker. Well, I meant to enjoy my share; I had the need and I didn't care if Bill had wallowed in you a hundred times. It would be easy. All I had to do was find the right words.

Intent on intersecting the line of last night's masturbatory fantasy, I was working out toward the three small islands. "Aren't we getting pretty far out?" you said at last.

"Heading for those islands yonder," I said. "Ever been there?"

A wariness creeping into the relaxed lines of your body, you said, "No. I haven't."

I took it as a cue. "We'll go ashore for a while," I said.

The exultant note I had failed to hide in my voice made you turn at once to measure me with a long look. I did not flinch, but let our eyes meet; I wanted to see in your eyes your understanding and consent. I was certain of it, too, for you said nothing, you only moved to bring down the mainsail, as I had shown you, when I raised the centerboard and ran the boat up on the sloping beach. You watched, then, while I placed the anchor, and came ashore when I beckoned.

We stood together on the beach while you gazed about as though we were indeed stranded on a desert island. I was beginning to sweat, now that reality had intersected with dream. There was a surge of anticipation in my loins, and suddenly I possessed the boldness of certainty.

"Come on," I said, taking your hand. You did not resist, but followed obediently into the security of duned and hollowed sea oats. My heart was thumping painfully. I was committed now; no way to return to the security of innocence. At a clearing in the tall sea grass—so like the clearing in my dream I felt a thrill of recognition—I stopped. Taking away your hand, you stood beside me. A million times since I have wondered what you were thinking. I know what was in my mind: I had it now, all that a man could desire. If only I could accomplish the primal deed without making a fool of myself.

Even then, I believe, you didn't know. Oh yes, your instinct had tried to warn you. There was in you a wariness. But your innocence was as real as mine. With all our warm, inchoate needs and desires, with our adult sexual equipment, we were yet, and would be for a long time, no more than children. Babes on an island.

I can't believe, though, what I said. But I did say it.
"Is this all right?"

You looked at me, so puzzled I couldn't believe it. "All right for what?"

Impossible to utter my meaning in real words. Even with my evasion, I had to look away. "You know."

An edge came into your voice. "I don't have the faintest idea what you're talking about."

Knowing, from all I knew about you—*All you got to do is ask*—that you were lying, I became angry. "Well, we're going to do it, aren't we? Isn't that why we came out here in the first place?"

Becoming, suddenly, very still, you listened all over again to every word I had spoken, from the beginning "Hi!" until now, while I faced you shamefaced and stubborn.

"Do what?"

You spoke in a soft voice. But you knew now, in your tone no dodging of the issue. You were facing my invitation as directly as you were looking into my eyes.

I was not as brave. "You know," I muttered.

"No. You'll have to tell me."

I have not described your voice. Knowing you had been reared in Pass Robin, I had been surprised that your accent was not as marked as in the other natives. A trace of it showed, true, but only enough to make lilting and musical your shades and turns of speech. Only later did I learn that as a little girl, determined to erase the speech marks of your birthplace, you had imitated movie stars and radio personalities. Self-conscious and strained for a long time, you had endured ridicule and scornful aping; but you had persevered until it became such a natural part of yourself that it was, finally, accepted.

I listened now to your low, musical tones because I

didn't want to hear the words with which you were daring me. Yes, I thought to myself. A dare. If I can say it, I can have it.

"All right," I said then. "Fuck."

The word resonated through you. I doubt that a male had yet spoken it in your hearing. Believing I could not say it, you had thought yourself safe—and you would have been if I had not, from Bill, known about you. But now I had voiced the word, and the fact of the word echoed deeply inside you. Maybe, in that second of time, you wanted it as badly as I. Certainly the possibility showed in your eyes. For you had your own needs and hungers, didn't you, you were sixteen as I was seventeen, you had shaped so often your own inchoate fantasies.

You said, "So that's what you meant all along. Like everybody else."

I was brave now. "What else?" Letting the urgency boil over, I came closer, taking your arms in the grip of my hands, ready to press you backward to the earth, ready to mount you. "So come on."

"No."

Anger. Disappointment. And anger again. I had considered it settled now: you would sink beneath me, your legs would open, you would accept me with gratitude, and so I would have accomplished the needful deed that burned in my flesh.

"What do you mean, no?" I demanded.

For the first time, you turned away. Your voice trembled. "Just what I said. No."

"Now listen!" I was breathing hard, as though I had been running for a long mile.

You were entirely away, showing only your back. "Will you . . . take me back to the mainland? Now?"

"I will not," I said. "Not until we've ..." I braced myself. "Not before we fuck."

The word jarred you again. When your eyes came again to my face, they were large pools. "I didn't ... I didn't think you'd be like this," you said in a trembling voice. "You're not being fair."

Your eyes, your voice, made me a coward again. "But Bill told me ... Bill said ..."

You grasped the meaning so quickly it must not have been the first time you had faced it. Your green eyes went dark, very dark, a deep suffering moved across your face. In my arrogant innocence I had thrown all of Pass Robin at you; the status of your family, the greedy eyes of the men and boys when you walked down the street, the jealous whispers of girls who would never have a tenth part of your beauty. Oh yes, you knew it, you felt it all.

"So he told you ... I did that ... with him."

"And why would he want to lie?" I said harshly. "So what's all the big difference between me and everybody else?"

You turned me off the way a light bulb is blinked out at the snap of a switch. Walking blindly, you stumbled away, while I stood dumb and aching in my tracks. I understood now, dimly I knew that in my rampant erotic drive I had been heedless of you except as a warm hole for my maleness.

I didn't try to follow. I went, instead, back to the boat, wading out and climbing aboard, to wait patiently through the agony of time until you could bring yourself to face me again. You would have to endure my presence long enough to get back to the mainland, at least, no matter what you thought of me.

It was a long wait. With the boat out of the wind

under the shelter of the island, I was sweating and uncomfortable. But only by showing myself ready could I hope to communicate my abject willingness to perform whatever you wished me to perform.

Finally, recognizing necessity, you came slowly out of hiding to stand at the rippling edge of water. Getting to my feet, I began to make myself busy about the boat.

"Come here," you said.

I straightened in surprise. I could only obey; I waded ashore, but with no wild hopes that you had yielded. Standing before you, I saw that you had wept, and that you had conquered the weeping. I saw you, for the first time, as a person—and I liked you, your courage and your meaning, I believe in that moment I began to love. Even as somewhere down under the love, the respect, the liking, abided still the lust for your body.

"Come on," you said again, and turned to lead me. Going directly to the place I had chosen for lovemaking, you sat down, tucking the yellow dress behind your legs. Looking into my face, you said, "Sit down."

I sat down. You looked, not at me, but straight ahead into emptiness while you told me. "You must know. I have not ... done it. If anybody tells you ... I've done it ... with him ... he is lying." You turned your head, giving me a full view of yourself. "I've ... wanted to. So bad, sometimes, that I ..." You folded your arms around your knees, hugging tightly. "Some nights, I can't get to sleep. But I can't, I can't let myself...." Your voice broke then healed itself with a rush of strength. "If I don't get out of this town, I'll *die*. Just *die*. And if I let somebody do that to me ..."

"Leslie," I said, "it's all right. Believe me, I didn't ..."

You wouldn't let me lie, either. "But you did," you said. "So I've got a right to tell you, haven't I? I've never been able to tell anyone ..."

"Leslie ..."

Your voice hardened along the edges. "I won't live my life here. I won't. I won't marry one of these boys, and have babies, and get old and fat, like Mama. So I've got to be careful, I can't give in to anybody. Not even to ... to myself."

I was uncomfortable. "Where is it that you want to go, Leslie?"

"I don't know. I don't care. Just away, that's all. Away." You stopped, holding yourself still. "Bill ... I kissed him once. I won't lie about it. After a school dance. I kissed him, and he put his hand on me." You shuddered, a long steady shudder from head to toe. "I nearly ... oh God, I wanted to, I needed to. If he hadn't put his hand right on me, he wouldn't have needed to tell a lie. But ..." You drew a deep breath. "I kissed him. But that's all. A kiss." You were looking at me. "Do you believe I'm telling the truth?"

"Yes," I said.

You kept on looking into my face. "I'll kiss you, too, if that's what you want. Because I kissed him."

I wanted as much of you as Bill had had. I shouldn't have. But I sat still while you leaned into me, put your mouth on mine. Your lips were tight and dry. I did not touch you and you did not touch me. Your lips were hot in their dryness, and the instant before you pulled away a shudder of desire rippled through you.

But I knew you now, I knew you truly; so I stood

up and held out my hands, saying, "Come on, Leslie. I'll take you back to the mainland now."

You looked up at me for a long, fraught minute. Then, putting both hands into mine, trustingly, you let me pull you to your feet.

From the way our first day, in which we had become friends if not lovers, had ended, I believed that we would go on together. Indeed, when you walked away from the dock—I guess you didn't know you were supposed to help with the Tender Loving Care of the boat—I didn't have the feeling that you were going away mad. For you paused, looking back, to say, "You never did tell me your name."

"Russell," I said. "Russell Walford."

In my confidence I didn't ask if you would come tomorrow. But, though I anticipated all day, you did not come. Even after I knew it, I couldn't make my-self go sailing alone, but waited glumly, hopelessly, stubbornly, until the sun had gone down. As I waited again the next day.

On the third day, I sailed; but not carefree. Instead, I slanted westward, staying close inshore, until I came in sight of your house. When its tall, yellow sides were in view, I tacked out to cruise by at some dis-tance, scanning avidly for a sight of you. The waters were so shoal that even with a centerboard I ran the risk of going aground, but heedlessly, all day long, I tacked back and forth, yearning for a glimpse of your yellow dress.

I have never known if you saw me that first day. You did not show yourself. The house, its yellow paint weathered, stood high on stilts, the blind win-dows staring. Occasionally I saw people moving about, but not you. I would have known you even at the distance.

The next day I borrowed Father's bird-watching binoculars—without telling him. No one at all in sight this early in the morning. With the magnification I could see a couple of dogs on the front porch. The yard, scant of grass and bare of ornamental shrubbery, was cluttered with the debris of shabby seacoast living; a stove-in rowboat, a stretched net, tin cans and old tires. This close-up view of the place where you lived depressed me; it made me realize acutely your hunger for escape. Your Pass Robin was not at all my Pass Robin, a lazy, sleepy, lovely place to spend the endless summers between school endings and school beginnings.

Your father emerged, putting on an old felt hat, and walked away down the path toward town. Wearing overalls and a gray work shirt, he moved with a careless, shambling gait, his shoulders rounded. He was picking his teeth as he went. Next, a boil of kids erupted into the yard, four or five boys and girls, and began racketing back and forth, screaming in play. Your brothers. Your sisters. I tried to count them but it was like counting chickens, they moiled about so.

Then—you came. You were wearing white today, fresh and pressed. I had captured you in the field of vision before you had finished sitting down. As I gazed, my breath locked in my throat, for you slowly turned your head, giving my distant boat a long, slow scan. You must have known it was me, for you did not look again.

I could see you so plainly. You were sedate in the chair, your hands linked in your lap, your legs close together. You must have remained so for an hour. I went too far west, tacked and came back. I went too far east, tacked again. Then, as the sun climbed the sky, the morning breeze died, so that the boat lay dead in the water, rolling gently, the sails drooping. In the still heat, though I was in the shade of the mainsail, I began to sweat. You continued to sit as though posing, giving me only your profile. I dwelled on it, studying your face minutely for as long as my arms could support the heavy binoculars, remembering the lovely texture of your skin, not the least sign of a freckle even with your red hair but smooth, creamy, unblemished.

Your mother—she must be your mother, I decided—came to the front door. Out of curiosity, I put the glasses on her. A short, thick woman, her legs sturdy, her face plump. She was wearing a gingham dress that hung unevenly against her calves. She must have spoken sharply, for your head snapped around defensively and I saw your lips move as you answered. Without looking again toward the boat, you rose and disappeared into the house.

I wondered how two such people as your mother and father could have given birth to a girl like you. I know now it must have been a miracle of the genes, where the whole adds up to a thousand times more than the sum of the parts. But who knows—perhaps your mother was beautiful, too, before the childbearing and the cheap, starchy meals of a poverty-stricken lifetime had caught up with her. Perhaps your father had been a handsome man before the hard labor of commercial fishing had misshapen his body.

At high, hot noon I ate the sandwich and drank the Coke I had provided for my vigil. But I didn't see you again until nearly sundown, when you came to the edge of the porch to call the children. Swarming in from their various places of play, they clustered about you. Watching you chivy them into the house, I hoped you would look out to sea, acknowledging my sentinel presence. But you did not.

Next day, I was on station for the third time. Did I intend to spend the entire summer coasting tediously back and forth at the edge of shoal water, feeding my soul on an occcasional glimpse of you? I didn't know. I could only live the days as my heart—and my flesh—commanded.

Soon, you came to the porch. You stood for a moment, gazing out to sea. Surely you must recognize the boat. But without a sign you went to your straight chair, to present your profile to my magnified gazing. But I detected today a difference; you couldn't find yesterday's comfortable stillness in your sitting. You had to hold yourself quiet when your father emerged, to stand picking his teeth and talking to you for a moment before disappearing down the path toward town. And when your mother came to sweep the front porch, you went into the house and returned with some sewing. I watched you try to concentrate on the task. But after only a few stitches your hands dropped into your lap while you sat gazing straight before you. At last, abruptly, you stood up, threw the cloth into the chair, and came to the seaward edge of the porch, where you stood for a moment, looking out toward me. Then, with a switch of your skirt—you were wearing the white dress again, I didn't like it as much as the yellow—you went down the porch steps and walked away from the house.

I decided you meant to walk to Pass Robin to drink a Coke and check the mail. I even considered, on the premise that you would pass that way, trying a quick run home to my dock. But when you emerged from behind the house, you were moving westward, walking quickly along the road.

I had a breeze today, slight but steady, so there was no problem in keeping pace with you. The road, beyond the point, ran close to the beach for a stretch, only a fringe of growth occasionally concealing your progress. At the place where the road curved inland, you left it, walking along the beach. Still you did not look my way. A quarter of a mile from your house, you came to an abandoned dock. The pelicans roosting on the pilings launched clumsily into the air, one by one, as you picked your way with care over the rotting boards.

I couldn't figure it out. So I coasted in slowly, watching you erect and still at the edge of the dock. Only when your arm lifted, beckoning, did I understand that you wanted me to come to you. My heart thumping, I sprang into action, trimming the sails to take the boat into the narrow twisting channel I could read on the water. I had to tack sharply, twice, and once the centerboard scraped a sandbar, shuddering the boat, so I had to snatch it to keep from going aground.

Catching the line I threw you, you stood holding it, gazing down at me. You were silhouetted against the sky and I could see your legs through the shadowing of the thin white dress. You were so lovely, gazing down with such a cloudy face.

"Going sailing with me?" I said happily, as yet unaware.

"Do you want to get me in trouble?" Your voice

was low, without anger. Your green eyes were
opaque with darkness.

"What do you mean?"

"Sailing back and forth out there all day. They're
not dumb, you know, they'll notice sooner or later."
You paused. "Then I'll be in trouble."

"I won't do it any more," I said contritely. "Honest." I held up one hand. "Now come on. Let's sail
out to our island."

You drew away. "No. I won't do that." Your voice
came sharply, almost fearfully.

I studied you. "You're too pale for a Pass Robin
girl. You don't get nearly enough sun. Come on.
Don't you want a nice tan?"

You tossed your head. "I wouldn't look like one of
those summer girls for anything. They work so hard
at those tans, when all it does is make them ugly."

"Leslie," I said. "I won't try . . . you know."

"Gee, thanks." I could read the defensiveness in
your tone. "Not that it would do you any good if
you did."

"Then there's no reason we can't go sailing."

You looked away. "I don't care much about
sailing."

"But you loved it," I protested. "I know you did."

"It's silly, all that work just for fun. Just silly, that's
all."

I wondered why you had bothered to walk all the
way down here, and wave me into dock, if this was
how you meant to be. I firmed my determination.

"All right, then, we won't go sailing. Can I come
up there on the dock?"

You regarded me steadily for a long moment. "All
right," you said indifferently. "If you want to."

We talked for a long time, remember, sitting side by side. I can't recall all we said, so I don't suppose it matters. It was simply the exploration of each other that counted. I remember I spoke first about the house where you lived, so exposed on the point, and how was it when a hurricane came along? You said you'd seen the storm tide all the way across the point, the family having to wade out, single file and holding hands, to spend a night or two nights in the high school gym. It was scary, and tiring, but fun.

"There's always a lot of people there, families with babies and grandmothers, and the young people organizing games." You turned defensive again. "Our house is as old as yours, even if it isn't on high ground."

"Well, I didn't know you *liked* the place."

"I don't," you said moodily. "I hate it."

Trying to cheer you up, I asked where you meant to go when you left Pass Robin. But you didn't want to talk about it, it only made you restless, so that you began to fret about going home before they began to wonder. I begged you to stay, and you stayed. The next time you said it was time to leave, noon was on us, so we shared my sandwich and lukewarm Coke, sitting companionably on a very chancy plank at the very edge of the dock and letting our legs dangle.

It was a beautiful time. Accustomed to each other now, we were comfortable and easy; once, I remember, you lay back, shading your hands over your eyes, and I sat leaning over you. Though we only kept talking, I believe that, given the courage to make the attempt, I could have put the palm of my hand between your relaxed thighs. Certainly I thought of it, gazing down on the tender shapes of your body left unguarded by the covering of your eyes, and surely you knew that I was thinking of touching you. But I didn't want to make any more mistakes; by now I had found something I couldn't risk losing. I needed your companionship, today, far more than anything else.

And I won. At least, I think I did. Maybe you won, or *we* won, I don't know. But there was surely a victory; over our youth, our inexperience, over your fears and my fears; for when at least you got to your feet, reluctantly yet with a determined movement, I was confident enough to mention sailing tomorrow.

We were both standing. You gave me that straight, steady look that searched me so deeply for honesty and truth. I met it squarely.

"Just sailing," I said. "We won't go to the island."

I heard your breath catch. "Promise?"

"I promise." Reaching out, I took your hand. "Listen, Leslie, I . . ."

You took your hand quickly away, and my heart sank. But you said, "All right, Russell. Tomorrow." It was the first time you had used my name; the sound of it in the rich, low tones of your voice made me tremble.

"Fine," I said, hoping the tremor didn't show in the words. "Come as early as you can."

"Wait a minute. I don't . . ." You hesitated. "Somebody'll see me. Can you . . . pick me up here?"

I studied the water dubiously. "If the tide's right. But if it's out . . ."

"If the water's low, I'll come there. All right?"

"Wonderful," I said.

And, with a sudden glow in your eyes, a quick smile that took away my breath; "I love sailing, Russell. I just love it."

I had to take your hand again. "Leslie . . ."

"Hush now. Just hush."

I hushed. It was in my heart to say it, say it all, but I obeyed because I knew you were not ready, yet, to listen. So then you said, "I've got to go," and, turning, walked away without looking back. I watched you, remembering you, remembering the tender shapes of your body through the thin, white opacity of your dress. And I ached with love and with lust.

As we had needed the day of companionate conversation on the old dock, we needed also that week together in the innocence of saltwater sailing, of bright sky and white clouds and a steady wind, of mirrorlike floating upon a mirrorlike gulf in the absence of wind; the sweat on our bodies in the still heat, the hunger in our bellies when we broke out the sandwiches. Because youth needs time to come to love; and, beyond love, a further time to accomplish lust. So young, so innocent, we had no real conception what it was we sought in each other. I could not truly imagine taking you, my love, any more than you could imagine how it would be to feel me probing your body. Wandering so innocently along the precipices of ourselves, we were really in no danger at all.

There were also the serious conversations. I had to make you understand that I was discontent, also. I, also, yearned to escape from family, find time and space in which to show Father and Mother that I had something on the ball. But with Mother an accomplished painter, Father a thinker and a writer, what was left for me to do that would impress them?

"But it must be wonderful to live with people like your parents," you said wistfully. "Nobody in my house ever talks, except about the price of fish and how in the world they'll manage to buy shoes and school books when fall comes." You shuddered delicately. "Or fight. They drink beer on Saturday nights, then they fight. I'll bet your parents never fight."

"Not like that," I said. "When they're angry with each other, they just don't speak at all, except to be polite at the dinner table." I brooded for a minute. "Maybe it's better to fight like your folks, instead of all that distance and silence. I don't know."

"What do you want, Russell?" you asked me, so quietly that I had to hunt for the answer even though the answer was not in me.

"I want *people*," I said passionately. "I want people who care about sharing things, not all turned in on themselves like they are. I want turmoil, and excitement, and . . ." I stopped, floundering. "I don't know," I said sadly. I looked at you. "Except—I know I've got something, Leslie." I put my hand against my chest. "Something in *here*. And it's better than what they've got!"

You can only say such truths when you are seventeen years old and in love. And only when the girl loves you, when she clasps your hand in both of hers and cries, "I know you do, Russell. And I know you'll find out what it is, too!"

"What about you?" I said. "What is it that you want more than anything else?"

You withdrew into that quiet stillness of yours. Your mouth drooped, your eyes lost their excited sparkle. "I don't know." Your voice was almost sullen. "I haven't even thought about it much. Not lately, anyway."

"There must be *something*."

You began picking at a loose thread on your overalls. You always wore overalls now when we went sailing, remember? "Just to be like other people," you said, the words heavily reluctant. "Just to live in a clean, beautiful house, on a clean and beautiful street." Lifting your head, you stared at me defiantly. "I want a husband and I want children and I want to have my own car to drive to the store and buy things." Your voice had become passionate in its certitude. "Just to be like everybody else. Without people sneering at you because your mama is fat and ugly and your daddy won't work any more than he has to." Your mouth trembled, your voice dropped lower. "Not to have people say cheap things about you—and to you—just because you're a Dollard."

"Leslie," I said. "Don't."

"You ought to know it." The stubborn need to say it was strong, undeniable. "I can't even let a boy take me to a movie, Russell, because every time he'll ask me to ... do it. Just like that, flat out, without even kissing me first, or trying to make me *want* to do it. 'How about it,' they'll say, like asking if I'd like to go for a hamburger and a malted milk. 'Come on, for Christ's sake, you can put out for me, too, can't you?' And then, even when I won't, they'll brag, they'll claim to have got it because they think everybody else got it—and so the next time it's just that much worse." Your face became rebellious. "They don't treat the other girls that way. They let the other girls lead them around like they had a ring in their nose." Your voice broke. "But me ..."

"You ought to kill them!" I said.

You looked at me hopelessly. "You can't beat them.

All you can do is get away from them." Doubling your fist, you pounded it twice on your knee. "And I will. I'll go where nobody knows me, I'll be *nice*, I'll marry a nice man and have his children. I'll live so well, every day of my life, that nobody will ever know how I was raised."

Taking you by the shoulders, I laid my mouth on your sweet mouth. It was not meant to be a passionate kiss, only loving and kind. But you put your arms around my waist, your nails digging into my back, and held me so fiercely that I couldn't breathe. Yet, all the while, your mouth stayed closed, with a hard, resistant line that bruised my mouth. When we drew away, we could not look at each other. Searching desperately for escape from the mutual dilemma, I scanned the water, spotted a wind flaw sweeping toward us.

"Breeze coming on the starboard bow," I said. "Stand by on the lines."

As soon as we were trimmed away and sailing again, you came to sit beside me in the cockpit. In a moment, you took my hand into your hand. You held it for a long time. But we did not talk, for we both realized that we had sailed dangerously over a dangerous reef in our relationship.

The next day was different. Because you were different. Though you crewed with all the quickly learned efficiency and skill, you were silent, and you would not look at me. Once we were well out from shore, and sailing free, you went forward to sit in the bow.

All I could do was allow you the solitude you craved, hoping that sooner or later you would emerge on the other side of your troubled thinking and become again my Leslie, my sailing companion. So alone I handled the boat while you sat hunched in the bow, both arms wrapped around your knees, holding yourself in a tight, repressed knot.

Toward noon, the luffy breeze quit completely, leaving the boat dead in the water, sails flapping idly. I remained in the cockpit. You remained in the bow. We were as far away from each other as it was possible to be in the small boat. In the continuing silence of ourselves, I drooped into my own melancholy. I couldn't understand why the world should be so constituted that so few people could have what they truly wanted, yet were saddled with such great burdens. So absorbed in my own gloom, I was not aware you had moved until, standing over me, you spoke in a quiet, fatal voice.

"What?" I said, looking up.

"We might as well go ashore for a while," you said again. "There won't be a breeze for a long time. It's so hot out here without a wind."

I gazed about in astonishment. As though aware of our secret desires, the boat had drifted close inshore to the middle island. The island where we had been before. Quietly, as quietly as you, I searched into your face. It was a decision you had made. I recognized the decision. I found the paddle and began moving us closer inshore. When the water was shallow enough, you went over the side with the bowline and pulled from the beach. I went over the side, also, at the last moment, and between us we beached the boat high and dry. Trotting out the anchor, I dug it carefully into the sand.

"Let's find some shade, if there is any," you said.

"Bring the boat cushions. I don't want to sit on the ground."

You spoke in such an ordinary voice I couldn't believe it. Silently, I took the three cushions from the cockpit. As you walked ahead of me into the island growth, the wet legs of your overalls flapped about your ankles. Going on past the place we had stopped before, you headed for the cluster of cabbage palms that crowned the highest point of land. There was shade under the palms, but no breeze. I dropped the cushions. Kicking one into position, you sat down on it. I sat on another, not too near, not too far. High overhead a sea gull screeched at another gull, raucous and hateful. Taking off my straw hat, I wiped sweat from my forehead and fanned myself.

"Sure hot today, all right," I said into the emptiness surrounding us. "Hottest day yet, I think."

You were not looking at me. "Russell. You'll go away from Pass Robin in September, won't you? You always go away in September."

"Yes," I said. I sighed. "Back to school."

"Will you come back next summer?"

"Sure," I said. "I suppose so. We always do."

You turned toward me. "But you'll be eighteen. So you won't have to come back unless you want to."

I was uncomfortable under the intense scrutiny. "Well, I always have. Of course, I'll be graduated by then, getting ready to go to college. So I might not." I thought I knew what you were worrying about. "But I'll be here, Leslie, I promise you. We'll have all next summer, too."

Your eyes were dark. You were sitting with your legs braced, leaning toward me; your hands were clenched into fists. The stance of your body was pure anger; but in your face showed only the abiding sadness of your beauty. That—and more, something I could not read. Gazing now, as intensely as you, I discovered the first flaw I had ever found in your beauty. There were dark rings etched faintly under your eyes.

I said, before I thought, "You didn't sleep last night, did you? You didn't sleep at all."

"No," you said tensely. "I didn't." Your mouth twisted. "I guess it shows."

"Leslie," I said, "what's the matter?"

I might as well not have spoken for all the resonance it made in you. You were still looking at me steadily, your eyes direct, seeing . . . even cold in their seeing.

"So there's just from now until September, isn't there? That is, if you'll promise not to come to Pass Robin next year."

"What do you mean?"

Reaching for the other boat cushion, you placed it carefully behind you. Lying back on it, you moved your legs farther apart. You were looking straight up into the infinite blue depths of the Gulf Coast sky.

"So I can let you do it, can't I?" you said slowly. "Because it wouldn't count. It would just be now, it wouldn't last in you and it wouldn't last in me."

A thrill of mingled fear and excitement shot through me. I had put the idea so far away that I couldn't grasp it so quickly and bring it back again into the realm of possibility.

I took refuge in words. "What do you mean, it wouldn't count?"

You turned your head. "It wouldn't be like those

Pass Robin boys. You wouldn't tell anybody, would you? You wouldn't brag about it."

The very idea stirred an answering anger. The anger was also a refuge. "Of course I wouldn't, Leslie. Why, that's the meanest, nastiest thing ..." I stopped myself. "Listen. When Bill said it about you, that time ... I wouldn't go sailing with him any more. I picked a fight just so I wouldn't have to."

I might as well have kept silent. You were following your own meaning, not my distractions.

"So you can do it, Russell. Right now. If you want to."

I stared. You were looking, not at me, but straight up again. The bladed shadows of the palm fronds shifted on your face from a momentary movement of wind. It was very quiet here in the palm grove, though far away I heard the call of a seabird. I watched your breasts move gently with your breathing, and an aching tenderness came into me. You had come to me so suddenly, and I did not know how to cope with it. All this past week, we had been safe. But now I was afraid.

"Then you have done it," I said. It was the only reasonable statement I could find for your actions.

You didn't move. "No. But I will. With you."

"Because it won't count." I looked away. "Leslie, I ..." A hard lump had come into my throat; the words were not easy to say. "I've never, either. I ..."

"That doesn't matter," you said. "I don't mind." Even in that moment, I tasted the strange texture of that statement.

My voice trembled. "But saying it doesn't count ... that's not how it ought to be."

Your eyes were lost in blue depths of sky. Your

voice came dreamily. "It can't count, Russell. You'll go away and you won't come back. Then, somehow or other, I'll go away, too. So it won't matter to the man I marry, he'll never know it unless I tell him, he'll go right on and marry me and buy me the nice house and all. And the girl you marry, she won't care, men are expected to have done it already. It won't make any more difference in your life than it will in mine."

"Listen, Leslie," I said hoarsely, "if you think I'll forget you . . . If you think I can just go away next September after I . . . after we . . ."

Your voice came quick and sharp and angry. "For God's sake, Russell, quit talking about it. Just do it, that's all. Do it, damn it!"

So absorbed in the intricacies of response, I didn't even have a hard-on. I couldn't believe that it was happening. Yet I didn't mean to let it happen the way you wanted it. The tenderness and the love were ripe in me; I wanted, far more than I wanted to lay you, to say something that would allow you to cry. For surely you needed to weep.

"No," I said. "Not unless you want to, too."

Bringing your eyes back from blue infinity, you looked at me. In that moment, I'm sure, you hated me for my slowness, my ignorance, my innocence. You needed a man rampant with lust, ruthless to sweep you along in the ruthless tide of your own feelings. But I was ruled by something beyond simple inexperience. Loving you more deeply than I myself realized, I could not allow you to establish this limited premise for a first lovemaking.

"Do you think I'm doing it for you?" A hard, cold edge to your words. "I'm doing it because I can, with you, without getting caught in a trap." You paused, breathing hard. "Do you understand now? Do you?"

So paralyzed by the intricate wash and ebb of feeling and sensation, I could not have made the move. So it would have ended, then and there, leaving between us only the hostility of incomprehension. But you snarled suddenly, a sound more than a meaning, so that I did not understand the words until you had said them again.

"Touch me. Shut up and touch me!"

Involuntarily, I put my hand into your crotch. Through the thick denim fabric I could sense only dimly the arch of pubic bone, the shape of mount. I pressed harder. Your eyes had gone far away again, as you savored the pressure. But it was not enough. Pushing away my hand impatiently, you opened the buttons of the fly. Then, grasping my wrist, you guided my hand through the folds of cloth, pressing it warmly against the warm flesh. Still a thin fabric barred intimacy. But when my middle finger found the moist groove, a shudder rippled through you. We were both breathing hard.

But, because my hand remained quiescent, it was still not enough. So you twisted away again, swiftly unbuckling the overalls, and before I could catch that last lost breath, you had pushed them to your knees, taking with them the underpants so that you emerged naked from the waist down, leaving only the salt-stained shirt to cover your breasts.

You were on your back again; this time an arm was folded over your eyes as you revealed your nakedness. I gazed. Your belly gleamed in its lovely slantings into your loins. The red gold pubic hair, so secret until now, was ripe and thick. My penis

throbbed suddenly, a thrusting rigidity trapped painfully by the restraining fabric of denim pants.

"Russell." you said. "Look at me."

"I'm looking," I said. I moved closer. Having had
no experience in such matters, I did not know that I
was gazing, in that moment, upon the most beautiful
female organ I would ever see in my time upon earth.
The twinned lips were firm, rounded, there was a
sweet entrenchment into your thighs. As your legs
shifted, opening you slightly, the inward flesh revealed itself brightly, the tiny crimson tip of erect
clitoris peeking out of the enfolding tissue. Your
mount was well defined, the arch of muscle and bone
both revealing it and shaping it ready to receive male
assault. The warm waves of sensation washing through
me made me so dizzy I swayed over you. I wanted to
talk, to say something, to tell you. But no words were
capable for the massive tenderness, the huge need I
felt to satisfy, not myself, but you.

You waited a long time, a minute at least, two minutes, for my initiative. Then you said, your voice low
and trembling, "Touch me again now. Touch me.
Please."

"Leslie," I said hoarsely. "We *can't.*"

"Please, Russell. Don't make me beg. Just ... touch
me."

I put my hand on your revealed nakedness. Of itself
it cupped your mount, cherishing it wholly as your
body curled against it, lifting toward and shrinking
away from in the same movement. My greedy eyes
saw the sweat on your belly, my hand could feel your
quickened breathing. The sweat, gathering, began to
roll in beads along the gradients of your flesh until

your navel was filled with a tiny pool of salty water, glistening as a ray of sun found it.

I didn't need to decide what to do. Without my volition, my hand turned, sliding the middle finger sweetly into the sweet slit. The gasp of the intimate groping echoed in your straining body, for the tip of my finger, having found the tiny clitoris, was sating itself there; and it quickened you, you were pumping my finger, your whole lower body involved in the intricate convolution of a mountingly urgent rhythm.

It was not yet enough. Your hand came down to stop my hand. "Now," you said.

"Leslie," I said, my voice shaking.

Your demand rose. "Now, damn it. Do it to me. Now."

So much more your initiative than mine. My hands found the war-surplus belt buckle, opened it, I had to get to my feet to slide out of the tight dungarees, and so, when I was naked, I stood naked over you. Surging in me now, like a high tide, was a pride of maleness, so that I hungered for you to uncover your eyes and view my great organ, rampant and ready. But you didn't look at me; behind the shield of your arm, your eyes were squeezed shut. But your flesh anticipated me, your knees were opening a space between your thighs to be filled with my body, my tool, my enormous, rampant lust.

I plunged to my knees between your knees, the sand gritting harshly against my skin. With one hand under each thigh, lifting your legs, I leaned into you, I began the steady, slow, confident approach that would thrust my instrument into the receiving warmth. But there . . . it stopped.

I couldn't have stopped. I had gone past the point

of no return. But you stopped; somewhere inside your head a saneness must have kept vigil, cueing a female caution.

"You didn't put on anything."

"What?" I said.

You didn't move to draw away, you held yourself ready. But you said, "You've got to put it on first."

Aware of your meaning now, I drew back on my haunches. "Leslie, I don't have anything."

Troubled now, desperate. "We can't do it if you won't put it on, Russell. That would really ruin it, wouldn't it? But, for God's sake, hurry!"

"Leslie, I'm not lying. I don't have anything."

You became impatient. "You just want to . . . Boys always carry them. That's the first thing they tell you, they've got a rubber and so you're not taking any chances. They all tell you that, just like it's the only reason to keep a girl from giving it to them. Why, they even show it, like it was a temptation. . . ."

Your voice ran down. Still now in the flesh, silent, there came a shrinking withdrawal, as though a cramp, agonizing in its painfulness, had gripped your wanton body.

"You really don't have one."

"No," I said. "I never thought . . ."

"Oh God," you said. Turning on your side, you curled in on yourself, putting both hands between your gripped thighs and rocking back and forth. Watching your agony, desire ebbed as rapidly as it had come. My penis drooped shamefully, my knees ached from the bruising of the hard-grained sand.

"I'm sorry," I said. "I didn't know. I just didn't think . . ."

You did not reply, but lay deep within yourself;

and instead of lessening, as I had lessened, your frustration seemed to grow with your self-involved rhythm—until at last you turned open again, abruptly, violently, and your eyes were no longer shielded but wide and wild.

"All right. Do it your way." Your voice was angry in its desperate weakness of need. "Get in me, I don't care, just get in me. I don't give a damn any more, I just don't give a damn, so do it, do it to me, hurry up and do it."

With the crazy talking, you had raised up, your arms were dragging me down, your legs were locking behind my legs, holding me tight against nakedness. But, because my penis was still down, there was in me, as in you a moment before, a whispering sanity.

"No, Leslie," I said. "I won't."

Holding me clasped, your eyes glaring into my eyes, you began to thrust your mount against my limp organ. You were crazy with the need. But I knew you, I loved you far more than I lusted for your body. In an effort to encage your angry lust with my tender love, I cradled you in my arms, saying, "No, Leslie. I won't let you. I won't."

Saying it over and over again, my voice low and steady and filled with love, I eased your strife until at last your body began to slacken its grip on my body. Then I could put my hands on your face, holding it between my two palms and saying it now directly into your hearing until at last it began to penetrate and we lay quietly, looking into each other's eyes. And if we have ever loved each other, my lovely darling, through all these beautiful and terrible years, it was in that beautiful and terrible moment.

"All right," you said at last, your voice as subdued as your body. "I'm all right now, Russell."

I rolled sideways, taking the weight of my nakedness away from your nakedness, and we lay still. For a bleak minute, you gazed deeply into the deep blue infinity of sky.

"Give me your hand," you said then.

I took your hand in mine. But that was not what you wanted; instead, you guided my hand into your crotch. Fearful that you were starting all over, I held it still. But then, understanding, I pressed two fingers into the warm slit. The feeling surged in me again, a hard shaping, my penis ready; but I forced myself to hold to the limits of duty. Still, as my fingers penetrated more deeply, finding your vagina wet and warm, I rolled against your hip, my instrument pumping against the outside of your thigh. You didn't like the penetration; with your hand you guided my hand back to the clitoris and established a rotary twirling that brought you quickly to a writhing, panting, gasping peak even as the frantic press and slide of my tool against your leg dangled me over the hanging edge of unaccomplished orgasm.

You were already slipping down the far slope of fulfillment. But your instinct, though as untutored about my orgasm as I about yours—I hadn't even known a woman could seek and fulfill the pattern of need and accomplishment and release—led you to find me. You shuddered, lightly, as your fingers, closing about my penis, realized tactilely its warmth and turgid thickness. And its hungering need; you began stroking, slowly at first and then swiftly. Your eyes were closed, and you had withdrawn the warm gift of your thigh—but when I came you kept your fingers wrapped tightly, you let the gush flow warmly over your hand as you kept up the stroke, so excruciatingly easeful now, until I was utterly ebbed.

Abruptly, immediately, you sat up, holding your palm to look at it. A curious expression showed in your eyes, the wry, bitter fleetingness that only a woman who has lived a hundred years, and known countless men, should realize. Yet you were only sixteen years old and, in spite of yourself, in spite of me, still a virgin.

"I'm sorry, Leslie," I said.

Leaning to wipe your hand on my dungarees, crumpled in the sand, you said in a remote voice, "It's all right."

"We can do it tomorrow," I said hopelessly. "Tomorrow I'll buy some rubbers, I'll . . . that is, if you still want to."

Your eyes were beautiful as they saw me again. Your face so lovely, too, though in it no glow of excitement, of enthusiasm, only an utter sadness of realization.

A male, in prideful maleness I had to say, "We *will* do it tomorrow." Then I had to make sure. "Promise?"

"I promise." But your answer was almost indifferent.

You lived through those days also, of course; you have your own memories. But I am recounting in detail not so much for you as for myself. For both of us. Because you could not have known my feelings, any more than I could have known yours. So perhaps both of us will understand more, not simply of ourselves but of each other. I remain acutely aware that in my ignorance I surely misinterpreted your motives and your reasons and your feelings. Indeed, it would be a miracle if I could succeed in telling you the truth of myself in those times, much less the truth of you.

I wonder if you have ever known how much it hurt to know that you could make the decision only on the promise of a summertime romance? Perhaps, wise beyond your experience, you recognized the unbridgeable chasm that separated what you were from what I was. I, in my youth so much younger than yours, wanted to believe in a great love, an enduring love. I did not want to contemplate the bitter truth of an ending at this very moment of beginning. So what deep bitterness must have dwelt in your soul; for it is the way of a woman, far more than a man, to need to believe in permanence. But it hurt more deeply than you can ever know. And so perhaps in the very beginning there grew the fatal seeds of our first ending.

It is my fond desire to make you remember in the reading, as vividly and immediately as I in the writing, the subtle and complex movement of those events taking place simultaneously within our bodies and within our souls. Yet I run a risk in evoking such immediate and direct cognition of those long-ago events. I may open old wounds, or make a new one. It is a risk I must take for myself, and so also for you.

I must utter this warning at this point—and perhaps, in your present condition of mind and soul and heart, you cannot undertake these risks. So, if you are going to throw away this letter unread, then do so now, before I tell you something I have never revealed, even during those times when we were making an honest effort to be fully truthful with each other.

The first time I took you was not any good.

At the last minute, my love, I did not believe that

you would be waiting on the old dock. But you were there, wearing the yellow dress instead of the overalls and boy's shirt that had become your accustomed sailing costume. You stepped aboard. I might as well have been a ferryman, with you for passenger, for all the communication that existed between us. You sat quietly, leaving the sailing to me; when we arrived, you waited ashore while I beached the boat. At the sheltered place you had chosen yesterday, I arranged the three boat cushions. You laid yourself down on them, immediately arching your hips to slip off the pants and put them aside. The yellow dress still covered your nakedness. I wanted to see you naked, but I did not dare ask for such favor.

Today, you did not cover your eyes with your arm, but looked up at me, directly yet remotely. "I'm ready."

I had to take off my pants while you watched. I turned away, showing only my buttocks; for, shame of shames, I didn't even have an erection. Your face was solemn, intent; all your deep quality dwelled in your eyes as with both hands you lifted the yellow dress, tucking it neatly under your chin, to reveal the golden bush between your naked thighs. Despite acute embarrassment, I began to get a rise as I gazed. Yesterday's memory was strong in me, not simply the sight, but the remembered sensation of touch. Your eyes remained glued to my organ, rigid now at an angled thrust and beginning to ache, while I found the rubber where I had placed it ready in my shirt pocket. In my clumsiness I dropped the thing in its silver wrapping and had to stoop awkwardly to pick it up. Raising your head, you followed me intently while I positioned it and peeled it back. Then, lying back, for the first time you began to look at the sky instead of at me.

"I'm ready," I said shakily.

"Then go on," you said. "Don't take all day."

The abrasive remark, almost scornful, dashed my eagerness. But doggedly I kneeled between your legs, spreading them more widely. I wanted to see your face as I entered you. But your head was flung back. To get your attention, I put my finger against your mount.

"Not that," you said, twitching away. "The other"

Obediently I leaned over you. Sensing my nearness, your hips lifted, pressing your mount against the head of my penis. With an instinctive wriggle, the puffy lips pressed, parted, took me in. Even with the rubber, I could feel intensely the heat of your body. I moved gently so that my shaft blunted against your clitoris. With a rotary motion, watching your face for a response, I pumped gently.

You had been holding yourself arched and still. Now, shifting jerkily, you raised your head to gaze down the length of your body. "You're not in yet," you said. "It's not there, anyway, Russell. Lower down."

The critical remark made me angry. "Let me do it my way," I said through gritted teeth. Even as I spoke, I took my penis in hand and forced it down, shoving hard at the same time, and a sigh moved through you. Still upright on my knees, I drove a few strokes. I could tell it was not satisfactory. You shifted uneasily, then tried to lift yourself to swallow me whole. I couldn't seem to get any deeper, something was in the way, I was bruising myself against the obstruction.

"What's the matter?" you said impatiently.

"How do I know what's the matter?" I said in anger and despair. "It's not me. It's you."

You were angry, too. "If you can't manage it, then quit."

I didn't quit. I just forgot about being gentle and loving. Letting my full weight come down, I drew back and thrust as hard as I could. I meant to hurt you. It did hurt, you cried out against the violation. But then I was in you, I was plunged to the hilt and your vagina was clenched around my throbbing organ like a cruel fist. No warmth, no welcome, only an utter recoiling and a frantic welcome battling each other for dominance. Pulling away, I plunged again, wanting to hear you cry out again. Because I was gazing into your face, I saw your teeth clamped on your lower lip, I saw how you hated me for violating your body. You hadn't expected it to be so painful, it was all a terrible shock to you both physically and mentally.

Shame flooded into me. I lay on you without moving, my tool buried deeply but no longer violent in the penetration. "What's the matter, Leslie?" I said gently.

You didn't look at me. "It hurts. God, how it hurts!"

I became alarmed. "Something's wrong. It's not supposed to, is it?"

"I guess so. Because it does."

"It's supposed to feel good."

"Well, I'm sorry! But it hurts. Just like a knife, straight up . . ."

I made a move to withdraw. "We'd better quit. I don't want to . . ."

YOU

Your hands clutched at my shoulders. "Just get it over with, that's all. Go ahead and get it done."

"But . . ."

"Damn it, I don't aim to quit with it half done. So fuck, damn you. Fuck."

For the first time, your voice had slipped unaware into the southern accent. Twanging harshly on my ear, it made of you a stranger. You were no longer the Leslie I loved, but simply a slit to be used. My ebbing erection restored as stern as ever, I began again, my eyes closed so I wouldn't have to see your face. With each strong thrust the wind gasped in your lungs. I had to take you now, I couldn't stop because I knew, I *knew*, that with the next stroke, or the next after that, your body would accept me, your flesh would warm and soften, your hips would begin to writhe in a responding rhythm.

It didn't happen. Remaining cold, though utterly quiescent, you took the increasingly stronger beat, unresisting but not participating. I had passed the point of caring about you, there was even something exciting about the anguished moaning sound I jolted out of your flesh with each thud of flesh against flesh. I was penis now, you were vagina; if you had died under me, I would have finished still.

It seemed to go on for a long time; again and again the orgasm began to build, but each time, at just the crucial point, it would slip a notch as my semen sensed the cold flesh that awaited its ejaculation. Maybe it was the rubber too, at least partly—but I believe most of it was knowing how unwelcome I was. I suppose, to you, it lasted a little beyond forever. But I couldn't help that, I needed a little warmth, a small invitation of the flesh or, horror of horrors, I would not be able to finish. Then you really would hate me, wouldn't you?

Then, in spite of your coldness, it began to be. It gathered so far back, and built so slowly, that I began to ache with the need, my breath gasping horribly in my lungs as though I were breathing flame. It surged, like a mighty dam bursting, and suddenly, in the very midst of coming, I saw the warm gentleness of your eyes; not reflected in your resisting flesh but only in your loving eyes as you watched the orgasm happen in my face.

I collapsed, flared briefly into final spasm; then I laid my head on your shoulder, my face turned, letting myself sink cradled into your cradling body. You lifted your arms to put both hands on my head, holding it as you murmured unvoiced words.

We lay together in that manner until a foolish pride captured me—I was a man now, I had taken a woman. But needing also your confirmation, I stirred to see your face, saying, "Was it good for you? Was it?"

"Yes," you said. "Yes. Of course it was."

Even in the dominance of pride, I knew you were lying. "But I hurt you."

Your hands were stroking on my head. "Yes. A little bit. But it was good, Russell. It really was."

Then, your hands still caressing, my tool still embedded limply inside your bruised body, you began to cry. Very quietly, so softly, the tears overflowed. Only for a minute; less than a minute. Then, putting your hands against my shoulders, pushing, you said, "Get up, Russell. You're too heavy."

We separated and, without looking, I stripped off the rubber and flung it away. "Are you all right?" I asked, made anxious all over again by the strained whiteness of your face.

"Sure," you said with an effort. "I'm fine."

Getting to your feet, the crumpled dress dropping to cover your nakedness, you stood with your legs tenderly apart. For the first time you were not beautiful. I had to come to you, now that I had used you so, and demonstrate all over again the tender love that had been your prior experience of me. Consenting to my arms about you for a brief moment, leaning your head on my shoulder, you were small and warm in my embrace.

"It'll be better next time," I said out of male confidence. "You'll get to like it. You'll see."

Raising your head, there were those thousand-year-old eyes again, woman eyes gazing deep into the man. "Yes," you said. "I suppose so."

"Just wait and see, Leslie. I know I'm right."

"Russell," you asked suddenly, "was it like you thought it would be?"

"Better," I said stoutly. "A thousand times better."

You were not listening to my lie. Looking down at your draggled dress, your used body, you put your hands instinctively to your tumbled hair. "I want to go home."

"It's early yet," I protested. "We've got lots of time." I felt bashful for having repetition so suddenly in mind. "We might even . . ."

"I want to go home," you said.

Aboard the boat, you went into the bow, remaining there, isolated, all the way to the mainland. The moment the bow touched the old dock, you stood up and stepped ashore. I watched you walk away without looking back, moving with a faint awkwardness from the sore bruising of your most tender flesh. I did not know if I would ever see you again.

When you came to me bright and early, that next bright and early morning, I couldn't believe you were the same draggled girl who had left me yesterday. You were wearing a new green dress, remember, and it made a happiness in me just to see you. Because you, your yesterday-used body, showed itself, by its poise and movement, as happy in every cell.

I felt pretty good myself, having come early awake to let myself out through the side porch to sit on the boat and watch the sunrise. I had always liked the Gulf Coast mornings. Today, however, there was not only a natural beauty in my young world, but, as well, a change in me that went to the deepest roots of being. Gazing out over the water, I savored the faint finger marks of morning breeze flawing the quiet surface. A pelican dived with seeming awkwardness, dropping like a lead weight. But he got his fish. I snuffed at the air, still fresh and without heat, my nostrils attempting unsuccessfully to sort out the various aromas of sand and sea that marked this first day in which I was an accomplished man. I yearned to come to you, but it was too early to think about coasting down to the old dock. A faint cloud of apprehension shadowed my happiness; maybe you wouldn't want to see me. Maybe . . .

At that moment, I saw you. You couldn't have counted on finding me at this hour so soon after sunrise; surely you, as I, had been unable to hold yourself away from the fresh new world we had made for ourselves. Stopping, you looked at me as I looked at you. Then, tilting your head provocatively, you said, "May I come aboard?" Hastily catching the bowline,

I pulled the boat inshore. Moving with that new body-happiness, you came to me, put your hand on my arm.

That is all. Your hand on my bare arm. But, from the very warmth and weight and shape, I knew that you were mine. Your smile was beautiful, so warm and loving, as you said, "Good morning, Russell."

I ached to put my arms around you. But I only said, "Good morning, Leslie."

You would never again be the girl you had been yesterday. Your soul was lifted, there was in you only love and warmth and tenderness. Devouring you with my eyes, I knew suddenly that until this moment I had not seen you happy.

Your hand resting on my arm, you looked toward our island distant yonder on the edge of our place-in-time. "I've never been sailing at this time of day," you said. "Can we go sailing, Russell?"

"Sure," I said hastily. "No reason why not." I scanned the water. "There's a little breeze . . . it'll be luffy, but that won't matter." I was already scrambling to cast off the lines. You stood watching, not helping as I had taught you. I didn't mind. I knew you were remembering; it was a most wonderful remembrance that glowed in you.

"Can I take her out?" you said. "You've never let me take her out."

"Sure," I said. "You be captain. I'll be crew."

I watched as you handled the boat. You knew the course I followed, if the wind allowed, to skirt the first shoal, and then the quick tack to avoid the old sunken hull. Looking up, I saw the sails taut and true; not a luffing snap had sounded as you threaded the shallows. I came back to the cockpit. "Couldn't have done it better myself." You smiled at the compliment but, so busy sailing the boat, you had no time for me.

The morning breeze, like so many morning breezes, was untrustworthy. When it dropped, we were halfway between mainland and our secret island. Sailing, we had spoken only the technical, necessary language. But now there was time, and need, and love.

"Leslie," I said, "is everything . . . all right?"

"Everything's wonderful."

You answered as solemnly as I had asked the question. But your eyes were smiling.

I fumbled for the right words. "But . . . it did hurt, didn't it? It hurt pretty bad."

"You always want to talk too much," you said. "We don't have to talk about it, Russell."

You wished to contain it quietly, secretly. But somehow, I felt, talking would make it as real today as it had been yesterday. I yearned to detail the scope and run of my feelings, I wanted to hear you tell minutely how it had been for you. So I kept on trying to encompass the deed with words.

"You're all right now, aren't you?"

Perhaps you read my need; at least, you yielded to it. "I'm . . . sore yet." Your eyes darkened, a residual flutter of pain straining the physical and spiritual happiness of this new day in which you were a new woman. "I . . . bled, Russell. So bad it scared me."

Perhaps I'm not quite a hopeless case. At least, I did the right thing; I quit talking and put my arm around your shoulders. You moved your head, wanting me to kiss you. I kissed you, your lips firm yet soft against my lips. When I put my other hand over the lovely cup of your breast, you did not hinder me. Beneath us, the boat rocked gently and, swooping down, a gull screamed as though resenting our presence.

Taking away your mouth, you turned your face into my neck. "Russell."

The word breathed against my skin. I put my hand under your skirt, moved it into your crotch. Your legs clamped tight against the search, though you did not move away. The reaction, I know now, must have been purely involuntary.

"Don't," you said muffled into my neck. "Please don't."

I was baffled. Until now the texture of the day had been only affection and reminiscence. Suddenly it had become necessary to prove it all over again. If I couldn't touch you now, if I couldn't have you—at least, have your consent if not the deed—yesterday had not happened at all.

"Why not?"

You shuddered. Your voice was a shaky whisper. "Don't . . . touch me, Russell. Not until we can . . ."

So that was all. I looked toward the islands. The wind was down, the water utterly still. For the first time I wished fervently for an auxiliary motor.

I needed, had to have, confirmation and a renewed accomplishment. "We can do it here. Inside the day cabin." I kept watching your face. "That is . . . if we're going to do it again at all."

You became quiet, still, as you returned my look. Then you turned your head, surveying the expanse of gulf. We were the only sailboat out this early in the day; on the western horizon a commercial fisherman, stained and disreputable, was coming in, following the channel markers. You studied the day cabin dubiously. Then, putting your hand against my cheek, smiling wistfully, you said, "Can't you wait?"

I put my hand over yours, holding it warm against my skin. "I don't want to wait. Not unless I have to."

Your fingers had moved to cover my lips, as though reading the words with the sensitive tips. Beyond beauty, beyond time, you were a woman recognizing and accepting the heedless urgency of your man.

"All right."

I rarely used the day cabin; its tiny space was a clutter of spare line, an extra anchor, half-empty paint buckets left from last summer's major refurbishing. The best I could manage, in my passionate haste, was to clear enough room for the three boat cushions. I was sweating from the closeness when I emerged, the outside air suddenly cool on my skin. You ducked into the cabin.

I waited outside while, kneeling on the cushions, you took off the new green dress. Folding it carefully, you placed it safely atop a bulk of canvas. Still kneeling, your back to me, you reached behind to unhook the bra. My breath caught; I would have your breasts this time. You wriggled out of your pants and, turning, lay down on the cushions.

I took a last look. Safe enough. I entered the day cabin, going to my knees to avoid bumping my head, and began to unbutton my shirt. You were lying with your head toward the bow, your knees drawn up because there was not enough room to stretch out. I looked at the shaping of your flesh, waiting for my penetration. I looked at your breasts. They were lovely, small breasts, with nipples like pink buds. I would put one hand on each when I mounted you; they would be naked against my palms. Then I looked at your face. Yes. Your mouth was waiting too, your eyes, so large and luminous in the shadowiness. I began to ache with the enormous erection. I would bury myself in you, I would die in you, my senses would swoon with the heat of your flesh.

"You'd better not get undressed," you said. "If another boat came, you might have to show yourself topside."

I hesitated. I wanted to be as naked as you were. But it was only prudent. "Just my shirt, then," I said.

The condoms were in my wallet. I had to lean over you to get them out of my tight hip pocket. I unbuttoned my fly. I had to bend my engorged tool to spring it free of the restraining cloth. You watched, smiling slightly, while I stripped a condom of its silver foil and sheathed my instrument. Ready at last, I came between your lifted knees. Leaning on one elbow, I put the other hand on your breast. You held me off, gently, with a hand against my bare chest.

"Be easy, Russell. As easy as you can. I'm still sore."

Determined on a gentleness I had forgotten in yesterday's angry frenzy, I moved cautiously against your loins. I came at you wrong; my organ felt the harsh brush of golden pubic hair, then slid, with a bruising of its rigid tenderness, along the slope of your belly. Pulling back, I tried again, and again missed the enfolding warmth of your liquid vagina. The tiny cabin cramped us, made everything difficult.

"Wait."

I waited. You put your hand to my tool, taking it delicately between thumb and one finger, making at the same time a subtle adjustment to accommodate its slanting entrance. In your eyes I saw the quietly intent alertness to the voices of your flesh as the sheathed head probed your warmth and wetness. The tumescent organ, tasting of your flesh, involuntarily poised itself to plunge recklessly. Recognizing the fierce animal urge, you closed your eyes, wincing in involuntary anticipation of pain.

"Be easy," you said despairingly.

You, as well as I, expected my rampantly independent instrument to refuse obedience. But it surprised both of us; I lowered myself into you with restrained care.

With an incredibly detailed sensation, I could feel the folds of flesh parting in sequence as I followed the tender path. When I reached the tight place I did not rip at it, as I had done yesterday, but pressed gently until that barrier yielded also, allowing passage into the utter depths beyond. Your eyes flew open, startled with the delight of this deep involvement that had extorted no ransom of pain and violation. Your arms rose to encircle my head, pulling my face down into the warm fragrance of your neck, and I could feel the deepest, strongest muscles of your vagina gripping warmly my rigid staff, an intricate pulsation of movement excruciating in its tenderness and passion. There might as well have not been the sheath of rubber interposing between my flesh and your flesh.

We lay quietly. The boat rocked gently, with a dreamlike slap of tiny waves against the hull. "All right?" I whispered into the fragrant warmth of your neck. Your arms tightened. "Yes."

It was not necessary to pump. It was enough, for this minute, to dwell in you in this quiet stillness. When I raised my head out of the loving cage of your arms, arching my chest to gaze down into your face, your eyes smiled, your lips quirked in affectionate response to my expression. I began a gentle stroking. Your face tightened as it remembered pain; your eyes closed again.

Stopping, I said, "Does it still hurt, Leslie?"

You didn't open your eyes. But you said, "No. Go on."

I went on, quicker than before but gentle still because your face remained tense, waiting for the pain but willing to pay the price. Pain did not come; instead, almost without transition, with eyes still closed and a faint smile on your lips, your face was dreaming a living dream of lovemaking.

You did not respond any more than you had yesterday. I had not brought you nearly that far, into a hot gush of lust, an uncontrollable commitment to an intricate spasm of vagina. Your vagina warmed, but not much; lubricated, but only a little. Your most needful flesh remained ignorant of its own needs and desires. You allowed sex not out of passion but because of love; and as I stroked more and more strongly, hitching into the stride and rhythm of increasingly imminent orgasm, you dreamed of the act of love, your eyes closed and your face remote, your hands holding to my shoulders but without a clutching need for your own fulfillment.

Even when I came, I did not rampage ruthlessly in your flesh, but ejaculated in long, slow pulses going on forever, it seemed, while, eyes open now, lips parted in a slight smile, you received it, loving this thing you had made me do.

Again, I had to ask. "Are you all right?"

For answer you took my head in your hands and

kissed me with warm, soft lips. Then, tucking my face into your neck, you held me crooningly close, your hands in my hair. As you continued in the caress, your body settled under me, spreading and opening in a manner impossible to describe, so that somehow I sank more deeply into your flesh. It was an enormously female cherishing of my finished male body that I have not known from any other woman. And, though I did not know it then as I know now, in all these first lovemakings it was your only reward.

Only when we were topside again did we discover that we were ravenously hungry. Neither of us, this morning, had waited for breakfast.

That, my old love, was, for me at least, the real beginning. It made me sure of you, as you were already sure of me. The beginning; from which we went on together, voyaging through day after day of our sensuous and innocent love. Only June now, we had July and August to be measured out by a daily act of love, placing a red letter into our summer's calendar with each discharge of come. In my memory, these couplings blend one into the next; yet each was distinctly and subtly different, as the textures of your flesh seemed to change, the shape of your mouth, the emotions and meanings that dwelt so mysteriously in your green eyes.

There came into being also certain constant understandings, from your nature or from mine. Though my hands were affectionate of you, you never liked to be touched casually, but only with intent. Sitting side by side in the cockpit, sailing with a fair breeze, so often you would lean your weight against me—but if I should put my palm between your shoulder blades, a place I loved to touch, you would twitch away. I asked you more than once, remember, why you were like that. Your always answer was that my touch made you desire me; so there was no time for touching while sailing or eating or swimming, any of the casual intercourses of our day. I sensed within this assertion a certain reserve, but I could only accept your inviolate sense of yourself.

Though we made love almost every day, often twice and sometimes three times, your flesh failed to learn turbulent consummations. I suppose you did not know, as I did not know, that the female can reach an ecstatic state of total surrender and, not expecting such release, you did not strive for it. You were simply acquiescent as you lay beneath me, your face remote in your private dream of sensuousness as I plowed you with my fleshly plow. Warm, yes, liquid with your sweet lubrications—with each added experience and anticipation your golden depths became more quickly liquefied, until at last, even at entrance, I could count on a glowing wet heat—but never, of its own nature, greedy and needful. Only rarely did you move, and then abruptly, abortively, as much a surprise to you as to me.

I blazed with lust. Each accomplishment of panting ejaculation only fired me toward the next event. Perhaps it seemed to you it was all love on your side, all lust on mine. Certainly I loved you; but I needed you, too, I used your compliant body again and again without assuaging the basic need. You did not seem to mind, certainly you honored my lust as you honored my tool, you experienced a sweet fulfillment when, my semen pumped with ever-renewed passion into the catch trap of the condom, you could wrap my head in your arms, your fingers stroking, stroking, stroking with an infinitely tender love. I came to feel that was all you needed, the intercourse itself only a necessary preliminary, a female granting of male lustiness, to the awaited moment when my body, peaceful and finished, lay with its own sated acquiescence upon your body.

Occasionally—not often, no more than four or five times throughout the entire summer—you would take my hand, when I rolled my weight away, and place it on your mount. I understood, then, that I was to caress your clitoris, first a tender up-and-down stroke and then, when your hand clutched strongly at my wrist, with an insistent twirling until your loins were writhing. Then, as you never did during actual intercourse, your breath would pant, your lips drawn back in a ferocious grimace, until, plunging immediately from the highest peak, you would curl in on yourself. You were always ashamed when it happened. Turning away from me, you would lie with your face hidden, your crotch hidden also by the withdrawn curling inward of your body. After these times, you did not cherish me tenderly, you would get abruptly away from me, and for a long time you would not speak at all. This, too, I did not understand; I could only accept.

Once, I remember, I had the brilliant idea of putting my hand on your vagina before entering you, instead of afterward. You let me touch you but, the moment I began the twirling motion that always brought you to orgasm, you grabbed at my hand with both of yours, a blazing anger flooding into your eyes. Snatching up your clothes, you fled beyond the cabbage palms, and all my coaxing could not persuade you. I did not understand; I could only accept.

There was also this constant; we developed no sexual games. I don't know why. There is a playfulness in sex, a childlike enjoyment of fun and games, even an innocent—sometimes not so innocent—sampling of strange tastes and preliminary teasings. We were children, with a child's inquisitiveness inside our nearly adult bodies. But—such was not our way. You never exhibited the least desire to inspect closely the workings of my sexual apparatus. I thought once or twice, I must admit, of parting your nether lips to examine with curious eyes those wonderful arrangements I knew only by sensuous touch. But I understood, without asking, that you would resist with outrage and anger this visual violation. So I did not try it.

Our sex was not oral. Our kisses were chaste, for your mouth did not open to mine, in what was then called French kissing, and there was no use of tongues. Though my hands were free of your breasts, I did not put my mouth on them. The idea of going down on each other was, of course, utterly alien.

I don't know how children are nowadays. But you and I, with a direct and simplicity-minded innocence of flesh and spirit, simply made love. Between acts, we did all that one does to enjoy a summer on the water. Sailing mostly, of course, for you loved sailing even more than I. But we swam every day. You always brought along your bathing suit now—I still remember the black latex suit, all one piece and far more modest of your lithe body than the flimsy dresses your wore. Though you had once scorned the sun-dark summer girls, with every day spent on the water you became more deeply tanned. How vividly I remember the golden glow of your skin, so spectacularly without blemish, in combination with your red gold hair and your deeply green eyes.

There in the solitude of the seaward beach of our island, swimming was not a sexual game. Though we might well have just made love, our naked bodies hot and close, you would invariably disappear behind a bush to get into your bathing suit, while I changed behind another. For swimming I used, remember, a pair of dungarees stagged off jaggedly just above the knee, though you considered it scandalous to go swimming without a proper suit.

You were marvelous in the water. The black suit shaped to the lines of your body like a second skin, you were a sleek otter, beneath the surface as much as on top, sinking with a white flicker of feet and coming up so far away, after what seemed far too long, that often, in spite of myself, I was anxious for your safety. When you floated on your back, resting, your face would show much the same dreaminess of sensation I saw so often during lovemaking. It was as though, immersed in the water, you were yet far away in a dream of swimming, so that you experienced it, as you experienced the sensation of sex, on two levels at once. Sometimes the dream would capture you so totally that I would have to call your attention to how far out we were drifting. You always turned reluctantly, but obediently, and with long, slow strokes swam back into safer waters.

There was also—it began immediately with that second lovemaking in the day cabin—another element in our daily love that puzzled me . . . not only then but for long after. I suppose I have something more than my natural quota of male density about the female kind. I was a middle-aged man before I realized the simple truth that a woman—any woman, every-woman—has an enormous natural capacity to domesti-cate any sexual situation, no matter how bizarre. I have seen it so often that I know it must be a funda-mental truth of the sexes. A man will proceed with a fine recklessness to establish a clandestine relationship. But the moment it is successfully established, he will begin to fret himself with the dangers of discovery; each accomplished episode will make him that much more cautious until, at the end, he will abandon the arrangement simply because he cannot endure the strain.

But a woman—any woman, everywoman—no matter how timorously she has entered into the clandestine intrigue, makes it immediately a normal part of life. Accepting utterly the shameful dodges and devices necessary to maintain the relationship, not for one second does she look back in regret, nor forward in fear. It is simply a thing that she does, as natural as sleep or child care.

I know now, as I did not know then, that within the secret realm of our innocent love you passed through dark and intricate textures of feeling. There dwelled in your mind, and were shadowed forth in your eyes, obscure reticences and shieldings, advances and retreats and turnings aside. Our love, that to me was as sunny and open and natural as a Gulf Coast summer day, was to you, like an imperfect gem, dan-gerously shadowed and flawed.

This was your own truth, kept secret even from me. For outwardly—I must tell you, my darling, how greatly your daily demeanor astonished me. It was my constant intent to keep you and me secret unto our-selves. Never once, for instance, did it occur to me to

take you to the drugstore for a Coke. But you? . . .
you waited at the old dock for our daily meeting no
longer. You came openly, in calm certitude, to the
place below our house where I docked the boat. You
had domesticated the situation; you did not care who
knew about us. I couldn't understand. Had you not
wept bitter tears because braggart boys had told lies?
Hadn't you sensed the greedy male eyes gloating over
your body, while you cringed inwardly with the sure
knowledge of their lewd thinking?

One day, during our very first week together, Bill
came walking along the path while we were tied up at
the dock; you were sunbathing in the bow, while I
scraped some scaling paint.

Bill's long stride hesitated when he saw us together,
then came on with a slower step. His eyes were on
you, his face speaking plainly the evil direction of his
thoughts. When he glanced at me, a sneer showed itself so unmistakably that in spite of my burning
shame I started forward angrily. Ignoring my provoc-
ative reaction, he went on toward Pass Robin, leaving me staring after him, my mind a hot turmoil of
shame and anger. I knew, as well as if I had already
heard the words, the contemptuous news he would
spread gleefully in the town.

But you. Even as he had observed your telltale
presence on my sailboat with such an immediate assumption, your eyes had drifted indifferently across
him. Your mouth was even shaped to reply if he had
spoken a greeting. After he was gone, leaving me fum-
ing and fretting, you turned on your stomach, cradling your head on your arms, and apparently went to
sleep. Because you made no comment, then or afterward; we never spoke of the incident.

YOU

I suppose, in a quiet village such as Pass Robin, it would have been impossible, anyway, to keep ourselves secret. Pass Robin was two separate towns—the natives and the summer visitors—but they were not strangers to each other. We must have been, now that I look back on it, an immediate scandal. You were, after all, the most beautiful girl Pass Robin had ever seen. Though sprung from the matrix of a native tribe of fishermen and so belonging to Pass Robin in that unique way of belonging that adheres only to small southern towns, you were—armored in your serene reserve, your self-sufficient inwardness, as well as in your natural perfection of face and figure—an exotic bird of passage among them.

I was also noteworthy, though not in my own right. The Walfords were not transients—indeed, most of the summer visitors were as permanent as the natives. Mother and Father, though the basis of their fame remained obscure in Pass Robin's understanding, were the most illustrious figures that had ever graced the town. Because their summers were spent in work, they had traditionally held the Walfords aloof from the bridge parties and genteel teas and picnic expeditions that were the staples of Pass Robin's social life. But they were equally recognized and respected among the summer people—though as much for the Walford lineage as for their personal achievements. Indeed, our annual arrival and departure was hailed in the columns of the Pass Robin *Gazette*, our weekly newspaper, as the beginning and the end of the summer season.

Though, in pattern with the Walford aloofness, I had few acquaintances and no friends among the summer young people—after all, for years before you

79

came along I had sailed habitually with Bill, son of
Pass Robin's carpenter—it would be duly noted that I
had involved myself foolishly with the daughter of a
commercial fishermen . . . and that could be for only
one reason, couldn't it?

Certainly, I discovered quickly, Mother and Father
were aware of our liaison. Your family must have
known, too, but if you suffered recrimination and
chastisement, you never revealed it. No. You came to
me serenely, day after day, without a hint of such
probable family difficulties. But perhaps you moved
among them so inviolate in the armor of yourself that
they were barred from derogatory comment.

I, certainly, was not inviolate. In the second week
of our love, Mother came to me in the kitchen—having returned ravenously hungry from a long day with
you, I was making a stack of peanut butter sandwiches.

"Well, hello," she said. "I'm glad to see that you
touch home base often enough not to starve to death,
anyway."

I took a large bite of the first sandwich. "Been
sailing," I mumbled.

Mother crossed to the refrigerator, opened it, took
out the water bottle. She found a glass, poured. drank
from it thirstily. She placed the glass on the counter.

"Who's the girl?" she asked. "Do I know her?"

She spoke casually; but something in her tone made
me look at her. My mother was a formidable woman,
big of frame, but shapely and light on her feet. There
was no beauty in her; she was, rather, what people
call handsome, or distinguished. A good face, but the
features were too bold for a woman—a blade of a
nose, a high, white, pure forehead, and two deep lines

chiseled from the flanges of her nose to the corners of her mouth. Her eyes, though kind, were the seeing eyes of a painter.

"No," I said carefully. "I don't think so."

Picking up the glass, she again drank deeply, put it down empty. "She does have a name, though, doesn't she?" she said dryly.

She must have known the whole story, at least about you. And enough about me to guess accurately at the rest of it. Not only a painter but a mother—the changes in me must have been as plain as day.

"Leslie Dollard," I said. I took a quick bite of the sandwich to keep from having to say more. The mouthful of bread and peanut butter stuck dryly to the roof of my mouth.

"Dollard?" Mother said. A frown wrinkle carved itself between her eyes. "I don't seem to recall the name. Have they taken someone's house for the summer?"

I understand now in this moment of writing about it, that she sought primarily to find out if I had to lie about you. Maybe she was even hoping I would lie, for prevarication would reveal at least a guilty awareness of what I was doing.

Putting down the bitten sandwich, I looked at Mother. "Leslie has lived here all her life. Her father's a commercial fisherman. They live in that yellow house down on the point."

She studied me. Her expression was quizzical, as though I had surprised her. Without further word, she turned her back, in considered deliberation it seemed, and went away, leaving me with a sinking feeling in the pit of my stomach. I knew what it was like to go up against her disapproval. I wasn't hungry any more; leaving the sandwiches on the counter, I went upstairs to my room.

At dinner that night—for once we were alone in the family, the houseguest had departed yesterday and the new famous visitor wouldn't arrive until tomorrow—I was wary. But Mother only talked amiably, to my father and to me, of how her work had gone today. Relaxing, I started an argument—a discussion, we never *argued* in our house—with Father about the relative merits of stage and screen. Knowing Father disliked movies, I held out stubbornly for the thesis that films could be art.

Only after Mother had poured the coffee did she launch her subtle attack. "Russell has a new friend," she told Father as though imparting a treasured bit of news. "He goes sailing with her every day now." She turned toward me. "What *was* her name, Russell?"

"Leslie," I said, though I understood she knew it perfectly well.

"Yes. Leslie," Mother said brightly. "Carl, I suppose she's Russell's first real sweetheart." She glanced at me. "You've never had a girl friend at school, have you, Russell? Oh, I'm not talking about dances, that sort of thing. A *real* girl friend."

"No," I muttered. "I haven't."

Father, knowing my mother's ways well, was studying me. I tried to meet his eyes, but failed.

"Do we know her people?" he inquired, apparently having located the area of concern.

Mother laughed. A natural, genuine laugh. "Oh, *you* probably do, Carl ... after all, you halfway grew up in Pass Robin, just like Russell. Dollard. That's it, isn't it, son?"

Father was as formidable in his way as Mother in

hers. In a day when beards were rare, he wore a
neatly trimmed spade, black but grizzled with gray.
Behind it showed a flat-lipped, strong mouth under an
almost-menacing luxuriance of eyebrow. Yet his eyes
gleamed with a mild tolerance and amusement at almost all that he observed. He was tall—I had inherited
from him my own leanness—but there was a certain
fragility in his long limbs.

Father's eyes, when he was not tolerantly amused,
had a way of holding you pinned like a butterfly to a
board.

"Dollard?" he said. "That's a mean bunch, son. I
saw Ben Dollard almost kill a man, once, right
downtown in front of the drugstore. Oh, it must have
been twenty years ago. He would be a murderer today if the fellow hadn't run. Ben was after him with a
knife that looked as long as your arm." He stopped
talking. He was still looking at me. "Would he, by
any chance, be your friend's father?"

I turned away my head. "I don't know. I just know
Leslie, not her family."

"Does she live down there in that yellow house on
the point?"

"Yes," I admitted unwillingly.

Father swung his head to stare at Mother. She was
silent now, content to let him handle the problem.
"That's old Ben, all right. Meanest man in Pass Robin,
bar none." Father shifted his heavy chair, angling it to
one side so he could stretch his legs. "Son, if you'll
take my advice, you won't have much to do with
those people."

I decided, foolishly, to see if I could make his eyes
again show amusement. "Father, the critics have al-

ways praised you as a principled egalitarian. Do I detect a slight note of elitism in your remarks?"

Father grunted. "I don't hold it against a man if he labors for a living with the strength of his body," he said, the words coming in precise spaces. "I know that commercial fishing is hard labor. It warps a man's body, it weathers his hide. Just about your age, I worked all one summer on a fishing boat." He stopped. He looked at Mother. He looked back at me.

"It's not that Ben Dollard was born poor, and reared poor, and will die poor. It's that he, all the Dollards, have a bad reputation. Ben now, and his father before him. That is something that will not change, son. It will not change."

Cowed now, I was completely on the defensive. "She's not like them," I said. "She's so different you wouldn't guess in a million years that . . ." I stopped, floundering.

"It is not wise, son. Take the word of a man of experience, even though he happens to be your father." As though all was now settled, he said to Mother. "Can we have the second cup of coffee on the porch? It's a trifle warm in here, don't you think?"

I looked first at Father. Then I looked at Mother. Comfortably secure in their inherited money, in their long-recognized talents, they were so sure of their values. Only a long-engrained certainty could pronounce such sentences without appeal.

A saving anger rose in me. I got to my feet. "You don't know what you're talking about!" I burst out.

They stared, so astonished that, for the moment, they had no response.

I didn't give them time to recover. "You don't even *know* Leslie!" I cried. "How could you? You don't know what it's like to be born in a family like that and hate it. What it's like to be a fine, intelligent person whose only chance is to get out of it, leave Pass Robin just as soon as you can." I stopped, breathing hard. "And why? Because of people like you, that's why, sitting on their old money and their old family and condemning her just because she's a Dollard." A bitter edge had crept into my voice. "And do it so casually, it's so easy to damn her to hell and then ask for a second cup of coffee."

If my diatribe had shaken them, Mother, at least, recovered quickly. In her driest voice, she said, "Is that how she found you, Russell? Looking for a way out of Pass Robin?"

"That's not fair! She's . . ." I had to gulp the hard anger out of my throat. But then I threw it recklessly into their faces. "All right! If that's what she wants, she can have it. I'd do anything for her. Anything!"

Father's voice had changed. "Russell. There is no reason in anger. If you are so right, why must you be so angry?"

"Just listen to me," I began.

"I will not listen. I will not permit voices to be raised in anger in my house."

I knew I had gone too far. He had never used that final tone with me. "I'm sorry, Father," I said quietly. I looked at Mother. "But I won't stop seeing her just because you think I should."

The flat defiance held us in silence for a long minute as they stared at me. Wanting to tremble, wanting to weep, in my shame and anger; yet I would not let my eyes falter. At last, to avoid losing control, I turned and left the dining room. They made no attempt to stop me.

Later, much later, after Father had smoked his cigar—lying on the bed in my room, I could smell the fragrant drift of smoke upward from the front porch—he called to me. I rose to stand at the open window. "Yes, sir?"

"Come on down. Take a walk with me."

This would not be, I knew, Father's accustomed stroll before bedtime. We went side by side down the path to the dock. Father paused there, looking at the moon, bright in a sky with white clouds, shedding its light silvery on the water. My boat shifted groaning in its anchorage, masts black against the sky.

A match flared. Father, beyond his usual habit, was lighting a second cigar. The glare of the match snatched his bearded face momentarily out of shadow.

"Russell," he said, looking, not at me, but out to sea. "The first sweetheart I ever had was a Pass Robin girl."

I didn't say anything. He turned to look at me. "Come on. Let's sit on the boat."

I followed his lead, but did not sit down beside him. After settling himself comfortably, he puffed twice on the cigar. On the still air three separate clouds of smoke floated full-bodied.

"I loved the hell out of that girl. You wouldn't believe how I did love her." He chuckled quietly. "I'll tell you a little secret, son, that maybe you haven't learned yet. You'll never forget the first one. No matter what good things life might bring you, a secret place in your soul will always remember."

I didn't have anything to say.

"Maybe you find it hard to believe," he said after a thoughtful pause. "But I'm speaking the God's truth. I was maybe a year older than you are now. She was fifteen." He chuckled, fond reminiscence as thick in the air as the cigar smoke. "She loved me, too. Oh yes. *How* she loved me!"

I cleared my throat. "Then you . . . Then, Father, you ought to understand."

He put both hands on his knees. "I do understand, son. And I don't blame you for a minute. I wouldn't tell you this in front of your mother, you understand, but it's the greatest thing in the world for a growing boy. A gulf summer, a hot-blooded girl, and first love." He sighed. "I'll tell you the truth, Russell. Never have I been fucked like I was fucked by that fifteen-year-old Pass Robin girl. With a cock inside her, she was like a little animal. She taught me things I had never dreamed about." He sighed again. "Only fifteen years old, and had never been touched until I got hold of her."

I was so shocked that I was grateful for the darkness to hide my hot face. I would not have believed that my father could use such words. In a hoarse whisper, I said, "Listen."

He looked at me. His voice was very quiet, very real. "You're a man now, Russell. So I'm talking to you like a man. You have had this girl, haven't you?"

It was in my throat to deny it. But he would know my lie. Blindly, I turned away.

"You don't have to be ashamed," Father said. "Do you think I would have mentioned my first girl to you if I were ashamed of it? It's a natural thing, son. The most natural thing in the world."

The gentle tone of his words stopped me. Thinking that he truly did understand, I turned to him and said, "Father. I love her."

"Wonderful," he said. "That's what I'm trying to

tell you. Love her. Enjoy her. Learn from her. Because never again will there be another first time, another first woman. Because she is the first, isn't she?"

My heart was lifting. He was a wise man, a generous man. He had brought me away from Mother so that he could tell me these wise and generous truths.

"Thank you, Father," I said quietly. "When Mother started in on Leslie, I . . ."

"A woman doesn't understand," he said. "No woman, not even your mother. So don't expect understanding."

"Yes, sir," I said.

We were silent while Father smoked his cigar. Then he said musingly, "There's something about this Pass Robin pussy, boy, you won't find anywhere else. They don't have to learn how to fuck. They're *born* knowing. They've got hot blood, and hearts as wide open as a barn door." He leaned toward me. "So take it, son. All of it you can get. Enjoy it. Use it. Learn how to be a man. But . . ." He paused. He was suddenly staring at me through the darkness. "But remember. September, you'll be going back to school for your senior year. And she will be staying here. So it will end. It must end. You will go on to take your place in the world and she will remain behind to yield her ass to other men, to marry one of them eventually and breed a brood of brats."

He stood up. He came to me, putting his hand on my shoulder.

"That's all I'm trying to tell you, son. Fuck her to your heart's content. But, when the time comes, make very sure that it ends. Be content that she will always be a warm and secret memory—and hope fervently that ten years from now, when you are married and bringing your family to Pass Robin for the summer, that you won't meet her on the street and see what she has become."

I knew, now, what he was telling me. "No!" I cried in a strangled voice. "No!" And, crying out wordlessly the third time, my aching throat bursting with a random noise of anguish, I fled away from him.

I knew that Father, in spite of myself, had meant to make me hold you differently in my heart. I don't think he succeeded; or perhaps he did, in subtle but unmistakable ways. He was, after all, only outlining to me the selfsame conditions you had yourself established for our adventure—that September, looming closer with each passing day, was a great wall we could not even hope to climb over. You knew. And he knew. But I did not want to know.

It took a conscious effort to keep my acute awareness of familial disapproval from staining our bright world of water and sky and love and white sand. Every morning, coming down to the boat dock, I willed myself to leave their world utterly behind. And now I have to wonder if you were not doing the same thing, crossing the border between your two worlds without bag or baggage. If this was as true of you as it was of me, then, within the limpid honesty of our love, we were both practicing deception, weren't we? But out of love. Out of love.

Father did not speak again of my errant ways, but went about his daily routine of writing and meditation as though nothing had happened. Mother, more devious and, perhaps, out of her feminine distrust of females, more concerned, was another matter. Having surely sensed that Father's man-to-man talk had ended disastrously, she bided her time for a few days. But

one afternoon, hearing me in the kitchen—I always
came home from our expeditions ravenously hungry—she called me into her studio. She used the back
porch, screened and windowed, as her place of work.
It had a good northern light, and she had furnished it
comfortably as her place in the house.

"I saw your friend yesterday," she said. She was
painting, laying down a background with broad,
smooth strokes, and because she had the easel turned
so the light would fall on it, I could see her only
shadowily against the open windows. "She's a lovely
thing. What did you say her name was?"

I was getting tired of that question. "Leslie," I said.

Mother glanced at me. It was hard to read her face
against the light, but she seemed to be frowning.
Shaking her head slightly, she said, "Are you sure?
Someone told me she was named Lessie Mae."

(Yes, I promised not to use your birth name in this
letter. But because Mother used it as a weapon, I can't
tell this part of the story without it.)

"All right," I said angrily. "She hates that name. Is
there any reason she can't call herself anything she
wants to?"

"No reason at all," Mother said soothingly. "I just
think it's . . . sad, don't you?"

The pineapple sandwich was getting soggy in my
hand. I was afraid it was dripping on the ancient ori-
ental rug that covered this half of the porch floor.
Mother, cocking her head, studied the canvas and laid
down a stroke or two. Then she dropped the brush
into the turpentine can with a clutch of other brushes
and took up a rag to wipe her hands.

"Well, she's so lovely, I can't blame you for falling
for her, whatever her name," she said lightly. "Not

just beauty, either. She has an *interesting* face. Do
you think she'd let me paint her?"

I recoiled from the idea of you and Mother spend-
ing time together in the intimacy of a series of sit-
tings. "No. I don't think she'd like that."

Mother was still wiping at her hands. "Of course, I
haven't done portraits for years. I haven't *wanted* to.
But, if she would sit for me . . . will you ask her for
me, Russell?"

The sandwich was feeling soggier and soggier. I
was desperate to get out of there—besides, if I could
mollify Mother by *seeming* to try . . . after all, I
wouldn't have to mention it, even.

"I'll ask her. But I don't think it'll do any good." I
turned, with an inward sigh of relief, to leave.

"Of course," Mother said thoughtfully, "what I'd
really like to do is paint her in the nude."

"Mother!" I said, so thoroughly scandalized that
the sandwich fell from my nerveless hand. I looked
down at it helplessly.

Mother's tone, ignoring my faux pas, was judi-
ciously professional. "She's not only a very lovely
girl, in an unusual and distinctive way. But just at this
time she's poised between being a girl and becoming a
woman. When that quality is gone, it will be lost forever. If anyone's going to paint her, it ought to be
now—and I mean very quickly, maybe even before
next week." Putting down the turpentine rag, she
came toward me. She looked at the sandwich oozing
pineapple juice on the rug, then at me.

"Ask her for me, Russell. After all, she can only say
no."

"If you think she'll pose naked . . ." I said hotly.
"What kind of girl do you think she is, anyway?"

"I see no reason why she'd mind," Mother said coolly. "After all . . ."

"After all, you're my mother," I said.

She smiled. "I'm a painter. If the sitting is successful, it will go into my fall show. Tell her . . . be sure to tell her that part of it." She hesitated. "Just talk about the portrait first. After she's used to the idea, then you can mention posing in the nude."

"I won't do it," I said. "My God, Mother, what would people think?"

Mother's voice was very soft. "You don't seem to be bothered much by what people might think." She shrugged. "Besides, it's her decision, isn't it? Not yours at all."

"If you want to look at her naked, you'll have to ask her yourself," I said. "I won't do your dirty work for you."

Mother sighed. "All right. I won't insist." She looked down at the sandwich. "What a mess you've made, Russell." Then, as I began to stoop after it, "Leave it alone, you'll only make it worse. I'll clean it up myself."

Blindly, I got out of there.

Foolishly, I believed that I had fended off the danger I sensed in Mother's intense desire to paint you naked—not only in your body but in your soul. But, still intent on cleaning up the mess I had made, she was waiting at the dock the next afternoon when we came in.

"Hello," she said in her most gracious voice. "Did you have a good sail?"

"It was all right," I said mistrustfully.

You were looking at Mother, knowing who she was. She made few concessions to the Gulf Coast heat; today she was wearing not only a dress too heavy and covering but, over it, a painting smock, fingerprinted and smeared from her labors. And Mother was looking at you in your overalls and boy's shirt. Only an hour ago, I was acutely aware, we had been making love. I had a feeling that Mother was thinking the same thing . . . but how could she know?

"So this is Leslie."

"Yes, Mrs. Walford," you said.

A mere male, I stood silently excluded.

"Come up to the house with me, child. I want to talk to you."

She left without waiting to see if you would follow. Without looking at me, you started up the path behind her. I hastily finished with the boat and caught up with you. We walked side by side. You kept your eyes on her figure moving steadily ahead of us. I sought for, but could not find, a means for deterring your obedience to her wishes.

Mother didn't enter by the front door, but took the path around the house. Opening the glassed-in door that led to her painting porch, she went inside. You followed without hesitation. Mother looked at all the chairs in the studio. Choosing one with heavy arms and brocaded seat and backrest, she placed it, at an angle to the window, before a canvas backdrop.

"Sit there, child."

"Mother," I said.

Both of you ignored me. You arranged yourself in the chair. Mother, picking up a piece of charcoal, began making a preliminary sketch. You gazed directly at her until she said, "Look out the window, child, not at me." You turned your head and gave yourself to her seeing eyes.

Anonymous

For two long and silent minutes, Mother worked intensively. Standing poised on the edge of bursting anger, I was restrained by your calm submission. Laying aside the charcoal, Mother stepped back to study what she had done. With satisfied abruptness, she nodded.

"I don't suppose Russell told you I asked to paint you, Leslie," she said.

You looked at me, your eyes wide and green. You looked at her again. You didn't say anything.

"I haven't done a portrait in ten years," Mother said. "I have not wished to do a portrait. Now—I do. Will you sit for me, Leslie? It won't take much of your time, not really. I am very quick when I'm right." She looked at the sketch on the easel. "I can be right with you."

For no more than the tick of a second, you sat still in the chair, the weight of her words on you. Then you got up and walked around the easel to see what she had done. She did not move aside; the two of you, mother and lover, were very close together.

You studied the charcoal sketch. I wanted to see it, too, but I didn't move. You looked into Mother's face. "I'll be very proud to sit for you, Mrs. Walford."

Mother grunted, whether from astonishment or pleasure I could not tell. I wanted to cry out, *Don't, Leslie. Don't, for God's sake.*

You had no idea what you were getting into. She'd have you trapped at least an hour every day—and in that time, I knew instinctively, she would be seeking constantly the way to destroy us. Seeing the danger so clearly, I couldn't understand why you remained serenely unaware.

"All right," Mother said briskly. "Same pose as before. Sit relaxed, and you won't get too tired. Thank goodness you don't have the least tendency to slump. We'll sketch in today, then tomorrow I'll start with oils."

You took your place. She began working. After a few minutes, without turning her head, she said, "Get out of here, Russell. We don't need you."

I sat on the front steps for a time, telling myself I'd go down to the boat and do some work. But I didn't. At last I went upstairs to lie down on the bed. Time passed very slowly. I got up, took a shower, and stretched out again. More time crept by. I kept imagining all that Mother would find to say, the little scars and bruises she could put into your mind. Twice, restlessly, I rose, determined, no matter how much Mother protested, to mount guard in the studio every minute you were there. Each time, realizing the futility of such tactics, I went back to the bed.

But I had a perfect right to make a sandwich, didn't I? I went downstairs into the kitchen, found the bread, laid out two slices. I started to open the refrigerator, then paused, looking toward the studio porch. Moving softly, I went to the door and leaned to listen. Not a sound. I put my hand on the two-way door and pushed. It opened silently. I slid through it sideways. Then—I stopped.

You were naked before my mother. She was not painting, simply looking. One hand on the back of the brocaded chair, you stood fully revealed in the fall of light from the enclosing windows. Your head was turned slightly, your face tilted downward, drooping from your neck; one foot placed behind the other. The nipple of one breast was etched sharply against the light. A horror-struck moment; yet I was sensuously aware of the flowing line of your naked body. I could read, in your shadowed profile and in the line of your neck, the sadness that has ever been an integral element of your loveliness.

Mother, without taking away her eyes, chose a narrow brush and took paint from the palette—she had to look at the palette, but her eyes returned directly to you—and made one long sweeping stroke down the canvas.

The movement jarred me out of stasis. "Mother!" I cried. And then, "Leslie!"

I heard your gasp, read in it the surprise and the horror as you turned toward me. Your lovely belly gleamed, the red gold glint of pubic hair, in the startled arch of discovery. Whirling as suddenly the other way, you darted behind a screen.

Mother sighed, put down her brush. "Well you've ruined it for today. Just when I found the line."

For the first time in my life, I think, my anger was cold instead of hot. "Mother, you didn't have the right to do this."

She avoided my eyes. "What do you mean, *right*? I asked Leslie, and she agreed." She lifted her voice. "You might as well get dressed, child. We'll start again tomorrow."

"But she doesn't know what you're up to," I said, still in that cold anger.

Mother made a small laugh. "Up to? I'm up to painting a picture. Perhaps the best I've done this year."

Wearing your overalls and boy's shirt, you came from behind the screen. Because you had let her do this thing to you, I gazed at you almost in loathing.

Recovered from your startled embarrassment, your eyes met mine innocently.

"Come on, let's get out of here," I said roughly.

I was leaving through the kitchen, the way I had come. You started to follow, but Mother said, her voice a trifle too smooth, "Why don't you use the outside door, Russell? It's so much handier."

I whirled abruptly, bumping into you, and started across the porch. You followed. I was glaring at Mother but she remained oblivious, studying the single line laid down on the canvas. She glanced up at the sound of the latch.

"Tomorrow, Leslie?" she asked. "As soon as you come in from . . . sailing?"

You heard the hesitation, the careful choice of word. But you merely answered, "Yes, Mrs. Walford."

Outside, I grabbed your wrist in a savage grip. "Why did you let her do it to you? Why?"

You gazed at me with those limpid green eyes. "Because she asked me. I didn't see any reason why not."

Baffled, frustrated, angry, the words sputtered in my mouth. "But . . . but . . . you don't know. You don't understand. Mother, she can . . ."

Removing your wrist from my grip, you rubbed it with the other hand. My hard grasp had bruised you. "Besides," you said serenely, "it'll be a much better painting. She'll have to do all of me."

You started around the house. I could only follow. You paused in the front yard, looking at the porch. Then you said, "I want to see what your house looks like inside."

I knew that Mother had deliberately kept me from taking you through the house from the studio porch.

Harshly, I said, "Come on, I'll show you," and led the way up the steps.

Though you must have read Mother's subtle prohibition also, you were completely at ease as you studied with care each room in turn; the living room, the small parlor off the other side of the hallway that was seldom used. You lingered longest in the dining room, so quietly elegant with its mahogany furniture, the gleam of silver and glass, in the afternoon shadows.

The door to Father's den opened. Looking quickly from me to you and back again, he grunted, whether of greeting or sheer surprise I couldn't tell.

"Father," I said. "This is Leslie."

He gazed at you. When his eyes came back to me, a gleam of envy showed plainly. For being young. For having, in my youth, enjoyed you in your youth. "Yes. Well." He lifted the papers in his hand in a gesture, turned to disappear.

"Mother is painting Leslie," I said carefully.

His eyes showed surprise, just for the flash of a second. Then, and I think wholly against his will, he looked at you again before he closed the door.

I was gratified by that encounter. Who wouldn't be?

Every day for three weeks, except Saturday and Sunday, you posed for Mother. As soon as we returned from sailing you would go on up to the house while I remained behind to TLC the boat. I would then come up, but only to fix a sandwich or two and go directly to my room. The sitting over, you left alone; I would lift my head when I heard the studio door open and close, and then I would come to the window to watch you walk down the slope, moving so wholly within yourself that never once did you look up to see me watching you.

I persisted in probing into the matter, but to no avail; you refused to discuss what, if anything, you and Mother talked about during the sitting. Every time I asked, you said she spoke only to tell you to rest for a moment, or to ask for a slightly different exposure. After much insistence on this truth, I decided the painting itself must be the weapon. So I wanted you to talk about the painting. But you replied, with the same quietness, that Mother had forbidden you to look at it until it was finished, saying it would only, by making you self-conscious, spoil the line. So I could only wait and watch.

When the painting was finished, you came no more to the house. The episode was ended, apparently without damage to our relationship, and I was content to leave it so. I never asked what you thought of Mother's work, though I knew, there at the end, you had viewed it. You did not volunteer your reaction. As for me—when Mother asked me to look at it, I refused. I couldn't take the risk of seeing you through my mother's eyes.

(You know, of course, that the painting was the hit of Mother's next New York show. Purchased on preview night, at a price that permanently raised the value of her work. *Leslie* quickly became a key canvas in her oeuvre. I saw it for the first time in Mother's retrospective at the Whitney two years after her death. A remarkable piece of work; in my opinion the best she ever did. So remarkably real, so remarkably kind. A painter's eye can be cruel, I know, but her eye was not cruel on you. She had caught with breathtaking accuracy the serenity and the sadness that shielded so beautifully your hard-held inwardness of self. She saw you truly, but with extraordinary kindness, showing in the lines of your body the faint reticences of girlhood ripened to the moment in time of becoming woman. Each element of your character was so tentatively balanced, one against the other, that it made a sudden ache in my throat for the lovely, tentative girl I had once known. I came to see it every day throughout the show; and on the last day I remembered at last the words you had spoken that had ended my frantic probing once and for all. I had said, "Don't you know what she can do to you? Don't you *know*?" and you had gazed upon me in that baffling serenity and replied, "She is a painter. So she can only paint what she sees.")

Becoming daily more aware of the insurmountable fact of September, looming higher and higher on the horizon of our love, we avoided talking about it. But more and more often you would go unpredictably into a mood of intense happiness, gay and laughing and loving; in the next minute your green eyes would be filled with shadows and the corners of your mouth would droop so unconsciously that it made my heart ache.

Intensity of feeling entered also into our lovemaking, the act becoming almost frantic as we strove to achieve a fulfillment that would somehow endure in us forever. Such striving, so incapable of surfeit, left in our flesh an eroding dissatisfaction, me with you and you with me, so that our coupling had lost its gentle and loving quality. Sometimes we seemed to be fighting each other instead of making love. So often now, instead of cradling my head with stroking hands, you quickly got out from under me, to sit aside within yourself.

One day, near the end of August, you said out of a long silence, "I wish I could leave Pass Robin when you do."

"Why can't you?"

"If I left now, I'd have to work as a waitress, something like that. I have to stay here until I finish high school."

"What kind of work will you be able to do then?"

"I'm taking typing." You straightened, looking at me. "I'm fast and I'm accurate. And, once I get a job, I can go to night school, learn shorthand . . ."

"So you want to work in an office."

You moved your shoulders impatiently. "I just want out of this town. And that's the quickest way."

I was depressed with the suddenly nearer reality of September. "But listen," I said. "You won't graduate until next June. I'll be here only a week after that." I was watching you now. "We could have all summer again, if you . . ."

Your voice was flat. "But you won't be back. You promised."

"I know I promised," I said. "But . . ."

You were gazing out over the water. "It would just be another summer, and then you'd be leaving again. And I'd still be here, wouldn't I?" Your whole body moved angrily under the impact of your thought.

"Listen." My voice was suddenly eager. "I'll be starting college after next summer. No reason why I can't go ahead and start with summer school. You could come there, wherever it is, and there are always a lot of office jobs in a college town." I was suddenly triumphant. "That way, I would keep my promise, and you'd be gone from Pass Robin." My voice came more harshly into my throat. "We could be together."

You looked at me. Your eyes were very green. "We can't even think about it. Because September is a promise, too."

Getting to your feet, you walked out into the water. After a few steps you launched yourself like an arrow, going straight out with rapid strokes. I sat watching. You went far out, and stayed for a long time.

Separation once spoken of, the time of departure seemed to rush upon us. Something had speeded up the universe, and with heartbreaking suddenness the next-to-last day was upon us. It was framed by three separate couplings, each more frantic than the last. I sought in you a climax that would last forever; it was not there, you could not give it to me. And you—you had not found even the first orgasm, much less the last, for neither of us, in our innocence, knew that it was possible. But your flesh, like mine, was striving for something to hold onto during the barren future.

We came in quiet and tired, and so late that the sun was setting. Silently I set about washing down the boat, thinking sadly that if tomorrow wasn't any better we might as well say good-bye right now.

You must have shared the dismal thought, for you said, "Russell. I don't want to see you tomorrow."

Immediately agitated by the prospect of losing our last hours together, I said, "You have to, Leslie. We can't . . ."

Unsmiling, you shook your head. "Not tomorrow. Tomorrow night. All night long."

The revolutionary concept slammed into me like a

fist. Assiduously maintaining the fiction of summer sports, sailing and swimming and sunbathing, we had never been together in the dark.

I said uncertainly, "Can you . . . Won't your people . . . won't they *know*?"

You tossed your head. "I don't care." Coming close, you put your hand on my forearm. Your eyes were glowing greenly. "There'll be a big moon, Russell. We'll have the whole night, alone on our island."

Unable to face the brilliance of your desire, I looked out toward our sanctuary. "There won't be any breeze, more than likely."

Your warm hand went away. "You're afraid. Of your parents."

I couldn't bear the insinuation. "Hell no, I'm not afraid. I'll do it if you will. But . . ." I hesitated, feeling it suddenly, recklessly possible. "I'll have to borrow a little motor."

Your hand was on my arm again, the grip suddenly fierce. "If we have to, we'll paddle the boat."

The entire morning was devoted to the search for a small outboard. I spent the afternoon trying to make it run for more than a few minutes at a time. Finally, in desperation, I lugged it to the marina to have the spark plug replaced and the carburetor adjusted. Exhausted, I ate a silent dinner. Mother and Father were silent, too, though they seemed concerned. When I left the house to go down to the boat, Father said after me, "Where are you going off to, Russell?"

I turned around. "We're leaving tomorrow, aren't we?" I didn't wait for his reply. I didn't care what they thought.

You were waiting, coming up out of the day cabin the moment my weight rocked the boat. In the touch of your hand I sensed a different level of love and meaning. We didn't speak, but went quickly to work to get under way.

The boat had no running lights, so we moved ghostly through the darkness betrayed only by the put-put-put of the three-horsepower motor. It made everything seem unreal to have the sound of the motor in our ears, to breathe the stink of gasoline. By the time we were halfway to the island, the moon began to show a full golden glow on the horizon. You were sitting close against me, warm and still. When the moon was above the horizon, showing us plainly the black bulks of the three islands, you raised one arm, pointing, and said, "Let's don't go to our island tonight. Let's go there instead." You had chosen the island most seaward of the three. I didn't question your decision, but swung the boat to make a landing on the other side.

Running the boat straight in toward shore, I cut the motor and quickly tilted the propeller out of the water. The boat grounded, grating softly against the sand. You were suddenly out of the boat and running away up the beach. Astonished, I stood up and yelled, "Hey!" but you paid no heed. Hastily I pulled the boat, set out the anchor firmly, and trotted after you. Even with the moonlight, I couldn't find you. But suddenly you came, naked and running, to catapult into my arms, holding me with a fierce strength as though something had frightened you.

"What's the matter?" I said, alarmed by these strange actions.

You clung to me. "Oh, love me tonight, Russell. Love me, love me good."

I began to laugh. "You know I love you good."

YOU

Laughing with me, you began to unbutton my shirt. "It's not fair, me naked and you not. Get it off."

I shed the shirt and took off my pants and shorts, dropping them in the sand. For a single moment, we gazed at each other. I had not seen you in moonlight. It gleamed silver against the slant of your belly, made dark and mysterious the sweet nest of pubic hair, it struck a gleam across the thrust of your breasts. I reached for you but you whirled away, fleeing, in the same startled moment, leaving behind only a silver ribbon of laughter.

You were showing me tonight a girl I had not known. Always hiding our nakedness in the cabbage palms, we had never romped and laughed openly on the beach. I stood watching you run, marveling at the stranger I would love tonight, and knowing suddenly how perfect it would be now, how right you had been to make our farewell in the moonlight and darkness. When I began to chase you, I had such an erection I could run only awkwardly.

You were impossible to capture. The first time I caught you, your lithe body twisted in my arms like an eel escaping my frantic grasp. You ran in the shallow edge of the water, throwing spray as bright and silver as your laughter. I caught you again, and again you wriggled free, even after I had tumbled us both to the earth. At last, exhausted, my hard-on finished from the exertion, I sat panting on the sand. You crept to me then, huddling in my arms to lay your head against my chest. We held each other tightly. I put my hand on your breast and you responded by somehow getting closer and smaller against me.

Suddenly, with a yelp, you slapped at yourself. In the same instant, I felt a fiery sting on my thighs, and simultaneously on my back. I slapped, as frantically as you, saying breathlessly, "Mosquitos! We forgot about mosquitoes." We both plunged to our feet, dancing in agony. The saltwater mosquitoes, vicious in their gnawing ferocity, were a swarming cloud around our naked bodies. "Into the water," I yelled. We ran together, splashing in until all but our heads were covered. Even then we had to duck under until they quit hovering hungrily over our heads.

We stood together, arms around each other's waist, half treading water. "Well, I guess that's that," I said glumly. "I didn't think about the darn mosquitoes."

"I ought to have," you admitted. You were silent for a moment. "Don't you have any citronella on the boat?"

In my mind I went over, item by item, the clutter inside the day cabin. "I think there's a bottle. I don't know whether it's empty or not."

"Let's go see."

We swam down toward the boat. I left you neck-deep in the water while I climbed aboard. I had prudently stowed a flashlight with fresh batteries; I found it and began searching. "Got it," I yelled triumphantly. "It's nearly full, too."

You waded in to meet me on the beach. Hastily at first, then with more care, we smeared each other with the ill-smelling stuff. I began to enjoy the sensation of your hands all over me, the silken texture of your skin under my palms. By the time we were finished, we were making love as much as protecting ourselves from the ravenous insects.

You put your nose against my chest, sniffing. "Oh, don't we smell wonderful, though?" you said, laughing again. The laughter ended in a sudden throaty murmur and your hand, greasy from the repellent, suddenly sought my erection. Putting my arms around you, I laid you back gently on the sand. You were still holding on, with both hands now; you had not done that before, you had always been shy of touching me there. I put one leg over your hips. You turned toward me, lifting your leg, reaching with your whole body even as you guided my tool with your hand.

"Wait a minute," I said. "The rubbers are in my pants. Let me ..."

"Be still," you whispered. "I want to feel you naked in me."

I pulled away in alarm. "Leslie! We can't ..."

Your loins were reaching hungrily. "I want to ... I've got to feel you ..."

I couldn't let you do it. I rolled away. "It won't take but a minute to get them. I promise. No more than a minute."

You subsided into inertia. You were on your back, your legs spread. You were looking up at the moon. You didn't say anything until I stood up. Your head shifted to look at me. "You can put it in naked without moving or anything, can't you? So I can feel it like that, for once?"

I was worried. "You think we ought to? It's pretty risky ..."

You were still looking at me. No, not at me. At my maleness, standing in rigid profile. "But you won't come if you hold still. Please, Russell. Just for a minute."

I was dubious. Just the thought of being naked in your naked flesh was bringing me close to the edge. "I'll try. If you want to. But, Leslie ..."

Your voice came in a whisper. "I can't let you go
without knowing what you feel like, really and truly
in me, naked and hard and hot . . ." You shivered suddenly, all over, and your knees lifted.

I could have resisted if your body hadn't been begging, too. But now I had to have it; I was captured,
also, by the ecstatic idea. However, I forced myself to
be careful, going into you very slowly until I heard
your delicious sigh of satisfaction. Even then I held
myself against quickening. The muscles of my thighs
were taut with the effort of holding still.

God. All this long summer of careful lovemaking,
flesh had not truly tasted flesh. Your vagina, hot and
moist and faintly pulsing, tempered against my naked
blade, your moisture was both strong and sweet. We
were both trembling, in a delicious small quivering. I
raised my head to look into your face. Your eyes
came to meet mine, and I drowned in them. The
moonlight full on your face, I could see the trembling
of your mouth, the sparkle of wetness on your eyelashes.

"Oh God," you whispered. "Yes."

I did not understand what began, then, for it had
not happened before. Without outside movement,
from me or from you, your vagina started fucking
my penis, a tiny, passionate hand gripped delicately
around the head of my prick and pulsing in tiny milking motions. You could feel yourself doing it, your
eyes were greedy to see in my face the effect it was
having on me. We seldom kissed in the act of love,
but your mouth was as soft and warm and ready as a
second vagina. I put my mouth on it and that was
fucking, too, in tune with the primal fucking; and

now, as we had not known before, we knew what kissing could be.

I had no strength to resist you, I accepted gratefully that great love even though with each pulse of your uterus I was brought nearer to the point of peril when I would no longer be able to keep myself from coming. But then safeguarding love burgeoned in me, alone with the lust, for you began something else, something also new, a deep-laid response of your own that almost frightened me. In gritted determination, I began to withdraw. Laying your legs over the calves of my legs, you gripped both hands into my shoulders, holding me inside you.

"I'm going to lose it," I whispered in agony.

"Lose it," you whispered. "I want it. Let it come."

The tiny suction of your vagina had ceased, allowing me to ebb a slight margin toward sanity. "I can't let you do it, Leslie," I said making a determined effort to get out.

You held me. "Russell. Do you love me?"

I stared into your moon-clear face. Our bodies, so deeply wedded, were slick, moist, from the mosquito repellent. I could smell the strong odor of citronella made pungent by the heat of our flesh.

"I love you enough not to . . ."

"Do you love me enough to quit thinking about me? To quit thinking about yourself? To think only of fucking?"

"But Leslie, you're the one! What if, this very last time, I put a baby in you?"

Your eyes went away, gazing deep into night sky. "Then that would mean I wasn't meant to leave Pass Robin, wouldn't it?" Your face changed. "But if I didn't get knocked up it'd be a sign . . ."

You looked into my face again, in your eyes a reckless boldness. Then it swept your whole body and you were suddenly writhing under me, engrossed in an intricately voluptuous pattern that could have only one ending point. Until tonight you had dared this only with my twirling finger.

Your lips peeled back in something that was half a smile, half a grimace. "Now try to take it away from me. Just try it."

You need not have issued the challenge. My flesh had already surrendered to the gasping moil of your fevered desire; I began to fuck, hips pounding against the writhing rise of your hips, so that they slapped together like a pair of hands. I laughed breathlessly when your head strained back, your lips peeling harshly to bare your teeth. We burst simultaneously into each other, your orgasm as frantic and forthright as my own. There were no more shields between you and yourself. As there were no shields between us.

Ebbing slowly out of that first great peak you had succeeded in climbing, you lay quietly under me at last, my head cradled gently in your cherishing arms. But there were, deep within, continuing spasms and reminiscences. Only when that, too, had come to an end did you speak.

"So that's it," you said, sighing. Then, your face shadowed, "And we found it only on the last night."

My arms tightened around you. "Please don't be sad."

You smiled quickly. "Who's sad, Russell? You'll fuck me again, won't you? Again, and then again. So there's nobody sad around here."

I have no idea how many times, that night, I brought you to orgasm. Time after time, after time, you began building it, down deep inside yourself, and brought it gasping and writhing to the surface. It was as though behind a secret door was stored all the orgasms you had failed to liberate all the long summer; now, one by one by one, they were let free to romp in your flesh, and in mine. For I came too, over and over again, more times than would seem possible, I am sure; for you were, all through that seeming eternity of blissful lovemaking, not only my lovely Leslie but also that strange girl—woman—you had revealed to me tonight. Wild in exuberant passion, you coupled and laughed, you demanded and you surrendered, in such a bewildering alternation of moods and hungers I could scarcely keep up with you.

In between, we romped on the beach, we swam, after swimming we tenderly consoled each other with citronella—and the odor of citronella is mingled inextricably with my memories of that time, so that even now a whiff of it will bring you erotically into my senses—and then seguing from the practical and sensuous rubbing of each other's skin into a newly refreshed and passionate embrace.

At the end, when the sun was threatening the eastern horizon with its first faint pinkness of light, we stood naked at the edge of water, holding hands, and gazed seaward. Our flesh was quiet, our love was large within us.

"We ought to take the boat and head south," I said. "It'd take some dodging around, but we could sail all the way to Australia if we wanted to." I turned my head, smiling. "Why don't we do it?"

Your eyes did not come to me in response, but remained fastened on the southern horizon. "Better yet, why don't we swim it?" You turned, not toward me but away, saying wearily, "Come on. Let's go home."

. . . And so this letter comes to an end, as we came to an end, hand in hand at the edge of deep water. I wonder if there will be an answer. Or have I dropped it into an emptiness without echo?

THE
SECOND
LETTER
to
him

Today your letter came. My first impulse was to throw it away unread; too bulky in the envelope not to have things in it I don't want to think about. Once having thought about them, I'd have to do something, wouldn't I? Wasn't that the intent behind your writing?

But—I am a woman. I have read your letter twice, and I don't know what it is you want me to do about these things you have made me remember. So I am choosing your remedy—I am writing a letter.

You wrote almost too well to be truthful. Surely we were not so young—surely the long days of that long summer were not the most beautiful days the world, and we, have lived through. But the truth is there in your words—not simply your truth, which

115

was only to be expected, but mine also. You were so painfully fair, darling. You remember those days too well; you saw them, and yourself, and me, far more clearly and honestly than I would have believed. It was exactly as I feared, the moment I held the heavy envelope with the gaudy foreign stamps in my hand—there was the pain of sadness in the reading as much as the happiness of remembering. Remembered pain and new pain—remembered happiness and new happiness. A potent emotional cocktail for a lady alone.

I must also tell you that there is much you did not know. I don't want to go back over that same ground—your memory of it, and your telling, can serve for us both—but I must tell you this much, at least.

I loved you, in spite of myself, the first day I saw you. The brightest, most vivid memory in my mind is that of you, there on your little boat with Bill, so tall and gangly and embarrassed and shy that it made my heart ache. You wrote that I didn't look at you. I may not have looked, but I *saw*—and that deep, uncontrollable, female thing in my heart elected you by unanimous vote.

Now, so quickly, I have surprised you, haven't I? Perhaps you will hesitate, wondering whether to read this heavy letter in response to yours. Perhaps you should not, and shall not. So I may well be writing for myself alone.

You see, Russell, the world to me, has always been divided into those who are my people and those who are not. My psychiatrist, in the years I had a psychiatrist, used to tell me such a concept was nothing but an ego trip. I'm sure he was right—but no matter. I don't mean that "my people" are those I love, or who love me. It is, at least, not that simple. My people are those who, I know instinctively, are vulnerable to me in any of several complex ways—my sex, my looks, my needs, my love, my friendship. Their vulnerability, of course, makes me also vulnerable—but only in a controlled and measured response I can always count on being able to handle. Bill was one of these, for example—and, strangely enough, your mother.

All those others who are "not my people" simply do not exist in my world. I armor myself against them, I walk among them unscathed. In a very direct and emotional way I feel myself invisible. For they cannot touch me.

You should have been one of my people. But you were not—and yet I was not invisible to you. From the first instant when I did not look at you as you sat on the boat gazing in such brash and awkward self-consciousness, you were a new species of animal in my world. Not only were you dangerously unpredictable—I was, in myself, unpredictable where you were concerned. All that long summer, Russell—yes, and long afterward, until I had put you entirely out of me—I did not know from one minute to the next what I would do, what I would say, what I would feel.

Russell, I knew as well as if I had heard the words what Bill was telling you about me. Just as I knew who you were, that you lived in the beautiful old summer bungalow with the moss-green roof. I envisioned you, with your famous parents, moving in far-off and fabulous surroundings, among far-off and fabulous people. So I was very much aware that you were *there*, so serious and shy, so ugly and so beautiful in your awkward gangliness. In that first minute, without impulse or foreknowledge, my secret heart elected you to be the one. That, my darling, is what you didn't know even at the writing of your letter. You had not the least chance of escaping my love.

Nor I. For a long time—ever since I was twelve—I had held clear in my secret thoughts the male wearing the first cock I would allow myself to know. I have always had that habit, that fault, of *planning* people, shaping how they will enter into my life, how long they will dwell within me, and the manner of their departure. A shabby little defense mechanism, my psychiatrist used to say, designed to protect myself against the unpredictability of people—and destined to fail, because people cannot be programmed.

I think he was wrong. I believe the mechanism was designed to protect me against myself—my basic uncontrollability, my errant and erratic impulses, my needs and hungers. Without it operating constantly in aid of my basic and most deepest need, I would never have escaped from Pass Robin, I would never have been *free*.

So my prior choice was always held clearly in mind. At first, of course, at twelve and thirteen, I elected movie stars to that office of service. Practical reality soon intervened, however, and they became real candidates, actual possibilities. For a time, I must tell you, it was Bill—though Bill, no more than any of the others, did not know it. During another period, when the fumbling insistence of boys only disgusted me, it was older, married men who would know what they were about. And then—it was you.

But not through any choice of my own—it was spontaneous, unexpected, and unalterable. It was frightening. So, on our first day together, when you tried to make Bill's whispered lies the truth, I hated you. Not because you tried—after all, you were not the first to try—but because I was so dangerously vulnerable. I knew, very well and very truly, that at any minute I might recklessly make Bill's lies come true. If you had been sure enough, competent enough, I could never have denied you—and myself.

But I'm going into it now, retelling with my own slants and meanings the story you told so well. I don't need to do that—I want to devote this reply to the succeeding events.

Your letter made me so glad. It hurt, in places, and very deeply. I cried once or twice—and it has been a very long time since I have been able to cry. But when I gaze back over those long reaches of time, when I . . .

No. This is how I must begin. Because you are a man, it will baffle you, and then it will hurt a little. Maybe more than a little—but let me tell the truth of myself, as you told the truth of yourself, and where you must stop reading, then stop. Please stop.

You had not been gone a week before I let Bill make love to me.

Now I will try to tell you why. Not the *why* as I knew it then, but as I know it only now, after reading your lovely letter.

I don't know whether men, in their youth, elect candidates, as I did, or simply yearn, as they seem to, for every random girl that passes their way. Bill, certainly, had elected me so long ago that it was beyond memory. Seemingly, he had always been there, waiting patiently for the hour of my consent. He must have made the choice the first time he ever saw me, when I was six and he was eight. His mother, I remember, came visiting my mother one day, bringing him along. Marching into the living room, he put his arms around me and tried to kiss me. I was so flustered I began to cry—not because of Bill, so much, but because my mother and his mother were laughing. When Bill's mother rescued me, scolding at him, Bill said, "But, Mama, she's so pretty."

For the brief span of two weeks, Bill had been also my deliberate choice. That's when I let him kiss me, once, after a school dance. I think Bill knew that he had had it and then, somehow, it had slipped away— and that is why he began to hate me, why he marked me forever in that town with his bragging tongue. His hatred grew worse when he knew that one Russell Walford, his old sailing buddy, was the successful candidate. We knew it, too, that first day, as clearly as I, for he knew me so well. You were the innocent and ignorant bystander.

So why, you must ask, did I allow Bill to follow you into me?—and so soon after. I can only tell you this: when Bill came to the house the very next Saturday night after your family's departure, wearing a suit and tie for the second time I could remember—the first had been the school dance—and asked me solemnly and formally before my parents to go to the movies with him, standing there in the doorway, looking into his dogged, earnest face, I understood within myself that Bill would achieve his heart's desire.

Why? you ask again. Of course. The why, I think, begins with the bargain I made with God ... no. Before then. Long before.

I have always valued myself. Seemingly, I was born

believing that my fate must count in the scheme of the universe. My earliest memory is the vivid idea I found in my head that I had been stolen away from my true parents. I didn't belong to these people at all, they were holding me captive, and living a daily lie to make me believe that I was blood of their blood. I daydreamed for hours at a time how my real mother and father would come one day to take me away. I had it worked out in detail, even to the color—a deep coral shade—of the beautiful dress my mother would wear, and how handsome and elegant my father would be. Picking their way disdainfully down the path from the dirt road, they would stand imperiously on the cluttered porch, Ben Dollard cringing before them. Contemptuously, my father would give him money instead of the punishment he richly deserved, and then Ben Dollard would scrape and bow, while false mama simpered with astonishment. I would walk away forever between my real father and my real mother, each with a protective hand on a shoulder; and so I would be rescued.

In time I came to know, of course, that it was only fantasy. Yet it remained unreal to be a Dollard. I could not even believe the ugly name they had given me; I found my true name in my heart and cherished it secretly. You were the first person in the world to whom I spoke my true name.

When I grew old enough to begin moving out from family to town, Pass Robin was equally unreal. The children I went to school with, the people on the streets—I moved among them invisibly, armored against all they could hope to do to me. I was too valuable and unique, destined to escape from Pass

Robin and become my true self. Though I did not
know, yet, what my true self should be.

Somehow your love, that summer, served to certify
my value. The son of a summer family known and respected for both ancestry and achievement; a boy
who went to a wonderful faraway school instead of
dwelling in the grubby halls of Pass Robin grammar
and high school; you, in your marvelously awkward
earnestness, saw me as I perceived myself, a person of
depths and value and meaning.

So that, when you went away—as I had known you
would go, I had to make you go if you wouldn't of
your own free will—I lost abruptly that total sense of
myself. I was only another hot-blooded Pass Robin
girl, pushed on her back by a summer boy and fucked
to a fare-thee-well—and grateful for the favor. In your
private school, so fabulous and faraway, you would
talk about me in the winter nights, and would revel
gloatingly in the envy of the other boys. And when
you found one day, as you would surely find, a cool,
elegant girl of your own kind, I would not even be a
memory.

There was also the bargain I had made with God—
or Something—on our last night together. Until then,
though you were a new species I didn't know how to
handle, I had held rigorously to my self-imposed limits. Deliberately making September the final bound-
ary, I would not, could not, allow the least possibility
beyond that fatal time.

Yet, when we came to the ending, I could not re-
strain myself from an utterly desperate attempt to encompass it all. So I made my bargain. I could, for
these few hours, forget my valuable self. I would wal-
low in the sensuality of surrender. And this night

would be a sign. If I was fated to waste all my days in Pass Robin, your seed would grow in me. If my womb emerged unscathed from our great abandon, it would be a glorious confirmation of my dream of escape.

Daring the bargain, I was free at last, within the limited scope of one night, to love you, to cherish you, to desire you, as I had not let myself do before. I wanted—I even accepted the wanting—to lose the bargain; I yearned to feel your seed planted in me. I would gladly have given the dream of a lifetime to cherish your child as I cherished you.

You wrote so truly of that night, Russell. Reading, I experienced all over again that first wonderful naked penetration of your maleness. All our summer days had been only foreplay to get me ready for the moment. Sick with ecstasy, my flesh quivered with the impact, so soft and so hard, so utterly real because you were naked in me. I dared God and nature that night—and when Bill stood in the presence of my parents, wearing his navy blue suit and his red tie and his solemn dignity, I did not know, yet, whether I had won or lost. I felt strongly in my flesh that, following not fate but my own deepest desire, I had been given the sign. Your seed, I truly believed, was planted in me, growing secretly even now, and so I belonged to Pass Robin, Pass Robin belonged to me. All my great dreams, all my rich valuation, had been a deceit practiced upon me by self and by God.

First of all, Bill had to demonstrate his new car. With a proud modesty, he told me he had gone to work for his father early in the summer, had saved every penny of his apprentice wages against the down payment. I remember that car. It was a black Chevrolet, with five years of hard traveling mirrored in its condition. But Bill had waxed and polished until the metal glowed with a remarkable luster; the interior was clean and neat, spoiled only by a faint odor of burning oil seeping in from the old engine. He was proud of it beyond belief—indeed, he must have felt that my ready acceptance of his invitation was the first triumph accruing to its possession.

He drove carefully, telling me all the while how she would open up, even daring to suggest that we would go out on the highway after the movie so he could demonstrate. Then, pulling back from enthusiasm, he carefully informed me he didn't plan to go back to school. What good would it do him to graduate? He could learn his father's trade, as he was already doing, and make money at the same time. Pretty soon I'd see him driving a brand-new car. He did not look at me as he said, "A carpenter makes good money, and there's always plenty of work. That's what I aim to do, Lessie Mae, so I might as well get started. The sooner I get started, the quicker I can . . ." He was too shy to say the rest of it. And I was too silent.

I tried to conceal my depression as he escorted me proudly into the theater to a gratifying rustle of attention. The reaction came not because of his limited vision—Bill, I knew, would be a valuable workman in his chosen trade, and for him it was a fulfillment, not a surrender to the circumstances of his life—but because of his terrible happiness on achieving a formally recognized date with me. He bought popcorn, and I let him hold my hand throughout the picture. I was glad of the convention of moviegoing. It meant I didn't have to seek inside my emptiness for a response to his enthusiasm.

Afterward, he suggested a milk shake. A certain anxiety, showing subtly through his generosity, made me understand that he was straining his budget. When I said I didn't want a milk shake, his face cleared.

"Come on then, let's drive around for a while. OK?"

"OK," I said.

He pretended to be driving randomly, even going out to the highway first to open up the old car until it was straining and rattling and the smell of burning oil came hotly into the passenger compartment. I knew all along he meant to park and pet, unless I could succeed in laying down a firm prohibition. But, when he nosed the car into a grove of water oaks a mile inland, I didn't say anything.

He sat looking straight ahead, his thick hands holding the steering wheel. "This is where all the summer kids park." His voice showed the tension inside him. Clearing his throat, he turned his head to look at me. "I reckon you know all about it, though. I reckon you've been out here with Russell."

"Russell didn't have a car," I said. "We just went sailing, all that."

"I imagine old Russell showed you a high time all summer, didn't he?"

An ugly note had sounded inside the words. I didn't try to answer him. He waited a minute; then, with daredevil determination, he put an arm over my shoulders. When I didn't resist, he pulled me toward him. I sat unresponsive in the circle of his embrace. It was hot in the car—the windows were up against the mosquitoes—and the smell of oil was heavy in my nostrils. Bill would be obliged to spend a great deal of his hard-earned money on oil to keep his beloved automobile running.

"Well, I've been waiting a pretty long time for my second kiss," he said, a rough edge showing in his voice. He was beginning to believe I *wanted* to be with him.

I didn't say anything. He waited. He shifted again, reached his other hand across me, turned my chin. I let him kiss me. It might have been a child's mouth on mine for all the feeling it gave me. He quit kissing me. We sat there in the darkness.

I could see the future laid out in front of us the way Bill wanted it. We would date regularly once a week, probably every Saturday night because that was the day he got paid, most often to see a movie. After the movie we would park. He would kiss me. He would try to put his hand on my breast. I wouldn't let him. We would kiss some more and the next week, when he put his hand on my breast, I would not move it away. Gradually, date by date, he would earn the right to fondle my naked breast. By that time I'd have to be thinking about it, wouldn't I? So when he made the try to touch me between the legs my defense would be fainthearted. And again, date by date and inch by inch, I would yield my body to his probing hand until at last I would lie back spread legged in the seat and let him relieve my panting need. I would go home half satisfied, he would go home with the stone ache.

So, at long last, at the point where I couldn't help myself any longer, I'd have to let him put it in me—all against my feeble female will—and so he would have finally conquered me. From then on he could have me any time he wanted, for I would belong to him. In the end he might even marry me—especially if I could contrive to get knocked up.

I sat up straight within the prison of his arm. You were still in me, my sweet love, your seed was surely growing in my womb, and I ached with the memory of your lovely maleness so hard and pumping—flooding me with the seed I had lusted for as passionately as I had lusted for the instrument of implantation. I had struck my bargain with God and I had lost. Bill, my fate in Pass Robin, had been waiting with the enormous patience of that stolid, limited boy who had chosen me when I was six years old.

But I could not—not for my sake, but for his own—allow him to believe that we were safely cradled now in the Pass Robin courting routine, so conventional and secure. For myself, though September had come, you were alive in me yet. By my own metes and bounds of love, you could not remain.

"Lessie Mae . . ." Bill said.

"Bill," I said, "do you have anything?"

I felt him stiffen against the blunt implication. He had painted me in Pass Robin legend as the easiest lay in town, but out of all Pass Robin he had not believed it. He had been prepared to love me honestly. But now—the change in him was subtle but unmistakable. I had unscrewed it and tossed it over to him. He was a man, wasn't he?—only something less than a man could refuse the gift of a piece of ass.

"Sure," he said, leaning to tap the door of the glove department. "Right in there."

"Will you be careful?" I said.

"Baby, I wouldn't knock you up for anything," he said. Then he put his hands on me.

I opened my legs. His thick, meaty hand, trembling, closed against my crotch, squeezing so hard that it hurt. He leaned against me, his face against my neck, and I listened to his hard breathing as his hand found its way under my pants. Though I was braced for it, when his finger came into me it was an astonishing violation. I pumped suddenly against his hand, then pulled away.

"Come on," I said. "Let's get into the back seat."

He didn't want to let me go until he had made sure of me. He knew, as all Pass Robin males, that once a woman has touched a man's erection she can't help herself. So, taking out his organ, he put my hand on it. I didn't resist, but let my fingers close. He was so different from you, darling. It was like a blunt, thick club in my cold hand. I forced my fingers into motion, teaching my flesh that I meant to let it enter into me, there where your seed dwelled. Suddenly in a hurry, he opened the car door, saying impatiently, "Come on. Come on."

Getting out of the car, I stood waiting, looking up at the sky, while he fumbled in the glove compartment. I couldn't see the sky, though; the trees were black overhead and there was not even a moon. Bill came to my side and politely opened the back door. Turning, I sat down on the edge of the seat cushion, stripping down my pants as I did so. I watched Bill putting on the rubber. I couldn't see him clearly in the darkness, but I knew the motions. When he came to me, I stopped him with a hand on his chest, saying, "Put on another one."

"What?" he said.

"I won't do it unless you wear two," I said. "One might break."

If there was going to be a baby, I had to know it was yours. But there was also, beyond that, a cruelness in the command. Poor Bill was suitably obedient. I watched him put on the second rubber, then lay back on the seat cushion, lifting my dress to bare my bottom. He came heavily on me, trying to stab me with his weapon. But we were not right; I had never made love in a car and I didn't know how. I had to slide back on the cushion, then slide back again, with Bill hunching after me, until my head was butted against the other door.

I couldn't make myself open to him. It was not just the cramped rear seat, the hot darkness, the smell of burned oil. I was holding you safe in me, I couldn't make myself let you go out of me and leave room for Bill. He banged and sweated and grunted, his thick tool bruising against my mount. He hadn't even taken off his suit coat, or loosened his tie. Taking charge, I tried to accommodate him, but it only frustrated him so that he swore at me in an angry, snarling voice. At last, by sheer stubborn persistence, his thick, twice-sheathed organ found me, pried me open inch by inch until he was wedged into my tight tunnel. He lay still, panting. I could feel it in me, but with the doubled safety between his seed and your seed it didn't feel like a man's living instrument, only a thick, cold piece of meat.

When he put his mouth on my mouth, I turned my head away. Stubbornly, stolidly, he began, banging his hips against my hips with an unvarying persistence so much like him that suddenly I wanted to cry. But I couldn't feel anything, I was cramped and sweaty and uncomfortable, I could only keep my head turned aside while I endured him. It went on for a long time, and when he came, I could scarcely sense that he had reached his orgasm. I knew it was over only when his laboring body collapsed its full weight, smothering me into the cushions, seat cushions, and I had to struggle suddenly to get air.

He wouldn't let me go. Clutching at me with both hands, he said, "You shouldn't have let me, Lessie Mae. I wanted to love you, I've loved you all my life. You shouldn't have let me."

He was crying. His head was buried in my shoulder, his whole body was shaking, I could feel the wetness of his tears on my neck. I couldn't help myself, I had to put my arms around his head, I had to hold him, stroking his hair while he wept and trembled, and I knew for the first time the enormous sadness a woman can feel for a man who has bled out his semen into her, leaving himself naked and vulnerable as he can rarely allow himself to be. Yes, Russell, for the first time—it was not a sadness I felt with you, but an enormous fulfillment. Even when—especially when—in your ignorance and mine you had gone off to good orgasm and left me behind.

At last Bill was quiet. But suddenly I suffered a terrible fright. I could feel his penis, thick and heavy and *there*; suddenly I imagined it as naked in me, broken through the double barrier by sheer stolid persistence. His seed was in me, and so I would never know, in all my long life in Pass Robin, whether it was him or whether it was you. In panic, I struggled out from underneath his stolid weight.

"What's the matter with you?" Bill said sullenly.

"It broke, didn't it?" I said bitterly. A long shudder

rippled through me. I bowed my head into my hands. But I could not cry.

Suddenly concerned, he examined himself carefully. "It's all right," he said reassuringly.

"Let me see," I said. "I've got to know."

Finding his limp tool with my hand, I fingered carefully over the slick sheathing of rubber, making very sure that he was telling the truth. Responding to my touch, he began to stiffen again, so I took my hand away.

"Let's go home," I said.

Bill made no effort to detain me in the back seat. But, once again behind the steering wheel, he didn't start the motor. He had something to say and he did not look at me as he said it, his voice slow with the calculated insult.

"You're pretty careful, aren't you?"

I couldn't see him in the darkness. "I have to be," I said in the same tone. "If you had made me pregnant, you wouldn't marry me, would you?"

He didn't answer. He already had the next words ready. "Were you that careful with old Russell? All summer long?"

Abrupt anger made me want to slap his face. Not because of myself—he had a right to me and because he had laid on me shaking and weeping, because he had accepted the comforting stroke of my hands, he had the need to be cruel. My anger was for you.

I held myself still. "No," I said. "I let him do anything he wanted to."

His head turned. "I reckon you wanted to get knocked up by him. Because then he'd have had to marry you. You'd have got your chance to live according to your own high and mighty notions. Ain't that right?"

"I didn't even think about it. I just let him do what he wanted."

Bill bowed his head on the steering wheel. His voice was strangled. "God damn you, Lessie Mae. God damn you." I didn't want him to cry again, because I couldn't do anything for him this time. Straightening violently, he fumbled for the ignition switch and started the motor into life. "Come on," he said, "Let's get the hell out of here."

Only after Bill had left me—he didn't escort me to the porch steps, merely stopped on the dirt road and reached over to swing open the car door—did I realize that I was naked under the dress. I had left my pants forgotten in the back seat of Bill's car. I shrugged and walked down the path toward the house. What difference did it make?

Bill didn't come back again. But others came, for Bill had the truth to brag about now, didn't he? He had to strut and gloat and know himself to be a man, or else he would remember how he had loved and hated me, how he had wept in my arms, how he had cursed me for my betrayal. Not for one second could he admit to himself that he had desired tedious courtship, night-by-night progress, and eventual certification, instead of a quick piece of tail.

So when I sat on the porch in the cool dusk I would hear cars going by slowly out there on the dirt road, the honk of a horn, the faint yell of a voice. The very first time I heard it, I understood its meaning. Three nights later—no, four—when I heard a car horn perform *shave-and-a-haircut* in a brisk and practiced pattern, I got up and walked down the porch steps.

"Is that Bill?" Mama said.

I didn't answer, but kept on walking.

"It must be old Bill," Daddy said, satisfaction in his voice. "Heard that shave-and-a-haircut, didn't you?"

I went on to the road. The car was already going slowly away, the driver leaning out to look back. When he saw me, he speeded up, made a rapid turn, and came back to stop beside me. I recognized one of Bill's friends, the best basketball player on the Pass Robin High School team. Leaning across the car, he unlatched the door and pushed it open. "Get in, Lessie Mae."

I got in. At the next crossing, he took the road out into the country. I sat looking straight ahead. Because he did not say anything, I didn't speak.

It was a different place from where Bill had taken me.

"Do you want to get into the back seat?" he said.

"That's the best way, isn't it?" I said.

"Well," he said, laughing freely and unself-consciously. "You ought to know."

I stared at him until he quit laughing. I kept on staring until he began to fidget. Finally he said hoarsely. "Well. How about it?"

"I was just waiting to be asked," I said and put my hand on the door handle.

He had a better car than Bill's. There was no odor of oil. He wanted to kiss first, and put his hands on me. I wouldn't let him have my mouth, but he nuzzled over my neck as I stretched halfway off the seat so his finger could get into my pants. His body was thin and hard, his muscles were stringy, they rippled with his movements. At this first sensing of his body, I was briefly afraid of being reminded of you, but no danger, he was too controlled and intense in his movements, a conscious athlete with conscious muscles. His organ was long and thin even in erection; I put my hand on it, meaning to know his instrument as I knew yours, and Bill's.

When he considered me ready, he positioned my hips with careful expertise. I waited for him, my head back and to one side. I didn't care whether he used a rubber or not. I wasn't thinking of you this time, but of those nights I had sat on the front porch listening to the call of car horns. Idly, I was wondering if I had come out to him only because he had played a perfect shave-and-a-haircut, signaling the presence of a practiced man.

I needed a practiced man, and this time I had one. Yes, he used a condom, putting it on not for my sake but for his own. But he was very quickly into me and oh he was good; he had tricks of teasing—stroking and pausing, a tantalizing pause that raised my loins seeking the next stroke, then suddenly going very deep, rolling his hips in a grinding motion. He knew he was good, too; he kept repeating in a smug voice, "How's that, baby? Like that, don't you, baby?" My silence forced him to a fiercer ingenuity as he demanded through clenched teeth, the words hissing into my ear, "You've got to like it now, baby. You've got to."

Even though he could tease my body into reaching after him, I held myself cold and far away, letting his lean, strength romp on me, feeling his slender, tensile tool slipping and sliding, gnawing with an increasing frenzy at my tenderest flesh. Finally he became invisible, I was so far away; and at last I could stroke him coldly, once and then twice, my vagina tightening on his penis, and he began to come though he struggled to hold it safe. With two economical, utterly planned, twitches, I finished him.

He got out immediately, perching like a tense, stork-legged bird on the edge of the seat to strip off the rubber and fling it out the window. Then he leaned close over me, his hand between my legs, two fingers probing deep, and said through his teeth, "You're a cold little bitch, aren't you? What does it take to get you started?"

"The right cock," I said, and started to sit up.

He pushed me down. "You're not through yet, baby," he said coldly. "You don't know what fucking is. Before I'm through with you, you'll be begging for it."

Oh, there was a cold streak in him to match my own. Five times he took me that night, his lean, strong body supple and tireless, his inventions and variations ever increasing in subtlety and scope. His thin instrument, forever confident of success, probed and teased in a thousand different patterns for the breach in my wall of not-feeling. And five times I absorbed all he had to offer. Feeling his body on my body, his organ in mine, I could yet drift further and further away, until at last I could strip him coldly, demanding his total surrender. And each time, helplessly, ragingly, he would begin to come, unable to hold it safe. And each time he returned a little more slowly, with a longer space for recuperation in between.

After the fifth orgasm he was used up, unable to move. The anger remained, although he could use it only in a whispering hiss of words into my ear as he sprawled wearily on me. "Bitch. Bitch. You cold bitch, your cunt is made out of ice." Putting my hands on his head, I held him as long as he would let me. It was only a few minutes, though, before he struggled up out of me, got out of the back seat, and went around to sit under the steering wheel.

I sat up, searching for my pants, and wriggled into them. All the time, I was watching his cold profile against the windshield. I got out of the back seat, opened the front door, and got in beside him. The instant the door was closed, he started the motor. When he let me out on the dirt road in front of the house, he stared at me through the window. "Jesus!" he said briefly, and drove away.

I don't remember how many men I went out to meet like that. I probably don't want to remember. Too many—but I had to get through a century of time, all the way to next June and graduation. Their faces were—and still remain—a blur, one man merging into the next. I remember only their instruments. I suppose few women realize the infinite variety of men's penises. There are bold ones and shy ones, long ones and short ones, thin and thick. Some are circumcised, some curve to the left or to the right. I became acquainted with tools that were slow to rise and quick to fall, and others quick to rise and slow to fall. In their infinite variations of style and mannerism, they are individualists all.

I hardly looked at the faces of those many men. I didn't want to know their faces. But always I put my hand to their penises, needing to learn them by touch. Perhaps I was looking for the twin to your lovely instrument—but I think that is an idea too simpleminded to fit the case. Only after learning their organs intimately by touch did I take them into my body, yielding myself, in my way, to their rampant individualities, bold or shy, stabbing in a leftward or rightward arc, or straight and true. After I had made each erection pour itself empty of seed, I could then, for a moment, a minute, five minutes, hold the man in my arms.

But each man only once—except for one. I made very sure they would not return a second time. The desired result was not difficult of accomplishment. I simply did not, could not, respond in any way that would satisfy them. I didn't have to hate them—simply, while lying within the grasp of their clutching arms, I would make myself invisible to these men who were not my people. With the utter frigidity thus achieved, coldly and deliberately I stripped them of their manhood. Somehow, no matter how stupid or insensitive, they knew within themselves that I had robbed them of more than their seed—and they could not endure it. Least of all could they endure the memory of lying cradled gently in my stroking arms after they had surrendered.

Soon, it was no longer the high school boys, but grown men, with thick, hairy bodies somehow so much heavier than the lighter-textured flesh of the boys. Their organs, too, were different, thicker, slower, surer of themselves. I shudder, now, to think of the dangers I walked blindly through. As I never knew what I would do, or refuse to do, they could never be certain of their piece of tail until they got it in me. At times I would approach the car, look into the waiting face, then turn to walk back to the house. Often I would get into the car, suffer the brief and silent ride, then simply sit inviolate, despite their importunities, until they took me home again. Once or twice it happened that, after I had acquainted my hand with the shape and size of the organ, I would say "No." Whatever the decision, it was mine, a yes or a no shaped somewhere inside me without the aid of conscious will or conscious thought. Silently enduring their frustrated rage, I faced down even threats of physical violence. My selection factor must have been very good; not one of all those angry men ever bruised me in my denial of their lust.

Perhaps those were the lucky ones, for I was cruel even when I allowed a penetration. I had to be cruel. I needed to weaken them in their malehood until they would let me hold them. I was cruelest of all to the only one to come back to me. The first time I sat in his car, he ejaculated the instant my hand touched him, then collapsed against me, utterly surrendered. But he returned the next night, and I went with him. He begged me not to touch him, even as his semen boiled over my gripping hand. It was a week, this time, before I saw him again. When he tried to make me promise to let him get it in me, I promised readily—and kept the faith until we were in the back seat and he was poised over me, his breathing like a bellows in the narrow space of the car. I couldn't help myself. I put down my hand, and his come sprayed wetly on my belly while he cursed me in a despairing voice. Even after that he wouldn't give up, but returned again and again, though he knew, must have known, that I would exploit his weakness. Never once did he succeed in entering me. Cruelty. A female cruelty, which is the worst kind.

It was always in the cars. I wouldn't consent to anything else. Once, four men came together, flashing a bottle of whiskey and a motel key, but a certain caution was watchful in me. I told them coldly, "No gang bangs. Come back one at a time if you want a piece of it." Without waiting for an answer, I went back to the house.

There were no rewards—I was not taken to movies or fed dinners, never provided a public escort. They made no attempt to be charming or romantic or interesting, they confided no secrets or ambitions. They knew me only as a piece of tail, capricious and unpredictable but so beautiful any man could enjoy bragging of having had me, and I knew them as penises, infinite in variety but inevitably vulnerable to my unerring instinct for the secret inadequacy that could be exploited to take away their male triumph.

During that long century of time between your departure from Pass Robin and my departure, I was defeated only once. Because I was defeated, I must tell it, Russell, I must show you that I was not utterly Diana—in spite of myself, Aphrodite remained also.

I knew about this man. I remembered, as I gazed into his face through the car window, that only a few weeks ago he had married a high school girl. On the second day of their honeymoon, the bride had come home alone on the bus from Panama City. She had not been seen in public since she had taken a taxi home from the bus station.

"Ain't you going to get in?" he said after I had stood long enough beside the car to remember that I knew these things.

"Of course," I said.

For the first time, instead of a quick lay in the back seat, I was taken to a roadhouse—what we called a honky-tonk in those days and in that place—forty

miles inland from Pass Robin. It was a raunchy building thrown up out of rough lumber. The dance floor
was uneven and unwaxed, so that dust rose from the
pounding feet. There was a three-piece band, guitar
and fiddle and bass fiddle, wearing shabby cowboy
clothes and playing Bob Wills's tunes.

He worked at making it a real date. We drank beer,
and danced. He was a small man, slight of body and
shorter than I. I had never danced much, but, with his
light-footed invention and sheer exuberance, he made
me feel that I was as good as he was. Betweentimes,
he sat across the table, in our corner booth, and held
both my hands, gazing romantically into my eyes as
he talked lightly and humorously, not at all put off by
my continuing lack of response.

In spite of myself, I began to have a good time.
Partly the beer, I suppose, because I wasn't accustomed to drinking—but it was also the music, the sensation of dancing lightly and gaily. I could float away
on the music. Away from him. Most of all, away
from myself.

We stayed until the place cosed. His arm about
me, he was tender and charming and gallant as we
staggered to the car. I was laughing by now, I
couldn't seem to stop laughing, and when he had in-
stalled me in the front seat, he kissed me for the first
time, before closing the door and going around to the
other side. The kiss was light and undemanding—simply fun, like everything else. As we began the long
drive back to Pass Robin, I let myself go into the
good body tiredness, putting my head back and closing my eyes. I was almost asleep, curled comfortably
in the seat, when I was startled awake by the car pulling off the pavement onto gravel. I sat up and looked

around. He had stopped on the service apron of a gas station. The station was closed for the night, leaving only one outside light burning, a high, glaring bulb that washed hard light into our faces.

I looked at the man. He looked at me. "It's fuck or suck, Lessie Mae," he said quietly. "Or I aim to beat the living shit out of you."

Russell, the thought that crossed my mind was, why didn't you and I think of that? For one second, I was lost in a puzzled regret. Such a natural, such an inevitable, thing; but in our innocence we had not even imagined the possibility. I understood "suck" immediately, you see, in all its meanings and implications—and yearned as quickly for the forever-lost taste of your penis in my mouth. I would never know it now, when I could have had it if I had only known about such things.

I was still looking at the man. The man was still looking at me. "Well?" he said. "Which is it going to be?"

"Both," I said.

I think he was astonished, as all the successful ones were, by my lack of resistance. They were habituated to, at the least, a pro forma protest and struggle before the girl let herself be overwhelmed by the great male aggression. He kept on looking at me. "Yes," he said. "Get down on the floor."

Sliding down, I turned to face him, the lower edge of the dashboard a hard ridge across my back. He angled his body across the seat.

"It's in there somewhere," he said. "Find it."

I put my hand on the zipper, pulled it. He was wearing jockey shorts. I could feel the hard lump of it, but I couldn't get it naked. So I unbuckled his belt

141

and pulled down his pants, his hips lifting to aid me. Bringing the shorts too, I pushed the wad of clothing below the bend of his knees. There was a strong wash of light in the car from the single high bulb. As I gazed at the revealed organ, I thought of the girl he had married. Unable to bear the need of the man to be sucked by his woman, she had fled homeward, shocked for life.

Perhaps I couldn't have done it this first time, either, if it had been a gross, hairy thing thrusting up in insolent demand. But it was like that of a child: small—no more than four inches long—fragile, almost delicate in its pink-headed cleanliness. The balls were a tight, smooth bag drawn close against the base of the stalk. He didn't have a full hard-on, only the anticipation of the lovely, small head just beginning to thrust up.

I looked up into his face. His lips were slightly parted, and there was no expectation of ridicule at the expense of his smallness. I returned to the tiny penis, nestled so sweetly in the folds of his flesh. There was an enormous vulnerability in its almost-unhaired nakedness. Leaning forward, I took him whole. There was nothing repellent in the sensation, nor the taste—the taste was strange, of course, so strange, yet somehow I had known it would have this flavor of the sea, rich and wild. I had smelled this taste when the tide had gone far out, letting the deep odors come up from the sea bottom.

He was coming to it, slowly but very surely, so I shaped my lips around the engorging bulb. I could feel the tiny ridges of the glans, so hard yet so tender, and he put both hands behind my head, holding me against him. His fingers were strong against the shape of my skull, cherishing me as I had so often cherished the heads of finished, defeated men.

He did not begin to climb to orgasm—this was more than enough, and he wanted me to go on forever. While he made all the sounds of gratification, I did go on forever, until after a long time he began to come to it, as a woman comes, voluptuously throughout his body. At the instant he focused into maleness, ready to come malely, his hands told me to stop. I looked up into his face, seeking instruction.

"You can finish me now, or we can fuck," he said. His voice no longer sounded with the hard peril of fuck or suck. "You don't have to fuck if you don't want to."

"Whatever you'd like best," I said.

"God, you were good!" he said. "Where did you learn to do it so good?"

"I've never done it before."

He did not believe me. He knew all about me, he had been told that if he wanted a nice piece of ass, all he had to do was drive down the dirt road and blow his horn. But suddenly he quit knowing that and, beginning to know me in the now, he leaned forward and kissed me. His mouth was soft and warm and I knew he wanted to sample the taste of his fluid on my mouth. There was a sweetness to his lips, a warmness, a flavor of stale beer.

"Let's fuck," he said. When we were out of the front seat, his legs thin and white in the wash of light, he said, "I want you naked, too."

I took off my clothes, while he removed the shirt and tie, and we got together into the back seat. The tiny instrument eased so gently into me that only after he had started did I realize he was not using a rubber. I no longer needed to think about safety; the men, more afraid of my random reputation than I of their random semen, always dressed themselves in condoms without waiting to be told.

I felt him naked, so small and sweet that he scarcely violated the intimate flesh where so many others, so much angrier and ruthless, had plunged out their pounding rhythms. I couldn't help myself—digging my fingernails into his naked back and crying out, a throatless cry, I went off into a linked series of spasms that, mounting from one to the next, swept through me against all possible resistance. He went with me, riding the violent whip of my body, and I could feel him beginning to reach back for his own orgasm. At my peak, he began to come, stride for stride, pumping a scalding come into my scalding flesh. I could hear the sounds that I was making, and the deep, rasping gasp of his breathing.

Ended, I lay crushed under him, trembling and panting and ashamed. It had happened only with you, only on that one night when I had made the bargain with God, or Something. I had made no bargain tonight. I had betrayed you, betrayed me, betrayed the bargain. The shame was all the more ineradicable because only in this past week had I learned, in the sign of my own blood, that I was meant to pass out of Pass Robin and become the person I wanted to become.

So, against my will, I had struck a new bargain. Why? Because I had known about his bride; because he had said, *Suck or fuck, or I'll beat the living shit out of you.* Even as he said it, I knew now in this after-self I had become, his tool had lain tiny and childlike and vulnerable in the crotch of his thighs.

The betrayal, the shame, did not end there. It was he who comforted me, his voice long toned and soothing in my ear as his hands stroked my sides in long, gentle strokes. When I felt him slide down on me, I didn't know what he was after; I believed he was escaping and my hands clutched to hold him. But it was not escape. He wanted to put his mouth on me.

Russell, why didn't you think of that? You didn't, in your innocence, any more than I had thought of the taste of maleness in my mouth. But he . . . he knew and, knowing, he did it. For me.

In the first moment, startled, I tensed against him. But then his tongue fluttered against my tiny penis, the clitoris, and helplessly I surrendered, though something in me did not want to surrender. Every cell in my body sensed him as he pressed his face deeply into my crotch. He inhaled deeply, snuffing up my odors, and my legs parted so wide that his face came deeply, wetly, into me. And, as his tongue stroked and probed, I began to come all over again, deeply and voluptuously and with an agonizing slowness.

I could not cradle him, I could only hold his head, the curled shape of his ears against my palms, while I writhed in the interminable coming that washed so greatly through me. Through it all his mouth stayed with me, his face buried wetly into the fragrant muff.

This man drove me crazy that night. I was helpless in his hands, tossed and turbulent on the tides of lust he could so effortlessly engender in me. When he was ready to enter me again, I was so open, so vulnerable, I could only respond, my helpless, greedy flesh his tender slave. I cried out in ecstasy, I wept in relief, and then, insatiably, rose up out of the dead ashes of

my burning self to be launched into orbit yet again.
And when he was used up, burned out, I put my head
again into his crotch, coaxing the pitiful remnant of
his tiny organ with infinite tenderness into one small
final orgasm, not for me this time though I wanted it,
but taking it in my mouth because I wanted more
than anything else to savor that sensation, too.

At the ultimate end of ourselves, I lay with my face
in his naked lap, breathing in his odor. Beyond shame
now; I had used up shame, and when he put his hands
strong fingered on my head, lifting me up, I leaned
weakly against him.

"Baby," he said, "you have got it all. There just
ain't any more."

"I don't need any more," I said. "You . . . you got it
all, too."

"And they told me you were a cold bitch. Good
God!"

I had to laugh, though shakily. He laughed also,
and there was a mutual tenderness in the rest of the
journey home. But when he stopped the car to let me
out, when he said, "Tomorrow night," I said, "No."

He looked at me, and the hard tone had returned to
his voice. "I'll be here. You'd better be waiting."

I was not waiting. The next night, when I heard the
sounding of the horn, I knew it was him; but, though
every cell of my hot flesh yearned to run to his
side, I held myself still by main force. Again the
next night, and the next; but, though I knew I would
lie in remembered lust through a hot, sleepless eternity, I would not let myself respond. The fourth time
I failed to answer, he came to the house. Standing in
the yard, he said, "Come on, Lessie Mae. I've been
waiting."

"No," I said. "I won't go." Seeing that he meant to come up on the porch after me, I called in a trembling voice, and Daddy came out of the house. "Make him go away, Daddy," I pleaded.

He went away, and he did not return again. Even if he had, I could not have yielded. It was not simply a denial of defeat at the hands of a male; he had struck a new bargain into my flesh and I had still to wait for the new sign of ultimate victory or ultimate defeat. That one man, Russell, was the only time I lost; and God, or Something, was good to me, for, rescued from that commitment, I was left free still to leave Pass Robin.

The time went on forever through the century of itself until June and graduation. But it did end, and I was indeed free. When I crossed the stage of the school auditorium to take the white roll of paper from the principal's hand—I had secretly persuaded him to engrave it with the new name I would bear from now on—I heard a snickering murmur in the audience of my peers and their parents. But I didn't care; tomorrow, as Leslie Dollar, I would leave Pass Robin forever on a Greyhound bus. It would have to be forever, because I had carefully fixed it so that I couldn't come back even if I should want to. I was invisible to Pass Robin—most of all to the multitude of males who had shoved their instruments into my cold welcoming, to spend their puny seed.

But, before I could end with Pass Robin, Bill had to happen one more time. At home after the graduation ceremony, I was taking off the white dress when I heard the horn. Though it was ended now, I did not hesitate, because I knew it had to be Bill.

When I reached the road, he dangled his left arm

out the car window, a filmy piece of cloth floating from one finger. "I've still got your panties, Lessie Mae," he said. "Thought you might want them back now."

I glanced at the garment in his hand. He was holding the pants with his finger through the crotch. They were dirty now, smeared and crumpled.

"I don't need them," I said.

He was still staring at me. His voice came roughly, with harsh edge and ugly overtone. "Get in the car."

I stood still, feeling the slight wind blow the white graduation dress against my thighs. With the sad truth that was in me, I said, "Bill, you don't really want me to, do you?"

His angry, baffled eyes wavering away, he clasped both hands on the steering wheel. It was a new car he was driving, no longer the oil-smelling heap in which he had once used me. His hands were thick and clumsy, I saw—but they would be clever with wood, wouldn't they? They'd have to be clever with wood.

"You're going away. Aren't you?"

"Yes," I said. "Tomorrow."

"Where?"

"I don't know."

The anger was no longer in him; only the hurt and the doubt. And a baffled question that would never be answered.

"Bill," I said, "if you really want to fuck me one more time, I'll let you. But it would be so much better if you didn't."

He muttered, "I guess you're right," and reached to turn the key. The new motor pulsed smoothly into life, ready to bear him away. He looked at me again, but only with a flicker of a glance. "Do good, Lessie Mae. Do good with yourself."

"Be happy, Bill," I said.

"Yeah, sure."

I didn't wait for him to drive away, but turned away myself. And so it was over, ended with, and I'd never have to do it again. For, when the Greyhound bus passed the city limits of Pass Robin, I was a new person. I did not know another man until I married Frank.

Celibacy was not a difficult accomplishment. I simply didn't want to make love. I suffered not even an occasional twitch of the flesh, to be assuaged with my own finger. Perhaps something in me believed that ladies who worked in offices did not have sex; and since I intended to be such a lady, I could be as cool and efficient and remote as they.

I had no trouble finding jobs; trouble came only when the boss reached the inevitable point of making a play. In the first year, I had to change jobs five times; a man can't let you work for him after you have refused him. I encountered that basic difficulty at the very beginning. The first city I came to out of Pass Robin, I was hired by the first employer who interviewed me. Of course, he added quickly, I would be on temporary status until he found out how good I could type, and whether I fitted into the office. That didn't bother me—I knew I was very fast and very accurate.

By the third day, I had found a place to live and was planning to enroll in night school to learn the other office skills. Late that afternoon, only an hour before quitting time, the boss gave me a thick sheaf of new work. When, at five o'clock, I was covering my

typewriter, he câme in hastily and said, without looking at me, "I do wish you would stay and finish that
proposal, Miss Dollar. I must have it first thing in the
morning."

I sat down, uncovered the typewriter, and went
back to work. When everyone else was gone for the
day, he came in again, standing behind me to see how
I was coming along.

"I'll be through in another hour," I said.

"I think you're going to do all right, Miss Dollar,"
he said in a hearty voice. "You are very fast, and very
efficient." His hands suddenly took my shoulders, one
on each side. "So nice to look at, too, and I'm sure
you're a warm, generous person who'll fit right into
the staff." His hands were gripping hard, and his
voice changed. "I'll take you out to dinner after
you're through. I can be generous and warm, too.
You'll see."

Getting out from under his hands, I backed against
the desk and looked at him. He was short and
sweating and, bulging the leg of his pants, I could see
the hard thickness of his erection.

"I'm sorry, Mr. Barker," I said. "I don't do that."

His eyes went flat with anger. Turning abruptly, he
said, "Be sure to finish, now, before you leave. I need
those papers in the morning." He did not speak to me
again until, at the end of the trial week, he paused by
my desk to inform me that he felt, given my extrordi-
nary looks and my manner, I was a disturbing factor
in the office and so he would have to let me go.

Five jobs in the first year, two in that city and
three in three others. But the next job lasted a full
year, and night school was teaching me the necessary
skills for advancement. This boss, however, turned

out to be only more subtle than the others; he waited until he was ready to offer me the position of private secretary before making his move. Nothing subtle about it then, though; he told me that he didn't like his wife, his wife didn't like him, so he counted on his private secretary to supply his sex life. So directly straightforward, I was tempted to accept the conditions and the job. I could have handled it. But I didn't, and so I moved on.

I went this time to a smaller city in the Midwest, in response to an attractive newspaper ad, and went to work for Frank. Frank, just then, was embroiled in divorce proceedings and he had no inclination to bother about me. Before long I had become an accepted and valued member of the staff, and I began to study accounting, because I had a feeling I could remain indefinitely in Frank's CPA office.

I worked for Frank for a year before he asked me to marry him. By that time I knew him to be a good man, a kind man, as steady and reliable and respected as his work. So I married Frank, I became quickly fond of him, I was happy to bear his children. We lived together as well as two people can, I think. Until you came back into my life.

I must tell this part very quickly, very simply. I shall not dwell on it, for I don't want to think about it any more than I can help. Can you understand that, Russell? But I must think about it, and so must you, for what happened is a part of you and a part of me.

This is what we did in that time.

It wouldn't have happened at all, I think, if only you had recognized me. After all, ten years had passed, and we were both very far away from Pass Robin. I had long since accepted the boundaries of my life in this midwestern city where you found me. Married to a good man, I had two nice children, I lived in a comfortable suburban home and drove a comfortable station wagon. Though I did not love Frank, he loved me. But I was fond of Frank, I could count on him, he was predictable in all things; I knew that he would want to make love on Tuesday night and Saturday morning, and he had planned each child as meticulously as he worked out a large office project.

Russell, this one thing you must understand—the goodness of the man I was married to. From the beginning, he understood that my affection for him was not love. Nor passion—it bothered him that he could not bring me to orgasm. He made love exactly the same way every time, cleanly and straightforwardly, beginning slowly and building slowly. He would make one sound, a long-drawn-out groan, as his semen spurted. His only quirk was that he liked to see me nude; he said I was more lovely naked than with clothes on. So he got into the habit of lying on the bed and watching me move naked about our bedroom, tidying up my clothes and his, perhaps emptying the ashtrays; and when I came to him, he was ready. It was the only foreplay we had between us.

You see, dear Russell? I was contented. I had found the shape of a life I could live inside, I had achieved everything I had left Pass Robin to seek. I had even learned, for Frank's sake, how to fake an orgasm ... this, within the last year before you came back into my life.

Then, that first night, you did not recognize me. I understand why, of course—I was totally out of context, and you were intent on beginning well your first independent chance to prove yourself in your chosen profession. But . . .

I hadn't wanted to try out for the play. Cora, my best friend, talked me into it. She told me, over and over again, how much better the community theater would be now, with the new resident director, and so I ought to get in on the ground floor of the new regime. In her enthusiasm for your professional qualifications she somehow failed to mention your name, so that I had no idea she was talking about you. I suppose it was meant to happen; for, given a prior warning, I would never have let you know that I lived in that random city you had come to out of the New York theater.

There must have been in me a tiny restlessness. I had not even thought about acting. Indeed, I had seen only two or three of the plays put on by the group. Cora, for a long time, had urged me to join, saying I was so much better looking than any of the women I would get leading parts immediately, whether I was much of an actress or not. I would never have a better chance; you had made open casting a matter of policy, over the jealous opposition of the regulars . . . and, who knows, I might be pretty good after all. So I came. I sat down with Cora to await my turn. I looked up on the stage. And there you were.

You had changed from the gangly, earnest boy I had loved so long ago. Lean still, and tall; you had learned the uses of charm rather than being naturally and instinctively charming. With a show of boyish earnestness, you had those ladies eating right out of your hand; yet the men liked you, too. They had already forgotten the battle Cora had told me about, over the question of open-call casting. I sat there

and watched you do it, somehow making each of the
regulars believe that his talent, his dedication to the
theater, would carry him through the upheaval of
the established pecking order. You were obviously
going to be an enormous success.

Please understand this, Russell. I saw you—I recognized you. But you were gone out of me. It had taken
many men, a lot of lovemaking, much time, and a
good marriage. But it had been so long since you had
dwelled in my flesh I couldn't remember what your
penis felt like, its shape and weight and thrust.

But then—I came up on the stage for my reading.
And you did not know me.

Maybe you didn't even look at me. I was, after all,
only one of many aspirants, variously eager or anxious
or confident, who yearned to emote under your direction. But I was *there*, wasn't I, you listened to my
voice reading the lines, you made me walk away and
come back, you were so devastatingly charming with
compliments that committed you to absolutely nothing: "Don't call me, I'll call you." All the time, concentrated single-mindedly on the immediate task of
establishing yourself firmly with this company of
stagestruck amateurs, you did not know that I was
me.

Going home in Cora's station wagon, the women,
their voices twittering in a nervously sexual chatter,
could talk only about your marvelous charm, your
authoritative presence, the enormous directorial talent
with which, in simply a word, a suggestion, you had
helped them in their reading. They were convinced
you were the greatest thing that had ever happened to
the Piercetown Community Playhouse.

I was so silent in their chattering midst that Cora,

noticing it, said as I got out of the car, "Didn't you like it, Leslie? Didn't you enjoy it at all?"

"I don't know," I said. "After all, I've never tried acting before."

That night—it was a Tuesday night—I gave Frank nothing but a hole. I could not cherish him afterward, nor let him touch me; I could only turn my back, the moment he was finished, and refuse to answer to his solicitude.

You see, my love, for the first time in my life I had been truly invisible. Ever since I could remember, I had practiced the art of making myself invisible. But never, never, never until that Tuesday night had another person succeeded in making me so, against my own striving will.

So when you called, three days later, to ask if I would take the second female lead, I knew I had truly earned the role. But I was wary. Looking candidly at the situation, I saw that it was not healthy. Simply and truthfully, I had too much to lose ... and for what? In my invisibility, I was gone out of you, as you were gone out of me. If I dwelled in your memory at all, it was only as the hot-blooded Pass Robin girl you had used to brighten one long dull summer of your youth.

I said, "I don't think I can take on such an important role. I have two children and I'm afraid I'm much too busy to consider it."

You gave me the boyish earnestness. "But, Mrs. Swenson, you're the only person who's *right* for the character." You waited for a response that did not come, then added, "If you've read the paly through, you know it's the meaty role, too. The lead has that silly, simpering business, you know, the coyness. But you'll have a couple of scenes that give you the opportunity to steal the show ... if you've got the talent to take advantage of it."

"That's just it. I haven't done any acting," I said, thinking, at the same time, that I was talking to you on the telephone for the first time in our lives. "I'd probably make a terrible botch of it."

"I heard you read, didn't I?" you said persuasively. "You have a natural quality, Mrs. Swenson, that is rare in an amateur actor. You have a *presence*. I can teach you the rest of it."

Pammy came tugging at my skirt, wanting a cookie. I told her to get it herself, but just one, and you were still talking.

"If you won't do it for me, Mrs. Swenson, it'll just *ruin* the production. Because, in my mind, you're cast in the role—and I can't believe anybody else in the part, no matter how good they might be. Do you understand that?"

I could visualize you so accurately you might as well have been standing at my side. I gripped the telephone with both hands, staring into space, and I didn't want you to quit talking. Your voice whispered into my ear so strangely familiar, so familiarly strange. And you did not know that I—*I*—was listening at the other end.

"Well," I said. "I don't know."

Your voice dropped. "Let me tell you a secret, Mrs. Swenson. This play is the most important play I'll ever direct in Piercetown. Why? Because, if it's not dead-on right, they'll start not to believe in me. So much of the theater, Mrs. Swenson, is simple faith. I've committed my fate to you in that role. So it's very much up to you whether I'm a failure in this town, or a success." Your voice became challenging. "I wouldn't have offered it if I had believed you were a coward."

You had no idea how much of a coward I was being. Suddenly, unexpectedly, it had hurt to be invisible to you. Then why was I so afraid of becoming visible again, afraid to let you know I was *there*? All the time we had been talking on the phone, I could have said, *Russell. It's me.* But I hadn't.

"All right," I heard myself saying. "I'll give it a try. But take warning—I might quit on you."

"Wonderful, wonderful." Your tone was warm, almost tender—you were, for God's sake, manipulating me. "I knew you'd do it, and I know you'll be great. Now, rehearsals start tonight, at eight. Don't worry about lines. We'll just talk about the play, begin to block it out. But don't fail to be here. I have some new ideas about interpretation that everyone must understand from the beginning."

Hanging up the phone, I knew that, at this successive moment, you were already calling someone else, talking warmly and boyishly and persuasively, seeking their consent and cooperation as you had sought mine. All a part of the job they had brought you from New York to do.

Talking, working, unaware; while I stood here with a steady, insistent tremor running through my flesh even as I looked about me, realizing all that I had gained in these ten years—and knowing that, simply because I had listened to the siren call of your voice on the telephone, it was not worth a dime to live this way with this man in this life. So it was my fault, wasn't it, right from the beginning? Because, the first night of rehearsals, I went up to you after the se̶s̶ where you stood momentarily alone to one side, and said: "Russell."

You heard me; the timbre of my voice rang a bell of memory somewhere inside you. But you didn't believe it. Your eyes flaring, you said, so tentatively, "Leslie?" and then, "My God!"

"Yes," I said. "Me."

You did the right thing then, the safe thing. Perceiving the peril so much more quickly than I, you whirled to Cora, standing nearby, and cried out, "My God, would you believe it? I've known this woman all my life, and I didn't even recognize her. She grew up where my family always spent the summer."

"Really?" Cora said. Like the others, she had been hoping for a chance to talk to you. "Why, that's incredible, Leslie. Absolutely incredible."

You told another, and then another, so excited and enthusiastic, and astonished by your poor memory, and we were safe now, protected by the conventions of old acquaintance openly acknowledged. We could even talk, quickly and quietly, enough to tell each other some of the things that had happened to us since our long-ago summer. By asking you to come to dinner, I managed to let you know about my husband and my children. You imparted to me—it struck a thrill into my bones—that you remained free by replying that, because you were a transient theatrical type living alone in a hotel room, you'd accept all the home-cooked meals Piercetown had to offer.

When at last no one was paying attention, you said in a lowered voice, "So you did it, Leslie. Just like you always said you would."

"Yes."

"And you're happy?"

YOU

"Frank is a fine man, Russell. A very good man. And ... the children are just great."

You didn't touch my hand, then, though you could have. "I'm glad for you."

"What about you? Why aren't you married?"

You laughed. "Oh, I got close once. A very nice girl, really, but she couldn't see the theater life. She thought it was shabby and disreputable—it was her idea that, after the wedding, I'd take a job in the family firm in Boston. By then, of course, I was pretty well committed to the theater. So ..." You shrugged elaborately, looking suitably solemn and dedicated, and then you smiled, spreading your hands. "So here I am."

I couldn't evade it any longer; I had to ask, because I needed to know. "Russell. Have I changed that much?"

You regarded me. "No. Not really." You hesitated. "No more than I have."

"Then why ... ?"

"Why didn't I recognize you?" Your gaze turned inward, focused on the puzzle. "I don't know. Maybe I didn't want to know it was you, because then I ..." You stopped. You looked at me again. "Can I see you? So we can talk?"

Russell, you accepted the denial of our old selves. You were absolutely circumspect; throughout the rehearsals, you were as tough and impersonal with me as with the rest of the cast. But it did no good. Though I made the strongest effort of my life to remain the same woman Frank had loved and trusted, he was already exhibiting a certain bewilderment. He knew that subtle changes were going on inside me, though he did not understand what he knew. You had come alive in me again. Every night I ached to experience all over again your lusty maleness. So, in spite of all resolution, in spite of my daily counting of blessings—it began.

People and circumstances conspired to bring it about. The night of the dress rehearsal, you beckoned me to the stand-up desk in the wings where you did so much of your work. Everybody else was milling around on the stage, as keyed up by the dress rehearsal as by a real performance. You talked to me quietly, changing for the tenth time a piece of business during my most important scene. I stood beside you, watching your hands in the pool of light from a tiny reading lamp and feeling moodily resentful that you were still giving me changes when two rehearsals ago you had frozen everybody else's performance. Do you remember, Russell? You were saying I should cross to the telephone, actually pick it up, then put it back on the hook, before speaking my last line and making my exit. With tomorrow night the opening, I was certain I wouldn't remember to do it, even though I agreed that three beats of pause would make my last words far more memorable. But what was so wrong about my performance that you hadn't frozen it with the others?

We were both totally concentrated, for the play had become as important to me as it was to you; I had discovered in myself an unexpected ambition, to create the character as wholly and truthfully as possible, along with a strong ego-belief that I could do it— was doing it. At that moment, Emma, playing the female lead, came to interrupt, putting her hand on your arm and saying, "Russell," and them something inconsequential; she had only wanted to touch you, claim your attention.

Watching her face, realizing she wasn't as dedicated to her role as I was to mine, I thought suddenly, One of these women will be fucking you before this play has finished its run. Admit it to themselves or not, that's their reason for being in the group; they all, every single one, want to lay down for the great New York theater director they've raised money from their husbands to bring to Piercetown Community Playhouse for a year. *So why the hell not me?* Emma went away reluctantly, her eyelashes fluttering as though still acting her stage role, and you were talking more hurriedly now, your eyes anxious because you sensed my resistance to the change. You explained all over again, with that enormous directorial patience of yours, how important it was for my final impression on the audience—and when I looked again they were all gone, leaving us alone in the theater, dark now except for a stage light, raw and naked, and the small desk lamp pooling its glow on your hands.

Solitude had not happened before. But it happened now, as though I had cued it. Just as it happened that I shaped my hand down the side of your leg and then, going down on my knees between you and the stand-up desk, I took it out and held it between my two hands, watching while it reared erect and ready.

The strange part of it, darling, was that I was not dwelling directly and immediately on you in that moment when I started the business that would destroy you and destroy me. The deed arrived so much more deviously, from a direction I had not guarded against. Suddenly in my mind—when I had thought I was only listening professionally to your professional direction—was the man who had said, "Fuck or suck," and how in that moment it had flashed through me, *Why didn't you and I think of that?* So it came about only by indirection—I wanted to taste you because, when I had tasted him, I had thought that thought about how I had never tasted you. That's perverse, isn't it?

With both hands pressing your buttocks, I took it into my mouth—and oh God, it was *your* cock, *my* cock, for no other man's flesh could have this sweet and bitter flavor. But then it turned perverse again, more bitter than sweet, for, as you grew so mightily in my mouth I had to slip my lips out to the head to keep from gagging, I remembered, with a terrible unavoidable recollection, that never once had I offered this kind treatment to the good man who was my husband. Then I did gag, with a sob both of agony and of release, and gobbled you up again, yearning to choke to death on your tool for I had thrown it all away now and I could not bear to realize something sweet and tender and wonderful in the midst of such betrayal as I was committing.

Both hands braced to the desk, holding firm against my greedy assault, you let me have my way with you. Then you started to move against my mouth, and it was like taking you in my vagina, for you probed the tissues of my mouth with the same hot urgency, and my hands on your buttocks could feel the ripple of your muscles as you drove yourself into me. You came quickly, in enormous quantity, as though you had been saving it for a long time, waiting for me, thinking of me every night as I had been thinking of you. It was mine—mine!—and my throat kept swallowing because I couldn't let a single drop escape.

YOU

Even after you were finished, I stayed with you, burying my face in the sweet dying away of your flesh, until you reached down with strong hands to lift me to my feet.

We stood gazing at each other in the dim light. And do you remember, darling, that we did not touch as I said, "What's your room number at the hotel?"

"Five-thirteen." Then you said, "You can't do that, Leslie. I won't let you do it." But I had already moved away from you, taking my coat from the stage-set sofa and swinging it about my shoulders as I went down the steps. Halfway down the side aisle, I paused, lifting my voice to reach you. "I probably won't remember that new business. But I'll try."

When I got home, Frank had decided to believe that a natural nervousness over my stage debut could adequately explain my recent strangeness; while I lay cold in my cold bed, my back turned, he fussed conscientiously, bringing a glass of warm milk to quiet my nerves and telling me over and over how great I'd be tomorrow night. While I lay cold, cold, in his bed, half of my mind remembering the shape and taste of you in my mouth, the other half shaping in sensuous suspense toward the moment in which it would again thrust its eager way into my warmly welcoming self.

It had to be in the afternoon. I didn't know that this common extramarital exigency was jocularly termed a "matinee." It was simply the only possible time: the kids would be in kindergarten until four, Frank never got home before five-thirty at the earliest, and the maid left the house at one. The evening would be devoted to the first performance and the following cast party; with the attendance of each performer's fans and family, it would be a mammoth affair, and you would be in utter demand during every moment. Only the afternoon could be ours.

You were living at the old downtown hotel, once Piercetown's most elegant edifice but now—superseded by motels sprawling alongside the highway bypasses—dingy, half empty, overshadowed by newer and taller buildings. Until a few years ago, it had still been called the Grange Hotel, but now it bore the grand misnomer, the Royalton. I left the station wagon in the parking lot behind Woolworth's—we suburban housewives learn the basic dodges very fast, don't we?—and walked the last two blocks. A cold, windy day; I hoped the threatened snow wouldn't start until late tonight, in the interest of getting a large crowd for your first Piercetown opening.

I had never been inside the Royalton. Meaning to use the stairs instead of the elevator, I entered at the side door and paused to reconnoiter. The stairs, as I had hoped, were just across a corridor. I looked toward the lobby. The desk clerk had his back turned, but a heavyset man wearing a narrow-brimmed hat, sitting in an armchair against one of the tall, ornate pillars, watched me as I took the three steps across the exposed width of space and opened the door that would lead me to you. I climbed steadily, keeping my hand away from the railing because it had not been dusted for a long time. Coming out on the fifth floor, I looked both ways, then followed the appropriate arrow to room five-thirteen. I knocked, and waited for you to open to me.

You must have been asleep; you were wearing only shorts, your hair was tousled, sleep and surprise showed in your eyes. Closing the door behind me, I walked against you, laying my hips tight against your hips, my arms clasping greedily your almost naked body. You bent your head to kiss me, your hands cupping against my ass, sending a delicate tremor through me with the total perception of their strength and passion. We clung together, wordless, until I felt in you an impulse toward speech. To forestall it, I pulled away—against my own will as much as yours—and walked to an armchair, where I put down my purse. Taking off my coat, I looked about the room, shabby, dingy, high ceilinged. Around the walls, a foot or so below the ceiling, was an ornate plaster molding. The drapes were closed, making a dimness that I was grateful for; not because I didn't want to see you clearly, but because the atmosphere made it more palatable that we meant to make love in the afternoon. I thought about the days of our youth, lit blazingly by the Gulf Coast sun. This ... dimness ... was more appropriate for the present circumstances of our pending passion.

You watched as I slowly took off my clothes, those heavy midwestern garments, and laid them on the chair on top of my coat. I kept my eyes on your bulging maleness, thrusting straight up against your belly under the knit cloth of your shorts. It jerked once or twice, straining to be liberated. I crossed the width of the room and laid down on the big bed. The covers were tossed back, and I could sense the warmth of your body lingering in the sheets.

You had not moved. "Leslie," you said, "do you think it's wise ... ?"

"Don't talk," I said. "Just fuck."

Putting your thumbs into the top of the jockey shorts, you pushed them down and stepped free. Gazing at last at your naked piece, a sickness of desire moved in my stomach. You were coming to me now, stooping like a hawk stoops over a doomed rabbit, and as I opened my arms and my legs, as I opened all of me, you came all the way into me in one great move.

I waited to explode. But I didn't go into orgasm and, holding my breath, I waited some more. And then I knew the debilitating truth. It wasn't going to be any good. Though inside me was your lovely instrument, so lovingly remembered, as in the time of the multitude of others I could only lie frozen and still, like this midwestern land would be tomorrow under tonight's snowstorm.

You knew, immediately. Shoved up into my unresponsive body, your rampant member began to lose its steam, even as you put your hands under my shoulders, lifting me, and pumped with an increasingly desperate franticness. It was no use. You dwindled to nothing, your energy ebbing until you lay still upon me; I lay looking up at the dingy ceiling. The plaster was yellowed and cracked with age, and there were cobwebs on the old chandelier.

Oh, darling, you tried so hard. Gathering up tenderness, you began to kiss me, between kisses telling me how it had been with you through all this absent time. As your hands teased at my breasts, you wallowed slowly in my flesh, gradually coming back to half an erection. At last, and it must have been in desperation, you slid down on me, putting your mouth where your penis was supposed to be. With the fluttering of your tongue against my clitoris, I pressed my head into the pillow and arched against your face; but even then the only thought in my mind was, *Who did he learn it with?* Then I remembered last night, and knew that you must have wondered the same thing about me.

Even when the spirit is absent, nature does finally have something to say. So, when you returned, it was with a new, good hard that wouldn't be discouraged. But it was only with relief on my part and, I'm sure, on yours as well, that you finally came, in a clenched, small orgasm, and we could quit.

I wanted to hold you, then, but you rolled away from me. As we lay gazing at the ceiling, the only sound was the slowly easing labor of your lungs. In less than a minute you sat up on the side of the bed, then went into the bathroom. From the sound of running water, I knew you were washing the taste and scent of me from your face. Coming back, you sat on the bed and put your hand on my naked belly. You watched me for a moment, then moved the hand inquiringly to my mount. I moved it with my hand, saying, "No." Then, looking into your dear face, "I'm sorry, Russell. I ... haven't had much practice at this sort of thing."

"I tried to tell you," you said. "You shouldn't have come. I shouldn't have let you stay."

"I had to," I said. "And because I had to, you couldn't deny me."

Lifting your hand, you moved it in the air above my flaccid body. "For ... this?"

The bitterness in those words made me want to cry. But I could not cry; I could only think that I needed to know the time, how long before I had to pick up the children at the kindergarten.

I sat up, putting my feet on the floor. We were side by side, naked. "For this, Russell," I said. "Even if that's all there is."

"I went to Pass Robin that next summer, even though it meant I was breaking my promise," you told me. "But you were gone. Nobody knew about you, where you were, anything." You shifted so that you could look at me. "People acted so ... strange ... when I asked about you. What happened, Leslie?"

"I fucked everything in Pass Robin before I left," I said.

I read the pain in your eyes. "Why?"

I moved my shoulders. "All so long ago, Russell, it's not worth talking about."

"I was back again the year I finished college. I was slated to get married, but I had to try one more time. By then, some people didn't even remember you. Bill remembered, all right, but he couldn't tell me anything."

"Bill," I said.

You smiled. "Bill was doing all right. He already had one kid, and another on the way. He was building a house for himself in his spare time."

"Bill," I said sadly. Then I looked at you. "You should have got married, Russell. Maybe not that Boston girl, but somebody."

You looked away. "I only came close that one time. I knew by then what it was going to take to make it in the theater." This time it was you who shrugged your shoulders. "There were girls. One of them was a very good girl. But even though I had long since quit ... thinking about that summertime of ours ... none of them counted, not even the good one."

Getting to your feet, you went across the room to pick up the cigarettes from the dresser. You gave me one, lit both. You didn't sit down again.

"And you? How in the hell did you ever get to a

place like Piercetown?" You made a small laugh. "Maybe you don't know it yet, but you're as out-of-place here as you were in Pass Robin."

"No," I said. "I'm in-place here, Russell. I really am. That's not why I had to come to you."

You were watching my face. "Your husband?"

"I told you. Frank is a good man. He loves me. We have been very good to each other." I lifted my eyes to look into your face; I wanted you to know my words to be the truth. "I have not done this, Russell. Not until now."

"And we won't let it happen again. Will we?"

"Yes," I said. "It will happen."

You moved your hand angrily. "Why? What the hell good is it? You brought it here today, didn't you, but you couldn't make it trot. Isn't that the truth?"

"Yes," I said. "It's the truth."

You were angrier with every word. "You've found what you wanted, back there in Pass Robin. In essence, and in detail. So why do you want to throw it away? Why take these chances? This isn't a very big city, you know. Just about day after tomorrow, everybody will know that the new resident director is fucking Mrs. Leslie Swenson. Didn't someone see you coming into the hotel? I'm sure they did."

I thought about the heavyset man in the lobby. But I was watching you as you moved in your anger, seeing how the bony, gangling body of the boy had matured into a man. Unconsciously, you handled yourself well, physically speaking. Your voice was rich and vibrant, you owned a confidence that you were good at your chosen work. You were no longer the boy, as I was no longer the girl. But the boy was still in me, the girl was still in you. That was the sim-

ple truth of the matter that you did not want to recognize. But I, the woman, not only recognized it—I
could also, somehow, accept it.

"If it's not me, it'll be one of the others in the company," I said. "They all want to have a whirl with
you, Russell. You're the best thing that's come down
their pike in a long time."

You were very angry now. "Oh no, they won't.
That's the first and last thing Harry Shaw warned me
about when he recommended me for this job." You
paused, breathing hard. " 'Whatever you do,' he told
me, 'don't make the mistake of screwing the females
in the company. This is your big chance, old buddy,
your first really good crack at building an independent reputation. So if you can't keep your cock out
of all that hungry pussy, you'd better not sign the
contract.' " You stared at me, glaring. "How was I to
know that I'd find you in a midwestern dump like
this? It's the last place in the world I would expect to
see you. I didn't even recognize you, for God's sake,
until you spoke my name."

"I'm sorry," I said.

You were quiet now. "What the hell do you want
with me? I'm no good for you. You're no good for
me. It was all faraway and long ago, and we're
both different people from what we were then."
You moved your arms too violently. "What about
me? OK. I know that's selfish thinking. But the minute the gossip starts, the company will start falling
apart. I'll lose control, I won't be the resident director
any more, I'll just be a random cock brought to town
to screw a few wives!" You made yourself stop. "I
can't blow this job, Leslie. I've not only got to have a
chance to direct; I've got to make a track record

while I'm doing it. That's the way it is. I'm giving
myself five years in the boondocks. For the record.
For the experience. Then, when I go back to New
York, I'll have a chance ... a chance, mind you, that's
all, just a *chance*. But a chance is all I need, because
I've *got* it, Leslie, I'm going to be the best there is."

I stood up. "Then you don't want me. Not ever
again."

"No," you said. "Good God, no! Not under these
circumstances."

"Then tell me how I can keep from coming to
you," I said. My voice sounded low, fatal, but it
reached you, it made you come and hold me, with
your arms so tight that it hurt. We held on to each
other while you said, "I don't know. I don't know."

Pulling abruptly away again, you escaped into the
bathroom. I heard you urinate, the flush of the john.
You came back, picked up your shorts, put them on.

"Leslie. You don't want to lose your husband. You
don't want to lose your children. You don't want to
lose the place you've made here for yourself." You
looked at me with tired and bitter eyes. "Remember
that you had to have it so badly that you could put
September out there in front of us, like a great wall
we could never hope to climb over? Even when we
were so much in love."

"No," I said. "I don't remember." Then I said, "If
you want me to go away with you, I'll go. Right
now, in this minute, with only the clothes I wore into
this room."

Your eyes were hot. "All right. Let's do it. If that's
what you want."

"It's not what I want. But I'll do it, if it's the only
way."

171

You turned away. "It's going to be a nasty business, Leslie. Every time you come to me, you'll feel like you felt today. It'll make you dirty, Leslie. It'll make *us* dirty, and small, we'll hurt each other and we'll hurt other people." You stopped. We looked at each other. "We began so much better than all this," you said sadly, hopelessly.

"Yes," I said. I found something inside me I had not expected to find. "I'll try not to come back, Russell. I will try. I promise."

"Not for my sake. For your own, Leslie, because I don't want to ..." You stopped. "All right. For both our sakes."

I ached inside, Russell, with the sadness of it all. Down under the uneasiness of this ugly, dingy hotel room, the prospect of having to walk down those stairs and sneak out the side door, that part of me that belonged to you, only to you, in the beginning and now and forever, ached with the sad futility of our lives. But even then I was glancing at my watch, seeing there was time to make love again if either of us had wanted it.

I said, "I've got to pick up the kids at kindergarten."

You watched as I got dressed, hurrying with quick efficiency though I tried not to feel the need of hurry. Ready, I picked up my purse. You looked at me.

"Are you going to be good tonight?"

I had forgotten that tonight I would make my stage debut. "I don't know," I said. "I suppose I'll stink."

Coming to me, you put both hands to my shoulders, gripping them. "You're the best in the company. You know that by now. You have to know it."

YOU

"But I . . . Why did you keep giving me new business, Russell, right up to last night? You know I've never acted before. I didn't even learn my lines until long after everybody else had theirs cold."

"Because you kept changing yourself, you were getting better. You hadn't opened it up at first but then you began to feel it." You stopped. You were looking into my eyes. "You have to be good now. You can't blow it. If you do, you'll have to blame it on . . . this."

"All right," I said. "I'll be the best I can be." I was looking into your eyes again, so tired, so sad. "Then I'll quit the company, Russell. I can't quit being in this town but I can at least get out of your way."

You put your arms around me, holding me very hard for a short minute. But you didn't kiss me and without the boon of your kiss I had to leave the hotel room, walk down the corridor past a maid carrying an armful of towels, who looked at me curiously. Downstairs, when I crossed the three-step corridor, the man with the small-brimmed hat was watching over the top of a newspaper. I got the station wagon out of the Woolworth parking lot and drove home, because there was still time to get through before I had to go to the kindergarten.

That night, after the first clandestine matinee of my life, I entered into the new experience, deep within my stagestruck heart, of making a performance and being rewarded by a swelling of applause when I took my separate bow. I remarked the venomous look Emma, the lead, gave me inside the brilliant smile she awarded the audience for her applause. Then Frank had surrounded me with red roses and glowing chatter about my marvelous performance, and his eyes

173

were as though he had not seen me before. While he had not the least suspicion of how truly stranger I had become.

But I can't deny—I didn't want to deny—the curious excitement of a fulfilled performance, the enthusiasm of the smell of flowers, of people kissing people in the swirling crush onstage. You were excited, too, with your great success; you were being kissed by all the women, your hand was shaken by every man, you had won Piercetown completely. Through it all, I did not look at you and you did not look at me. But we had to come together, however briefly, after you had congratulated everybody else. You held my cold hands and spoke the necessary words of praise. With Frank at my side, I had to say, "You haven't met my husband, have you? He simply refused to come to any of the rehearsals." You had to shake his hand and avoid his eyes, this man whose wife you had mounted a few hours before. Fortunately, Cora came, my best friend Cora, bubbling like the champagne in her glass. At least, I thought it fortunate until she said, "Frank, I'm sure Leslie has told you she practically grew up with this fellow. They've known each other for dog's years."

Frank looked at me. He was not a stupid man, simply decent and dull and predictable, and he remembered perfectly well that I had not mentioned old acquaintance. When he looked at you again, I stood between you wishing fervently you were the sort of man who could gaze into his eyes and smile and smile and smile. But you were not. I could not have loved you if you had been.

"Mr. Walford, I don't know anything about the

theater," Frank said in his quiet voice. "But Leslie is good, isn't she?"

"She's very good."

"She . . . sparkled," Frank said with painful precision. "I know I have to be prejudiced—after all, I'm her husband. But just standing onstage, in the scenes where she doesn't have anything to do, she comes right out at you." He paused, fumbling for the words. "She . . . she sparkles."

You looked at Frank then, your eyes meeting his eyes. "You're not being prejudiced, you're simply seeing the quality that's there. She does indeed sparkle."

Cora said, tittering, "Well, Leslie. Looks like you've got an admiration society going between these two men. I'd better break this up." She took your arm, leading you away.

Much later that night, after all the champagne and the midnight supper, finally served long after midnight, Frank said, as we were getting ready for bed, "Leslie, I couldn't believe that was you up there on that stage. I kept looking at you, but I couldn't believe it."

Having slid quickly into my nightgown, I pulled back the covers on my side. "Let's don't talk about it now. I'm dog tired. I didn't realize how tired."

Frank was buttoning his pajamas with his usual patterned meticulousness. "You were special, Leslie. Everybody knew it . . . the cast as well as the audience." He hesitated. "That Mr. Walford, he knew it too."

I got into bed and pulled the covers over me. Frank sat down on his side of the bed; I felt the mattress shift under his weight. Now he would take off his watch, place it carefully on the bedside table. He would clear his throat, he would cough, he would lie down. He would scratch his side, he would cough again, and he would turn out his light.

This sequence of actions always signified sleep. But tonight he did not follow the pattern. Instead he said, "I imagine he'll ask you to try out for the next production, too. Probably give you a bigger part, maybe even the lead. Will you take it?"

I had my back to him. It wasn't enough, so I reached up and turned out my light. "I don't think so," I said in the half darkness. "It just takes too much time to be worth it. After all, there are the children to think about."

"They'll all want you," Frank said in his heavy, unavoidable voice. "Mr. Walford would be a fool to let you get out of it."

"Well, I'm going to, I've already made up my mind about that," I said sharply. I waited for a minute, then I said, meaning more than Frank could know; "I really didn't like it, Frank. I really didn't."

"But you will. Just a little more experience, that's all you need." He paused. "In my opinion, Leslie, you ought to keep on with it. It can be the best contribution you've every made to the community."

I was staring at the opposite wall. "Do you really want me to, Frank? You know how much time it takes. You have to stay with the kids through evening rehearsals for weeks, or we have to find a baby-sitter when you can't get away from the office. Is it worth all that trouble?"

His voice came slowly, but surely. "You ought to find out what it's worth, Leslie. Find out how far you want to go with it."

He, though he did not quite know it himself, meant

also so much more than the acting. I could read the further meanings in the undertone of the words. "I don't need it," I said wearily. "And I don't want to talk about it." I made myself yawn. "I plan to be asleep in about ten seconds."

Frank turned out his light. I held myself stiff in the bed. This was not like him. He had not coughed, and scratched, and coughed again, he was not ready for slumber. He turned on the light again.

"I know you're tired, Leslie. But I would like to make love."

Frank had always signified desire by coming to bed without his pajama bottoms. He had not given the signal tonight. I had to turn over, look at him.

"Why, Frank?" I said.

He was not smiling. But his eyes were true on my face, and there was love in him. "It's not what you think," he said. "Just because it's been such a long time, every since rehearsals started. Not that at all."

I was still looking at him. "Then what is it?"

"I know you're exhausted, with all the excitement," he said apologetically. "You don't have to be enthusiastic, you can just let me."

"But why, Frank?"

His eyes changed. "I want to know what it's like to make love to the woman I saw up there on the stage. Will you let me make love to that woman?"

So few hours, Russell, since you had been inside me. Though my body had not welcomed you, the imprint of your presence was still in my flesh. Never in my life had I taken two men within the span of one day. But I couldn't deny him, Russell. I didn't have the right to deny him the use of my body; especially after he had asked me in this new way. Shifting to pull my nightgown up to my armpits, I managed a small smile. "Here she is, Frank. But I'm afraid it's just the same old wife you've always had."

He came to me slowly, so differently, so tentative. He had always loved to see me naked. But this time he put out the light, making us together in darkness. He put his broad, strong hands on my breasts. I could feel the faint trembling of his fingers. As I lay still under his touch, he stroked my belly, then cupped his palm to the inside of my thigh, moving down the shape of my leg all the way to my feet, then coming back up the other leg to touch me in the crotch.

His hands so gentle, he was like a blind man learning a room where he has never been. Only after a long time did he take off his pajamas, getting out of bed to do so. When he loomed over me, he was naked top and bottom, so it was going to be a new experience with Frank for me, too. I could feel the coarse hair on his chest tickling my breasts. I had opened my legs to take him in, my hands on each side of his thick, short-waisted torso. He was breathing lightly, he did not speak; I knew he was sensing me totally through the marvelous sensitivity of his organ. When he began, he moved almost languorously, not demanding the fervor of participation. Simply feeling his way blindly in a blind room, he was taking me all over again for the first time.

In spite of myself, I warmed toward his gentle love. He had anticipated that I would be different; perhaps he had believed that the experience of acting, an awakening of the soul, would awaken in me also a physical lust I had never found in all the years of our marriage.

I did not, could not, give him that. But I lay under
his weight, thinking of him solely, of all that we had
been together, and I warmed to him so that I felt
myself enfolding him deeply, so deeply, and within
me there was a deep movement of reaching up reciprocal to his downward strokes. When he came, it
was a long, slow event that went on and on and on, as
though he could not let himself end. But, once finished, he wouldn't let me hold him, he made no gesture of hand to mount to fetch me my usual small individual satisfaction. "Thank you, Leslie. Thank you,
my love," he whispered in the darkness and rolled
away, leaving me alone. He did not get up to hunt for
his pajamas in the dark; for the first and only time, he
went to sleep naked beside me. Quickly to sleep, very
quickly—long before I could close my burning eyes.

I believe Frank knew, so quickly. I believe Frank
was trying, in the only way he knew, to change as I
had changed, trying to make himself the man I
wanted. But Frank could be only Frank; it was his
only genius. In the following days he was, so much
more than ever before, the kind and decent and
thoughtful man who was so sure to get hurt.

Or maybe, without my quite knowing how, he did
succeed in holding me to the place he had made for
me in his town. At least, I did not come again to the
hotel room; though each afternoon, as the maid
prepared for departure, I told myself I couldn't endure another day without you. Caught in a sort of
limbo, I went about my daily duties and the regular
performances of our play. So perhaps it wasn't Frank
at all, but the play itself; with each succeeding performance I felt myself more deeply into the character, my body and my mind shaping with ever-increas-

ing eagerness and ease into her body, her mind. It was escapism; I yearned for the play never to end. Simply by sitting before a lighted mirror to put on makeup, simply by standing in the wings waiting for the first cue, I could become a better, more complete, person. I could read the audience's response; every night the applause came brighter, more readily, on my individual curtain call, for I was certified a great discovery in local drama by a rave review in the Piercetown newspaper. The reviews for the playhouse were always good, of course, but it was not necessary to single out a particular performance for fulsome praise.

Safe in limbo. I knew it couldn't last. Every afternoon I expected to find myself going in at the side door of the hotel, climbing the darkly lighted stairs, carefully avoiding the dusty handrail, to knock on the door of your room. You must have waited also, every afternoon—else you wouldn't have called, finally, one afternoon at a precise one-thirty.

The phone rang once. I picked it up. You said, "Leslie?" I said, "I'll be there, Russell. In fifteen minutes." Because the intimate tone of your voice tiny in the telephone earpiece must have been the signal my soul and my body were waiting for.

"No! You can't come to the hotel!" But then, "I've got to talk to you."

"All right," I said, remembering accurately that you didn't have a car. "I'll pick you up in Woolworth's parking lot."

So quickly clandestine, so immediately furtive; I was terrified that someone would see you getting into the station wagon. Driving with ill-timed haste, I bumped the curb turning out of the parking lot, and headed for a section of town that was not part of my daily routes. Only when, outside the city limits, we were cruising a narrow road with few houses did I draw a deep breath.

We had not talked until now. When you did speak, your topic was an utter surprise. "Leslie," you said, "I want you to do Blanche."

"Blanche?" I said blankly.

"Blanche DuBois." Your tone was almost impatient. "*Streetcar Named Desire.*"

All I knew was the movie. "Oh God, I can't do anything like that," I said. I didn't have to look at you; I was still driving. "Besides, I'm quitting. I thought you understood that."

"You can't quit," you said. "I need you. I've already booked the play."

Stubbornly I shook my head. "It's not just that I won't. I *can't.* I'm not that good."

"You've got everything but technique. I can teach you technique. But you'll have to study the role, Leslie. You must understand it down to your toenails."

Spotting a turnout ahead, beside a trash barrel, I pulled into it. Shifting sidewise in the seat, I looked at you. You would give me only your profile.

"Russell, if I don't quit the company, we'll fuck again. We can't work together that intimately without fucking." You didn't say anything. "Even quitting the playhouse, I'm not sure I can keep away from you. But I've got to try."

You still didn't look at me. "We've got to be together anyway, Leslie. That's why I decided you might as well do Blanche."

My breath caught. "I thought . . ."

Your voice came sharply. "We can't let the last

time stand." You looked at me, your eyes burning in equal parts of lust and anger. "We've got to find each other again, Leslie. We can't let ourselves remember *that* as our last love making for the rest of our lives."

My voice trembled. "Can we find each other, Russell? Can we? With all this?" I moved my hands helplessly, trying to show you *all this*.

"I don't know." Your voice trembled, too. "But I keep waiting, Leslie. Every afternoon, for hours. I lie there with a hard-on, waiting for your knock on the door. I masturbate it out of me, but then it comes up again, because I can't make myself quit waiting until I know it's too late . . . your husband's at home, and your children, you're busy with supper and getting ready to go to the theater." Your hands were over your face. "Then I see you, among all the other actors, and I have to be just an ordinary everyday charming resident director keeping an amateur actor up in the role. I have to treat you exactly like everybody else, when all the time I'm aching to . . ."

You stopped. I couldn't say anything. I was afraid you would cry, and if you cried I couldn't stand it.

"And he's there every night . . ." Taking your hands away from your face, you looked at me with agony showing naked in your eyes. "He knows, Leslie. *Knows*. I've already cost you that." You drew a shaky breath. "So what else can we lose?"

"We can't fuck just because he knows," I said tensely. "It's not enough. The only thing that can be enough . . . Do you *want* to, Russell? Do you want to?"

Your eyes came warm. "I dream every night about you. About us, on the most seaward of our islands, the night we were naked in the moonlight, when . . ."

It moved in me then—that enormous shift that had happened inside me the night I had made my bargain with God—for the very first time since. There was heat between my legs, my bowels yearned liquidly, for all in an instant the magic words of long-ago times had broken me out of limbo. In that moment of liberation, all that I had built here—the town, the children, Frank and the house, *everything*—did not count any more.

I reached to turn the ignition key. "We'll fuck. Right now. In fifteen minutes I can be in your room, and you can be in me."

You felt it then, as I was feeling it. It would be *right* now, beautifully right; we would have it again the way it had used to be. Happiness burst inside of me, so that I threw back my head, laughing gleefully as I stamped on the gas pedal so hard that the motor roared.

Then, miserably, you said. "I can't take you there. Not again."

My foot came off the throttle, idling the motor. "Why not? There's a side door, the stairs ... Like I did the first time."

You wouldn't look at me. "The man—I guess he was the security man—he spoke to me about you."

I was horrified. "Spoke to you?"

You nodded doggedly. "Oh, he was nice about it— as nice as he could be. Said he could understand how it was, a young fellow like me, single and in a strange city." You glanced at me almost defiantly. "But ... he told me he couldn't have local married ladies going in and out of the hotel like that. Nothing but trouble— for him, for the hotel ... and for me. Now, if I found myself a nice single girl, he reckoned he could wink and look the other way as quick as the next fellow. But married ladies . . ."

Tears were stinging my eyes. "Was he . . . did he wear a hat that looked too small for his size, with a narrow brim?"

"Yes."

"Oh God," I said. "He looked at me, coming and going. He knew . . . all the time . . . he knows who I am."

"Yes," you said. Staring into my face, your voice was very careful. "A motel. Will you go to a motel?"

I had to think about it; there was in me no immediate consent. My first impulse was to say to hell with it, town and husband and all. Why should we make the effort to keep ourselves a secret? Let us become scandal quickly, so that I could go away with you. Why should I care what Piercetown thought of me, now that I had found you again, and you had found me.

Frank. I owed Frank. So much. I shook my head. "Not a motel. Somebody would recognize this station wagon. I know it, it would have to happen . . ."

"So we can't fuck," you said quietly, fatally. "Not today."

I leaned toward you, and you leaned toward me. Our arms were about each other. I was weeping as you kissed me frantically all over my face; we were suddenly two greedy children whose candy has been stolen away. I had my hands inside your fly, holding the hard, hot shape of your maleness, and my dress was up to my waist, both your hands thrust through the waistband of the flimsy pants to caress me with trembling, probing fingers. The toot of a horn as a car sailed by, two boys and a blonde girl laughing and waving, making obscene gestures at us, so that we had to pull apart, trembling in our shamed and heedless lust.

"I'll rent a car tomorrow," you said quietly. "Where can I meet you?"

I pulled myself together. We must plan now, carefully and well and, oh, so guiltily. So the next day we were into that bit—after a sleepless night for me at least, driving with a fatal sense of helplessness all the way across town to a shopping center I had never entered before, parking and locking the station wagon, getting silently into your rented car to be driven to a place for clandestine lovemaking.

You had already rented the room, in the motel farthest from town, and somehow you had managed a room on the back, so that, with last night's customers already gone and tonight's not yet arrived, we were observed only by a man mowing grass in the buffer zone between parking space and the walkway.

The room was clean and plastic, the afternoon sun shadowed strongly through the drawn drapes. You had thought to bring a suitcase; oh yes, it was such good planning we might have been doing it for years. But none of it mattered—not the room, not Frank, not the children, not my station wagon secretly parked all the way across town—we *had* each other now and we were frantic as we stripped ourselves bare, tossing the clothing heedlessly, and as I went down on my back, my legs reaching to lock about your descending hips, your penis was plunging wildly into my savage box, and I was already shuddering into orgasm. Your weapon was a blade of hot iron in my flesh, and I could feel you beginning to come, too.

Though so desperately bitter and needful, it was a

great coming-together, a wild and reckless and heedless coupling such as I had never known, except for that one night on the seaward island. But we had been ignorant then, innocent even, and we were no longer innocent but clandestine and shabby. We were committed to, captured by, all the harsh betrayals of ourselves and of others, that left us only with this bitter boon of unassuaged flesh. Sex was all we had, could have, would have; and we both knew it. So, when you fell away out of me, I went with you, putting my head greedily into your crotch to gobble you up, tasting in my mouth the aroma of my own fluids, and loving it as I loved also the oyster taste of your maleness. With reciprocal frenzy, your hands clawed at my hips, drawing my loins down over your head, and your whole face pressed into my wet crotch. I pumped against your face, your lapping tongue, as we began to come again, simultaneously, and then again, and once again. The taste of your semen was bitter and sweet in my mouth.

Only then could we lie hip and thigh, holding each other, our hands stroking as we kissed, our mouths shaping gently together. We had it all at last, the greatness of the act and the guilt, tasting one as we tasted the other. It was all wrong, and it was right.

When we came to it again, we had receded into a certain gentleness. Because you had not quite recovered from the massive emissions—it's a wonder you could get it up at all—I took the top position, working in subtle inventions as your hands gripped my breasts. I watched your face and when it changed with a quickening, it quickened me, too, so that suddenly I was romping on you in a passionate frenzy of desire to squeeze your manhood off right to the roots. You had to come from far back, out of meager resources; feeling it, I began to screech through my lip-drawn teeth, a steady, keening sound like someone perishing in agony or in bliss. I collapsed over you, trembling, weeping, laughing, used up—and, in spite of all, fulfilled and happy. We had found a greatly complete event, so much more than we had achieved together in our innocent youth, because we had, each of us, brought so much more to it—all the pain and the love and the living that had passed through us during our years since parting.

"Love me, Leslie?" you said, finding tenderness at last. And tenderly I said, "Can you doubt it?" Then I sat up, still straddling you, your used member curled limply, sweetly, warmly, against me. Insatiably, I began to caress it with a gentle rocking of my hips; but time jarred suddenly and I snatched a frantic glance at my watch. "God, the kindergarten closes in fifteen minutes. I'll never make it."

We had to get dressed as frantically as we had undressed and flee, leaving, as the only mark of our sojourn in the room, the tangled sheets damp with our sweat and semen. All the way to the shopping center, I raged at every red light, and when you drew up behind my station wagon, I sprang out without a second to spare for a backward glance. Even then I arrived late, to be greeted by a resentful glare from the teacher, accompanied by an acerbic remark about picking up the children on time.

In this manner it began, my dear Russell, and so it continued. We had each other at last—but at what a cost! So many passionate matinees, harried by time and circumstance, in so many strange and plastic rooms, going from one motel to the next until we had used them all, then starting over again. With the frantic and desperate lust that was ruling our lives, we made love three and four times a week; we could not get to the end of sex where conversation and companionship dwelled. It was marvelously wonderful, as great as we had always known it would be, even in the days of our innocence when such abandonment was not in us. We even, in a cruel perversity, savored the bitterness of guilt and betrayal at the core of the sweet; we flaunted the shabby, tattered hems of our garment of bright happiness. There was not peace in us, nor quietness; from being merely frantic, we became increasingly desperate as the disquieting rage in your flesh pounded and sucked at the disquieting rage in mine, and was answered in kind.

We performed also, with devoted diligence, all the dirty little compromises and untruths that belonged to our clandestine affair. We agreed on a system of telephone signals; we were clever about finding safe places for me to leave the station wagon and get into your rented car. I, God rot me, deliberately allowed Frank his Tuesday night release, and Saturday mornings, in a calculated effort to allay his suspicion of my suddenly erratic pattern of behavior.

I could take him only by keeping my eyes open, gazing at the ceiling, while I concentrated on the idea it was you in me. Frank, poor decent loving soul, got better cooperation than he had ever had; and I learned more than I wanted to know about the whore that dwells in every woman's soul. Yes, I learned even that; by imagining him as you, glowing in my flesh, with a trick of the mind I could accept him. With practice and concentration, the trick became just real enough to make me come open and warm, as I would have with you, to the extent that, a number of times, I astonished him with a tense little orgasm; never the wild abandon I knew with you, but a suddenly uncontrollable writhing that was more a pain in the flesh than an ecstasy.

Frank was not stupid. It was he, rather than me, who suddenly ceased. One Tuesday night, quite simply and without a word, he signaled that he had no desire for me; he went peacefully to sleep while I lay awake, wanting him, in the perversity of human flesh, to want me. From that time forward until the end, Frank did not come again into our bed with his pajama bottoms removed.

By this time, we had started rehearsals for *Streetcar*. You had announced the cast, at the same meeting where you disclosed the new production, without conducting open call. Because I was the newest member of the company, there sprouted suddenly among the members a jealous suspicion, a not-very-quiet watchfulness, that engendered fractures and cliques, breaking the productive, confident unity you had established. Some of the people, like actors everywhere, expediently supported you—and me—in an effort to curry favor and fatter parts. Others found their fear of favoritism and secret relationship confirmed as you worked with me so assiduously, with such thoughtful understanding of me as well as of the role. Though we made the effort—both for the sake of maintaining discretion and for the sake of the production—we could not conceal our passionate commitment. Every moment in your vicinity, I had a sensation as if my flesh glowed; simply the touch of your hand, to guide me in a stage movement, shuddered in me as though you had bared yourself, ready to plunge.

The jealous awareness was first confined to the company. Inevitably, the whispered gossip reached the circle of supporters, then rippled in wider and more-encompassing circles throughout the upper-middle-class milieu Frank had brought me into by marriage. Though I might well achieve a blazing Blanche —I knew her more deeply and with a greater truth each day, every time you took me so frantically, so hopelessly, so lustfully, I realized her that much more—this second production under your aegis would be ragged and ill-proportioned. There were tiny rebellions in the cast, an occasional faint but unmistakable show of contempt for what was seen as your deliberate choice of a leading lady you could mount. Even worse, despite all professional resolution, you were subtly but unmistakably tilting the play toward Blanche, failing to give the other roles, Stanley and Stella especially, their proper weight.

Russell, you must have known it. You could not have helped knowing it. Day after day your whole reason and purpose for coming to Piercetown was being defeated. Doggedly you continued to exercise your charm, no longer infallible in its magic, to hold the company together. As opening night approached, in that irresistible rush of time that always besets rehearsals, you initiated a desperate effort to redress the balance of the play. But Emma, as Stella, had become undirectable in her jealous rage, the man playing Stanley had turned sullenly cynical. Only a new beginning, with an entirely new cast, could have retrieved the situation. But such a wholesale dismissal of members strong in their supportive commitment would have destroyed the Piercetown Community Playhouse.

Somehow, not only could we not stop; we could not even care. Moving daily in the midst of whispers, aware of the sidelong glances of malice—yes, and of envy, for I don't believe a single woman in the company, despite their midwestern scorn of my moral conduct, would have turned down my opportunity with you—I yet felt myself invisible and inviolate to everything and everybody but you. Even when Cora, my best friend, mustered up the courage one day to remark, out of the seeming blue, "Leslie, please be careful. Frank . . ." I only gazed at her with blank eyes and replied, "I don't know what you're talking about, Cora."

The possibility of stopping did not exist. Having given up the furtile search for peace and fulfillment in each other, we lusted to experience the deep, bitter, terrible lust that had swallowed up our love. In our desperation we had become reckless, careless, uncaring; after my little girl had suffered a fever and a sore throat for three long days, making it impossible for me to come to you, I whispered one night, as I got into my coat and scarf and gloves after rehearsal, "Stay. I'll be back as soon as the others have gone." As we writhed that night on Blanche's bed, a part of the set, our strained cries and harsh breathings echoed in the empty auditorium. Once we had dared that breach of decorum, of safety, there were other times when I left my station wagon sitting conspicuously alone in the parking lot while we made love, and came home late and depleted and without regret to Frank's increasing silence. That, too, had its subtle effect on the play; it was no longer simply Blanche's bed, in Blanche's room, but another place where you and I had made love.

I suppose, if it had not been for Frank, we would have ridden our wild horses all the way to utter disaster. We knew, by now, that we were doomed. We had destroyed each other. I had taken what was yours, you had taken what was mine. But there were no stops left in us; we could not even admit the possibility.

Frank, on the opening night, came with me to the theater. After the performance, the dear sweet soul came up on the stage with an enormous bouquet of red roses and told me quietly—everyone else, momentarily forgetful, had shouted their enthusiasms at me—that no one else in the world could have been the Blanch DuBois I had been that night. I scarcely listened, for I knew it of myself; I did not need Frank telling me, nor the audience in its storm of applause that had insisted on repeated curtail calls until I had lost count. I did need you. As I was waiting for you to come to me, Frank slipped away as inconspicuously as he had appeared.

He did not stay for the cast party so I, in the euphoria of an opening-night triumph, dared the most reckless gesture of all; I left with you, stating gaily that in the absence of my lamented husband I trusted no one else to be sober enough to drive me home. When I entered Frank's house, I had, for the first and only time, been thoroughly possessed by you in the back seat of a car. Sprawled open and wet and hot under you, feeling the steam pressure rising in me as you pounded and pounded, I thought of the cold flesh I had presented to all those miserable Pass Robin males; and when I began to come, I clawed your back to ribbons with my fingernails, while you left a mouth-shaped bruise on the side of my neck.

Frank was standing before the fireplace, a drink in his hand. That was strangely different. Frank drank very little, and never at this time of night.

"Did you lose the roses I gave you?" he said.

I stared at my hands. "I must have," I said. I tried to laugh. "I didn't realize I was *that* tight." I knew perfectly well I had left them trampled on the floor of your car.

Frank drank from his glass, looked at me again. Perhaps my appearance—draggled, depleted, guilty and unguilty—reminded him of the role I had played tonight. "You ought to be an actress," he said. "Why didn't you ever think of it, instead of working in an office?"

"I don't know," I said. "The possibility just never crossed my mind, I suppose."

His eyes had not left my face. "Leslie. Would he marry you? If you were free?"

Something congealed inside me. So this was it, what it felt like to know that you and I were coming to an end. Frank meant to end it. As well as possible. But end it, whatever it might take.

"I don't know," I said.

"Do you *want* to marry him?"

"I don't know," I said. "I haven't thought about it."

Frank emptied his glass, set it on the mantel. "You can't go on like this," he said, his voice quiet and careful and without heat. "I won't let you. Russell Walford will not produce another play in Pierce-town. I've already talked to three of the guys on the board, and they agree wholeheartedly." His lips twitched. "His contract will be bought out for the rest of the year. I'm putting up the money for the purpose."

"You can't do that to him," I said, stirred at last out of my frozen self.

"There's no way you can stop me," Frank said calmly. "Do you want a drink?"

"No," I said. Then I said, "I'll go with him."

Frank shook his head. "If you try that, I'll have to kill him. You don't want that. For him. For me. Or for yourself."

Gazing into Frank's eyes, I knew he was telling the truth of himself. He held my eyes for a long moment, then he made a drink with quick hands and thrust it into my grasp. "Here. You need this."

I drank from it, first only a sip that suddenly turned into a greedy gulp, so that the liquid over-flowed my mouth and dripped on my crumpled dress. I stared down at the dress, thinking dully that it was ruined, I'd never be able to wear it again. Not just the drink; ruined also in the back seat of your car. My fa-vorite long dress, too, a deep coral in color, draping so beautifully from a bodice line that showed off my neck and shoulders.

"So it's going to be your way," I said.

"This is a decent town, Leslie, made up of decent people. You owe them, Leslie. You owe me." He paused for a split second. "You owe your children."

"All right," I said, "Exactly what is your decent way for undecent people?"

The fatal bitterness in my voice gave him pause for a second. He stared at me, not in love, or compassion, though he had shown me so much love and com-passion; but simply to read whether I was going up the wall in my desperation. I could still, by sheer intransigence, destroy the decent plan for ending it that he had worked out so meticulously.

"He will go, right now, as soon as possible," Frank said. "The board will talk to him in the morning. You ..." He was watching me again. "You will remain in this house for three months. After that ... you can go anywhere, do anything, you wish. I won't lift a finger to stop you."

"Even if I ... go after him?" I said.

"Even if you go after him," he said steadily. He paused to fill his glass and drink from it. Now, for the first time, he could not look at me. "Leslie, that'll be three months in which you can think about ... think about things. If you want to consider staying, I mean. If you should decide that you'd like to stay ..."

My knees were suddenly weak. "Frank. You can't mean that. Not after ..."

He stood before me, heavy and stolid and so predictable ... except that this conversation, after theatrical performance and after sex, had not been at all predictable.

"I've never had very much of you," Frank told me. "But the small houseroom you gave me ... that's more woman than I ever had any right to expect. So ... yes, even after ..." His eyes were on me, and I knew he was looking at the mouth bruise on my neck. His voice choking to a stop, he cleared his throat with an effort. "You ought to know, Leslie, I came to the theater one night. Very late, that first night you didn't get home until so long after rehearsal. I ... standing in the back of the theater, I heard you ... with him. I ... discovered exactly how little of yourself you had allowed me, all these years."

As crumpled on the inside of my soul as my dress

was crumpled on my body, I covered my eyes with my hands. "Oh God," I said. "Frank."

His voice had steadied itself. "All right, a lot of it was my fault. I can't help it that I'm not half the man in bed that he is."

"Frank," I said. "Please. You were good in bed. Always. I just . . ."

He was not interested in a female massaging of the male ego. The words went steadily on as though I had not spoken. "I hope you *will* stay with me. I hope that when you've had time to think about it, what you have with me will count . . . enough, at least. If you can stay, I'll help in every way I can . . . I promise we'll never speak of . . . him." He turned away. "But I won't attempt to persuade you. I'll only say this; if you do go, the children remain with me. They won't be your children any longer."

I had not considered the children. It shook me, so that I yearned to go down on my knees before him, beg him to let me stay. But it was too late for that, too late to consider the children. Too late for anything. Frank had closed off all the options. I could only say, "All right, Frank. We'll do it your way." I took a step toward the stairs, then stopped. "I'm sorry, Frank."

For the last time ever, I think he put his kind eyes squarely on my face. "No," he said. "You're not sorry. So don't say it."

"Frank, he was the first one," I said. "The only one."

"I'm glad you told me that. I thought it was just . . . discontent." I went on, then, and halfway up the stairs Frank said, "I'll sleep in the guest room. I won't bother you," and I said, "Thank you, Frank," and went on to my empty bed.

Of course, darling, after the three months required by Frank's sense of decency, I had to leave. My house was empty, my life was empty, my heart was empty; I had let it all go for the sake of frantic sex—in motel rooms, in Blanche's stage-prop bed, that one last heedless coupling in the back seat of your rented car parked within a block of the house. It hurt more deeply than I had realized it would to leave the children. But after three months in that dead house, Frank as dead and finished as I was, I understood that it was the only decent thing I could do for them, too.

When the time came, I caught a train for New York. Frank transported me, and my single bag, to the station. He let me kiss the children and hold them close and warm for the last time. He even, as I stood on the moving platform, took my hand for a fleeting second. When I looked for the last time, he was leading the children away, one child clinging to each hand. I could not even weep. It was too late for weeping, even.

I meant to come to you, Russell. Out of that long-ago summer when I had been your girl with the golden cunt, out of these years in Piercetown I could not even label in my mind, you, the idea of you, was all I had left. Perhaps you wouldn't want me, perhaps by now you hated me for destroying you in your first real chance to practice your profession. Perhaps, more simply, we had burned it all out.

I didn't have the chance to find out. Very quickly, in the small world of the theater, I learned that you were in Europe. Because I had refused the alimony

Frank had offered, I didn't have the money to pursue you to the other side of the world where we might have the chance to begin again.

The end of that time. The end of this letter. It didn't come out bright and innocent and happy, like your letter, but as murky with guilt and shame as was the time itself. The best part of me is hoping that you have long since ceased to read it, there in that bright foreign island where you live now; and so I will not count on a reply.

Good-bye, my love. As poor old Bill once told me, "Do good with yourself," and, as I replied, "Be happy."

PS: I must tell you this; I have your mother's painting. When I married Paul, I made him buy it for me. It took a long search, and a great deal of money, to acquire it. It was the only wedding present I wanted.

THE
THIRD
LETTER
to

her

Your answer came as a surprise; not that you wrote the letter, nor that you mailed it after it was done—but that you went beyond the scope of my letter into the new time and the new place where we were no longer the hero and heroine but the villains. We all like to think of ourselves as the good guys, don't we? When those upright midwestern men came to discuss solemnly the termination of my contract, I was indignant and angry and self-defensive. It was not that I feared to face them; I did not dare face myself. I saw myself, and accepted their moral verdict, only when one member of the board, the man who had talked least, who had watched my antics most intently, remarked quietly that Frank Swenson was putting up the money to buy out my contract.

My letter spoke of us as innocents; you chose to write of us as evil. My letter stopped when it did because, I told myself, it was far too long already and, besides, that was another country. I expected an answer, if you answered at all, within the frame of reference I had laid down, there on the far side of September where we yet dwelled in Paradise. But, unflinchingly, you entered upon the evil time—for we were evil, not in what we did to each other, because we deserved each other, but for what we did to others.

So what does that leave me? Our third encounter—and I can't flinch from it, as you did not flinch.

But first I must tell you this, my love. There in Piercetown, where you should not have been and I should not have been, you were opaque to me. I understood with absolute clarity what you were doing to yourself, to me, to the innocent others; but somehow there was in me a suspension of insight, the avoidance of judgment. Knowing, in that time and that place, that you were evil, I aided and abetted the evil that was in you. Yet within you I perceived somehow the wonderful innocence of old we had shared through the summer days of Pass Robin. So, as we had once shared innocence, we now shared evil, so that it was my sin as much as yours, because I didn't know *why*. In the final analysis, I understood myself no better than I understood you. We all yearn to be the good guys forever.

In that winter town, you were a spring flower, totally unconscious that they, winter people, midland people, saw you as an exotic stranger from a land that was forever spring. There was in you an unconscious assumption of flowering and growth that they, in

202

their eternal winter, had lost. You went about in their city heedless of their eyes, uncaring of their judgment, weaving the pattern—unconscious only to you, only to me, for they knew, *they knew*—of destruction, with the energy and expertise of a spider making the web engrained in his nature by millennia of instinct.

How, then, could evil flower out of innocence? You had not changed; there remained in the woman of Piercetown the girl I had loved in my youth. It was that which I still loved; as it was the evil for which I lusted with a raging, heedless lust. Not understanding these things—then, nor for long after—I fled from that place. I scarcely paused in New York, for I could not bear the silent reproach of those who had believed in me, who had engineered the opportunity, who had awaited my return in triumph. I escaped to Europe—and it was a refugee's escape, for I had abandoned all ambition.

I was unlucky, in that economic necessity did not force me to a more limited option. Upon graduation from college, Father had settled on me a substantial portion of the family capital. At his death, and Mother's, I could count on receiving the rest of it. So for two years, three, I drifted footless in Europe, not even pondering what had happened, to me, or inside me, through you-in-Piercetown. If Eva had not come along, my fate would have remained the idle fate of an expatriate floating aimlessly from one pleasant foreign ambience to the next. For I didn't want to understand. I could not have endured understanding if understanding had come to me. You had been evil, and I had abetted your evil. I had been evil, too, aided by your commitment and connivance. Worst of all, I had enjoyed it, reveled in it; I had lusted after evil as I had lusted for your flesh.

Only now that I have read your letter, here in the peace and quiet that I have found for myself after our third adventure, have I caught at the hem of understanding. I will not try to tell it to you, by setting down on paper the part that you stopped before telling. For it must all be told, in substance and in detail. Mustn't it?

Let me state first the thesis of my understanding, as of this moment. We were, you and I, though still so greatly in love that we should have been immune, as immediately enthralled by the evil of lust as were those winter people among whom we acted it out, a morality play for their edification and benefit. Accepting the terms of the place, of the time, we wallowed in those imposed sexual conditions of lust and greed as my flesh wallowed in your lusting flesh. We patterned out their own dream pattern of clandestine behavior, their demeaning imaginations of motel rooms and the back seats of automobiles, of not-so-secret telephone signals and the thrilling clutch of hand on penis and finger in vagina at the snatched instant when no one, we thought, was looking.

Yes. We accepted it. We enjoyed it. We reveled in it. It was an indulgence of all the greed and lust and lack of conscious will that the human animal is heir to out of his unconscious animal past. And why? Because we could use it as a cloak to conceal the real events in which dwelled the underlying truth of ourselves.

All your life, my Leslie, you have been a rare and beautiful thing, enhusked inside one chrysalis after another. In the seventeenth summer of my youth I was privileged to break you out of the primal chrysalis of adolescence. Then, in the winter of Piercetown, my renewed presence was the catalyst that awakened you from the dormant state you had so instinctively sought and achieved. It was my task to make you aware, in the dead of winter, that spring yet existed. Change could come. Had to come.

The trouble is, you are, in all the stages, so rarely beautiful that everyone—me included—makes a desperate effort to hold you as you are in the moment of you that belongs to them. While you, with the serenity of foreknowledge, know the changes before they begin to happen.

No. This metaphor is becoming too elaborate to hold up. Let me put it plainly. When I came to Piercetown, the actress you were meant to become was awakening inside of you, ready to be born and take its rightful command of your destiny. It was not lust you sought, though you enjoyed so greatly the lust that you found. It was not evil that moved you, though you accepted the evil necessity of shattering the hard husk of being that held prisoner the new being you meant to become.

So all that evil, all that lust, all that hate and scandal that we left behind as the Piercetown memory of ourselves, were no more than the incidental shards of metamorphosis.

And me, you say? Simple. My task was twofold: to bring to you in that winter of yourself the seeds of possibility for your future self; and to drive you out of Piercetown as I had once driven you out of Pass Robin. You did not come to New York in search of me, my darling, but in search of your further self.

I am not saying that you never loved me. You did

love me. I am not saying that you did not lust for me, as I lusted for you. I am only telling you that, as I was your love, your lust, I was also your most willing instrument.

As, in a way, you were my instrument. For when I peeled back layer by layer those interleavings of yourself—even as my penis peeled back the intricate foldings of your vagina in so many passionate moments—and revealed you to yourself, I learned also, not simply to open; but, far more importantly, to recognize the possibilities of opening. To the limited extent that I made you an actress, you made me a director.

Which brings us to the third time around. If truth and meaning dwells in our third encounter, where can it be found? Did we do it all over again?—and I remember immediately the mythic saying, *the third time is the charm*—or was it new and different? Or simply meaningless. I don't know. So let me tell it with a plain telling and perhaps, just perhaps, we will find again a certain meaning at the end.

Ever since returning to New York after the long absence, I had remained distantly aware of news about you. I am sure, in our small world of the theater, you were aware of me in the same remote way, though I was on one coast and you were on the other. Every time I saw your name, I felt an obscure gratification. I made a point of going to see your pictures, sneaking away from Eva in the afternoons to sit with strangers in a theater and gaze at you performing on the screen. (You were good, darling, but the pictures, so often, were not good. Only two, I think, will be worth keeping.) You were so beautiful, up there bigger than life in Technicolor, that I would come out blinking into the late sunshine with a stone ache in my soul.

When Eva told me she had arranged for me to direct the motion picture of my new stage success, my first, purely involuntary, thought was that once again we would be in the same place at the same time. I could not decide, in the immediate realization, whether it was a consummation to be wished.

But, ready or not, here I came; Eva said it was time to direct a picture, so it was not to be avoided. Ever since Eva had picked me up in Europe and, after six months of love and therapy, had brought me back to the New York theater, she had planned the strategy and executed the design of my career. Eva not only had ample money of her own, but, as an agent and as a producer, had worked in the theater all her life. Eva and I had put together three hits in a row; then, after the disastrous flop of the musical, she did not allow me a moment of despair but insisted I should use the unavoidable hiatus to begin the study of films. We left New York again, not for Hollywood as we would have done in the old days, but for Europe once more. Starting all over again at the bottom, I worked on films in Italy, in Spain, in France. When she felt I was ready, Eva put up her own money for the short that won the prize at Cannes. Returning in triumph to New York, she found the new play; and when the movie offer came, we were ready.

I must tell you this, right in front; Eva is the best thing that ever happened to me. Five years older than I, no more than what you would call attractive, she was—and is—a woman with a sharp mind and a loving heart. If anybody could have saved me from my European refugee self, it was Eva. But I would not

Anonymous

marry her until I had directed a hit on Broadway.
Our relationship was loose and easy and understanding, based on love and respect and a decent display of
sex. When Eva gave of herself, she held nothing back.
I remember so well, the first play I directed, how I
came home after a frustrating day ready to give it up.

"But you can't do that," Eva said. "I worked too
hard to get it for you."

"I can't direct that bitch," I said. "She gets more
unreasonable every day."

Eva put down the script she was reading to look at
me. "Darling, you'll have to fuck her," she said.

I was startled. "What?"

Eva smiled. "I hoped you'd figure it out for yourself. Just ball her good, and she'll be like a piece of
pie in your hand. Can't you see that's what's wrong
with her? She can't believe you think she's any good
because you haven't shown any desire to roam around
in her pants. Darling, you're absolutely destroying her
self-confidence. Now, if you were gay, it wouldn't be
a problem, she wouldn't expect anything, she'd work
like a trouper. But since you're a man . . ." She
shrugged.

"But I don't have the least desire . . ."

"You want a performance, don't you?"

"Yes, but . . ." I stopped, staring at her. "And you
. . . you can sit there and calmly suggest . . ." We were
not married yet. But, in spiritual actuality, we were
married.

Eva shrugged again. "I want you to do what you
have to do to make a success out of this thing." She
smiled. "You might like it. I hear she's hell on wheels
with a cock."

The next afternoon, when the bitch went stamping

208

offstage, declaring she wouldn't come back until the male lead was replaced, I followed her into her dressing room. A fancy layout—as the core of the play, she demanded perquisites, including most of the money being paid to cast.

She was sitting on the couch, pouting. Gritting my teeth, I walked over, grabbed her by both ankles, and upended her. I must say, she fell expertly on her back, legs in air. I laughed. She was naked under the costume, and her pubic hair was dyed a deep purple. Not only that; chasing along the insides of her thighs, half a dozen delicately tattooed mice were scampering for safety. Still laughing, I unlimbered my club, plugged it into her mouse hole, and proceeded to beat her into submission with it. Eva was right; the talented bitch was Mary's little well-laid lamb from then on, and gave the performance of her career.

Even after Eva and I were formally married, our contract had no fidelity clause, so I was not violating intimate arrangements to think of you so promptly. Not that we solemnly averred to each other that jealousy would not exist, or that we would, as a matter of principle, seek sexual variety; it was simply our manner of marriage. Though we spent a great deal of time together, we were also often apart—so often in the company of the volatile and charming and childlike men and woman called players. I never had the impulse to inquire if Eva encountered demands or desires; I only know I was seldom moved to indulge, most often simply as an aid to work. We, Eva and I, needed each other in so many different ways we could have utter confidence that no other person, no matter what the circumstances, could move between

us. As I said in the beginning, Eva was the best thing
that ever happened to me.

I'm telling you these things so you will know fully
my situation at the time of our third coming together.
I was contented, I was successful, I was even happy.
Yet, the moment I knew that the circumstances of my
developing career would bring me into your vicinity,
I could not avoid thinking about you. Always you
had remained in the back of my mind, on the edge of
consciousness.

But I did not know you were married to Paul
Ruach until I walked into the restaurant to meet
Ruach for the first time, and saw you sitting with
him.

He stood up to shake hands. Paul Ruach was a
heavy man, broad but not fat, and astonishingly ugly.
His nose was an amorphous blob in the middle of his
face, his mouth large but firm lipped, his skin dark
and wrinkled. His hand was like a toad, even to the
clamminess, but a surprisingly firm strength was revealed in his grip.

"I'm glad to meet my new hotshot director at last,"
he said genially. "It's time the damned lawyers got
through talking so we can get to work making a picture."

Only as we sat down did he remember to introduce
me to you. "Darling, this is Russell Walford, you
know the name. He's directing my number one picture this year. Russ, this is my wife. Leslie Dollar, you
know the name."

You smiled. "I've known Russell for ages, darling.
Too many ages."

His shrewd eyes cut sharply to your face. "Don't
start telling me it's a small world."

"He got my cherry, darling," you said calmly. "Believe it or not."

Paul Ruach beamed. "Now isn't that nice!" he said. "Why, that makes it all one big happy family, doesn't it?" He forked a shrimp, put it in his wide mouth, took a swallow from the champagne glass. "Was she any good, Russ? She's Mary-Poppins-in-the-sack now, I can tell you that."

I glanced at you uncomfortably. For one thing, I had never been called "Russ" in my life. You appeared quite easy, smiling faintly, almost reminiscently, as you gazed into your glass of white wine. You weren't going to be any help at all.

And this was the man who held me and my picture in the palm of his hand. "She was the most beautiful girl you can imagine," I said.

Paul Ruach laughed. "She's the most beautiful *woman* you can imagine!" he said. "Why do you think I married her? Now come on, let's order you a drink and get down to business." He glanced at his wristwatch, ornate with diamonds. I watched the movement of his hand, thinking about it snugged into your warm crotch. "I've got twenty-five minutes. Not a second more."

For what was probably exactly twenty-three-and-a-half minutes, we ate and drank and talked about the picture. You were into the conversation, too, not merely decoration for Paul Ruach's table. He ate largely, and drank a bottle of champagne; you ate sparingly and sipped at your white wine. I don't remember what I ate, what I drank; I was thinking too hard about the conversation. That picture was of first importance to me.

Time up, Paul pushed back his plate, wiped his

mouth, glanced at his watch. He did not look at me, but at you. "Darling, what do you think?"

You didn't look up. "You were right, darling. I've already told you that."

His voice was insistent. "But I'm still right. Is that it?"

You gave him the flicker of an eye. "Still right, Paul."

He grunted, turned to me. "Russ, I'm giving you a free hand. As a general thing, I'm a pretty good fellow at looking over your shoulder. But I think, and Leslie thinks, that you've got what it takes. So I won't talk to you again until you deliver the answer print and I've had a chance to see it. But if the producer tries to give you a hard time, you call me."

"Thank you, Mr. Ruach," I said. "I appreciate the confidence."

He grunted again. "Just come in under the budget and on time. That's all I ask. And you can call me Paul. At least until I screen the answer print." He grunted again, put his hands on the table, shoved his chair back. He stood up, looking again at his watch. "I imagine you two will want to talk over some old times. See you tonight, darling. Ten minutes after eight."

He began to walk away, moving with a heavy waddle. The maître d' bowed, a waiter and a customer hastily cleared out of his path. Three tables away, he turned, lifting his voice without regard for the other people in the restaurant.

"Just remember one thing, Russ. You've got the first cut, but you don't have the final. You might get it, though, if everything works out." He disappeared through the door.

I looked at you, now that he was gone. "Thank you, Leslie. I know you must have had a lot to do with the freedom he's giving me."

You shook your head slightly. "Paul makes up his own mind."

"But he obviously respects your opinion."

"Yes. Paul respects my opinion."

I studied you. Oh, I had seen you, noted you; but now I took the survey necessary to bring me up-to-date with Leslie Dollar.

In so many ways, you had not changed at all. Still beautiful, still deep, still shifting inside yourself even as I gazed. Responding to my gaze. But you had changed, too; there was a sleek patina that had not been in you before.

I had known you as a girl; sixteen, virginal, ready to be awakened. I had known you as a full woman, married, a mother, and ready for clandestine sex. Now, this third time, the magic time, there was a certain . . . consciousness . . . in you, Leslie, you had not only come to know your beauty, you had learned to use it. You were using it now, not deliberately but unconsciously, so practiced and expert had you become, as we sat here among strangers. I don't know how to describe it; you were . . . no longer invisible to them. You knew it. You no longer . . . wished to be invisible.

With such intense scrutiny, I could read the infinitely tedious care that had been given your face this morning. It showed in the shape of your eyelids, the color of your mouth, the expensive disarray of hair. There was time now, years of time, to be contended with. But your eyes—your eyes had not changed, could not change, they were green and warm and seeing. Didn't somebody say that the eyes are the mirror of the soul?

"Well," I said. "Leslie."

"Well," you said, smiling as you answered with the word.

"Why him?" I said, gesturing with my head.

A small cloud gathered in the extraordinary clarity of your gaze. Your eyes knew what I meant. *All* that I meant.

"Women find power sexually attractive," you said. "You must have learned that by now, Russell." You smiled faintly. "If you haven't, you'll learn it very quickly out here. And enjoy the experience."

Yes. I knew. I had used it, so often and so deliberately. But could power be sexually attractive when the woman *knew* it was the power, not the man?

"I understand full well that he's one of the two or three most powerful men in the industry today," I said. "What surprised me was that you are married to him."

Your eyes were still dark. "Aside from everything else, about eighty percent of the time he's a very nice man."

"And the other twenty percent?"

You shrugged. "There are always dues to be paid."

I couldn't stop looking at you. I was trying to imagine you in the arms of that monstrous man, responding to the clammy touch of his toadlike hands, to the thrust of his brazen tool. You would respond. You would have to. Failing to respond, you would last about ten minutes in his life.

"Why did you tell him ... about us?"

You shrugged again. "Why not?" You hesitated. "He probably already knew it. Not because of me, but because he was interested in working with you. There's not much he doesn't know about the people who interest him."

I couldn't find an answer to that. You waited, but when you saw that I would not speak you went on, your voice very soft, very low.

"Paul Ruach is a great man in his way, Russell. The greatness lies in his need to do whatever it is he is doing with a concentration absolutely frightening. He does one thing at a time, within the scope of the time alloted to that one thing." Raising your eyes, you looked into my eyes. "In twenty-three-and-a-half minutes he decided to give you total control over your picture. I can't remember the last time that happened, because Paul doesn't trust anyone to be as good as he is. Hardly anyone." Your voice did not change, your eyes remained on my face without flinching. "He probably fucks better than you ever dreamed it possible to fuck a woman. When that marvelous cock of his comes into you, you are not only the only *woman* in the world, you're the only *thing* in the world. With all the force of his mind, with all the force of his body, with all the force of his spirit, he is thinking and feeling and performing the fucking of you." You shuddered. You actually shuddered. "A woman might not get it often, even married to him. Most of his women get it only once. But ..." You shuddered again. "But once you've had it, Russell, you can never forget it. It cannot be forgotten."

I had to say the words. "So you love him."

You shook your head briskly, decisively. "No."

"Feeling that way about him, you have to love him."

You smiled at my foolish statement. The patina on

you, I saw now, was a gloss of ancientness; not age. I don't mean that, but age-old woman, used so many times, and ready to be used again. By the right man. Only by the right man, for in this lay your free will, your independence, your ultimate meaning.

"I have enormous respect for Paul Ruach. I am one of the few people who understand exactly what it is he does; one of the even fewer who can help him at it. I share everything that Paul is, that Paul does. With me he does not have to divide himself—he can be whole. When he turns to me, it's because he doesn't have to lie and soothe and comfort and tease." You smiled, faintly still. "Sometimes I even like him. Sometimes I hate him." You were not looking at me any longer, but at your hands on the table. "He knows it all. He accepts it, as he accepts me. He makes me have to be whole, too."

I took a deep breath. "It must be quite an experience."

Laughing, you picked up your glass of white wine and emptied it. "You can say that in spades, darling. Now, what about you? Is your wife good for you? What's her name ... Eva?"

"Yes," I said. "She's great." I spread my hands. "What can I say? I wouldn't be sitting here, right this minute, if it were not for Eva. I wouldn't be the person that I am."

"Would I like her?"

I had not thought about it, but I didn't hesitate. "Yes. And Eva would like you."

We sat looking at each other. The restaurant around us was a buzz of talk, money and films and personalities; these were the big people, the movers and the shakers. We might as well have been, for that one instant, alone on our most seaward island.

"Leslie, can I see you?" I said.

You gave me your eyes for the breath of a second. "Do you want to? . . . after what I've just told you?"

"Yes."

You held yourself still for a moment. Then, shifting slightly in your seat, you enlisted the patina to intervene between us. I saw now that it was also a shield. Just for an instant you had lowered the shield. But now it was firmly in place again.

"Paul and I, we're into the group-sex thing," you said. "For quite a long time now."

"Good God, Leslie!" The words blurted out of me before I could stop them. "How could you let him do that to you?"

You glanced around, the waiter was alert, you put your fingertip on your empty glass and he poured it full in ten seconds flat. You looked at me, I said yes, I thought I would have another bourbon. Another ten seconds, and they remembered the sour mash though I had not been in this restaurant before. Power, I thought. The small uses of power. Looking at you from a remote distance now, the thought went on. And the large uses. Very large. To take a woman like you, so beautiful, so much inside yourself, and put you into a scene like that. Not only do it. Make you desire to accept it.

My thoughts must have showed plainly on my face. You sipped from the wine. "It came as no great surprise, Russell. He put it right up front. If I had to have him all to myself, it could be that way—for as long as it lasted. But, he told me plainly, he wouldn't promise more than a night, a weekend, a month, a year ... but if I wanted to go for the whole bit, I'd have to make up my mind I could not possess him. Even then it might not work. But if I was as good as he thought I was, I would become a part of him, he would become a part of me. We would be level with each other . . . and he had never been level with a woman in his life."

Your face brooded. "I thought about it. For a whole month. He left me alone to think. And then . . . I agreed."

Your eyes were on my eyes again. "It has been the right thing. We have kept the faith with each other. And right now . . ." Putting your elbow on the table, you curled your hand into a fist. "Right now there is not a woman in the industry, and damn few men, who can accomplish with a year's work what I can do in an idle moment. Because of me-and-Paul."

"But you don't act any more. Or very little."

"I make a picture when Paul Ruach says that I must, because no one else can do the job that needs to be done. It doesn't happen often. But it does happen." You smiled reminiscently. "What I've got is so much larger than playacting, Russell. Can't you see that?"

"Yes," I said. "So you have it all now. Everything you left Pass Robin—and Piercetown—to find."

"More than I ever dreamed."

"But there are dues."

Glancing at me, that quick flicker of eyes I had not seen in you until this meeting. "There are always dues, Russell. You know that as well as I do. Or you wouldn't be here, either."

"Is there . . . some part of you that still loves me?"

Your voice did not falter. "Yes. Some part will never stop loving you." You waited then. I knew you were waiting for me to say it too. But there was in my mind the great Paul Ruach, behind Paul, shadowy and vague and yet too real, all that I had ever heard or read about the group-sex scene. So I didn't say it.

You didn't wait more than a perceptible second before you began to make those unmistakable, subtle adjustments and movements that mean a woman is getting ready to make an exit. Stopping that, almost with an effort, you sat still again.

"So you see why I can't go sneaking off to a motel room where we can make love again, Russell. You can fuck me if you want to, to your heart's content and mine. But only there, in his house, within full view of Paul and Eva, of all the people who will be there doing the same thing."

"Eva . . ." I said, my throat choking.

Your voice was steady. "Yes. She'll have to come with you. We found out long ago that the surest route to trouble is to invite a man, or a woman, without the mate sharing also, open and aboveboard."

"I don't . . . think Eva would care for that sort of thing."

You could not repress a gleam of curiosity. "You mean . . . you've never done the group-sex thing? Neither of you?"

"I haven't," I said. "I don't know about her. If she had, though, I believe she would have talked about it."

"What makes you think she might not jump at the chance?" Your patina was shielding you again. "It's really very nice, once you get over the initial . . . shock . . . of the idea. If you have a good group of people. It depends so much on the people."

I tried to imagine it, and failed. "Well," I said uncertainly. "I'm glad I got to see you. I do appreciate you supporting me with Paul." I stopped. I said, "Do you want me to?"

Ready now, you stood up. The waiter was behind you, deftly shifting the chair. You leaned over the table, placing your clenched fist to bear your weight. I could feel your warm breath on my face.

"Yes," you whispered. "Oh God yes. Russell. *Yes!*"

You left then. But, before disappearing, you paused, almost exactly where Paul had halted before, to look back. I half expected you to call your parting word across the restaurant, as he had done. But you only gave me a long, enigmatic look, and continued onward.

When I arrived at the apartment Eva had found for us, I learned, with full force, that you were so much more now than you had been, for you had learned the uses of yourself, you knew the subtle ways of power. You had already called Eva on the telephone.

She met me at the door, a curious expression on her face. "How did lunch go?"

"I've got it all," I said. "Total control. The only requirements are to bring it within budget and on time. We'll talk about it again when he's seen the answer print."

"Good God!" Eva said. "Paul Ruach? I don't believe it."

"He's that kind of man," I said. "But I don't believe it, either." Aware that she was poised on the edge of something, I could feel a corresponding tension inside me.

"And she's that kind of woman," Eva said. "Leslie Dollar called me just a few minutes ago, to ask us to a party tonight. At their place."

220

I was immediately wary. "A party? I need to get to work. I've got to decide things I didn't expect to make the decision on. What kind of party?"

Eva was still watching me. "She explained the kind of party. Very carefully, so I'd know exactly what to expect."

"Oh God." There was nothing else to say, because you had put it right up to me, hadn't you? I walked through the living room into the bedroom, took off my tie and my coat, and threw them into a chair. After I had laid down, I looked up to see Eva standing there. She had come right along with me.

Slowly, almost fragilely, she lowered herself to the edge of the bed. "She's the one you told me about, isn't she? The time you got so drunk, after the terrible flop of your musical."

"Yes."

Eva took a deep breath. "I was praying you wouldn't lie. Because she told me. She said you had talked about fucking, and that's why she wanted you to come tonight. But I had to come along."

My hands braced behind my head, I was looking at the ceiling. "This is the sort of thing we don't need. She is Paul Ruach's wife, you know."

"She explained all that." Eva waited for a moment. She was watching me. "You're aching to go, aren't you? The idea of her is hot in your balls right now. Isn't that the truth?"

I sat up violently. "So what if it is?"

Eva gave me her long, level look. "Lie down," she said. "I want to tell you something."

I sank back to the pillow. My hands behind my head, I looked at the ceiling.

"I've not been unfaithful to you, Russell," Eva said.

"Never even wanted to be, except one time. You remember Carlos, don't you? Carlos decided he had to fuck me. When Carlos decides to fuck somebody, you wouldn't believe the ingenuity and enterprise he can put into the endeavor." Her voice became slightly insistent. "You do remember him, don't you? Carlos?"

"Yes," I said grudgingly. "A little man, dark, pencil moustache. That Carlos?"

"That Carlos. Subtle and persuasive, and he wouldn't give up. He just kept on and on, trying every way a man can try to put his cock inside a woman with her consent." She paused. "I used to laugh at him. It was so funny, all that earnestness, all that energy, all that dedication, directed solely toward screwing me. But then—as time went on, as Carlos went on—I quit laughing."

She drew a deep breath. "Instead, I suddenly found myself thinking about it. Yes, Russell. Without knowing exactly how it happened, Carlos had become a definite option in my life. After all, there was nothing to stop me. Knowing what you and I shared, a little flutter in the sack with Carlos couldn't disturb anything important. Even Carlos would have been horrified by that idea."

Her voice dropped. I turned my head to look at her. She was not looking at me. Her eyes were far away. With Carlos.

"It . . . almost happened. Remember, you were working so hard on the musical, you had flop sweat dripping from your bones, for days and then weeks you didn't know I was in the world. Carlos sensed his great opportunity. He was after me day and night. And then . . ."

She drew another deep breath. "One night he revealed a whole new approach. I was in the Algonquin with some people, there in the lobby on that big sofa against the pillar. Carlos came over, with that absolute insouciance of his inviting himself to join us, and sat down beside me. At the first opportunity, when everyone else's attention was diverted to a long story one man was telling, he showed me a key hidden in the palm of his hand, whispering that it was the key to a room upstairs. He had registered for the room the moment he had spotted me in the lobby.

"The conversation went on. Some people left, more people came, we had another drink and a better story. Every chance he got, Carlos gave me a glimpse of the key ... once even pressed it against my back so that I could feel the outline of it, rubbing it seductively between my shoulder blades."

Eva stood up, walking the length of the room and back again.

"It was working, Russell. He was making me so hot that I was grateful for the people with me. But then suddenly everybody was leaving, the drinking and the conference and the conversation had ended—and I said I couldn't go yet, I had to wait for someone else. So, of my own volition, I was alone with Carlos.

"Knowing I had deliberately remained behind, he changed his tactics again, beginning by describing to me, in a low, teasing voice, exactly how it would feel to get fucked by the great Carlos. Progressing by infinite and inventive detail, he took off my clothes piece by piece, he cherished me, he awakened me, he made me readier for a man than I had ever been in my life. He was utterly shameless, and absolutely effective. He knew he was winning, he was already living it in anticipation."

She was almost smiling now with the memory.

"Then, slowly, teasingly, he undressed himself, letting me see him, anticipate him. I was so damned hot, Russell, I couldn't stand it. I was wondering why I was still listening to a description of the event when I could, by simply going upstairs, have the real thing.

"Then—and he did it most dramatically, even though only verbally—he unfurled the great Cock of Carlos. 'Nine and a half inches,' he whispered, leaning toward me, his eyes gloating for my surprise. 'Measured and proved, Eva, measured and proved over and over again. Think of nine and a half inches of Spanish cock, Eva, being driven into your lovely pussy by the insatiable machine of Carlos!'

"I looked at him then, straight in the eye. I wanted it. Oh yes, he had got me ready, he had overwhelmed me. A finger against my body would have brought an orgasm, I was so ready. 'All right,' I told him. 'But you've got to prove the size. Or else it's no dice.'

"In absolute triumph, he whipped a foot-long ruler out of his breast pocket. 'You think Carlos is not prepared?' he said, almost hissing the words in his blazing enthusiasm. 'Carlos is a man of honor. You will be fucked tonight by a man of honor, my lady Eva.'

"So . . . we went upstairs. I sat on the bed, still in my clothes, watching Carlos undress. And good God, it *was* enormous. I'd never seen anything to match it in all my long life. I didn't *believe* such a tool could hang from a man."

Eva laughed shortly. It was almost a hurting sound. "But—it was not nine and one-half inches. It was only nine. Carlos measured it. Then I measured it. Carlos masturbated furiously, and it was still nine inches. I masturbated him, I even offered to go down on him,

224

but Carlos, utterly crestfallen, said that would not be fair, it would be cheating, he had promised nine and a half but the tiny little half wasn't there, he had over-reached himself, he had lied."

The short, hurting laugh again. "By that time, as I told him, I couldn't have cared less. I begged him to fuck me. I lay back on the bed and bared my steaming cunt, with my hand stroking his great cock I pleaded with him to put it in me. But Carlos, a man of honor, wouldn't hear of it; he was crushed, he was finished, he would probably commit suicide before the night was done, for no woman would ever again believe a word that Carlos had to say."

The hurting small laugh, and this time her face was twisted with the remembered pain. "That was it, Russell, my great adventure. Carlos, sitting sadly on the edge of the bed, masturbated until sadly, abjectly, he came. Then we went downstairs and I bought him a nightcap before he proceeded on his pilgrimage through what was left of what he declared would be a short, unhappy life."

I wanted to laugh at the story. At the same time, I wanted to cry. Eva, watching my reaction, smiled sadly. "I know. It's funny as hell."

Sitting beside me, she put her hand on my crotch. "I have not demanded fidelity, Russell. I am five years older than you are, and you are so often surrounded by these little animals, these children with hot bodies who not only would give you anything you asked just for the sake of a walk-on, they lust after you because you are Russell Walford. So often, it's even simpler than that; you are masculine, and there are few masculine men in their world. And beyond that ..." Her eyes were brooding now, her hand moving in my crotch. "You are damned attractive, sexually. You were attractive to me, weren't you, when I found you in Venice, picking you up so brazenly and taking you to bed without the faintest idea you had it in you to become the best director I've ever seen in my lifetime in the theater. I wasn't thinking about finding a man I could go partners with. No. I just wanted to get laid. So, if you should want another woman, a different piece of tail . . . who am I to say no?"

Her hand stopped. She sat looking at me. Her eyes were sad.

"But this is different now, and it will make a difference, Russell. What the difference will be, though, I can't tell."

"Come on," I said. "Take off your clothes. Let's fuck."

She might not have heard me. "You told me about her once, remember, when you were very drunk. The girl with the golden cunt, you called her that night, crying, and then you took me wanting it to be her instead." She sighed heavily, tremulously. "And now . . . You want to go tonight, don't you? And because of their rules, you're asking me to go, too. You're willing to let me fuck a stranger just so you can fuck her."

I was hurting for the pain that showed in her aching words. She was the good woman, not beautiful, not the greatest lay in the world but as simple and uncomplicated in bed as in her heart. For so long now, I had not needed any woman but her.

"Eva," I said. "Please. Let's fuck."

She put her hand on my instrument again, squeezed it through the cloth of my trousers. Then she took away her hand and stood up.

"No, Russell. I don't dare get between you and her now. I'll be trampled if I do."

I stared. I could not believe it yet. Not even in the mind, much less in the flesh.

"You'll go there ... with me? Just so I'll be free to ..."

Moving her head in that way of hers I knew so well, she put out her firm chin and laughed. "Hell, I might even like it. Maybe it's time I had some variety in my life." She looked at me with merry eyes. "I'll hunt for the biggest tool in town," she said. "Then I can lay there and pretend that it belongs to Carlos. Then Carlos will keep his perfect record, won't he, even if only by proxy."

I got up and put my arms around her, "You lovely woman," I said.

Her hands clung to me. "What else can I do? The minute you walked in, I knew you wanted it more than ... more than anything." Her voice went fierce "So use it, damn it. Make it good. Make it worth the dues." Pushing abruptly away from me, she walked out of the bedroom.

I was impressed, not by the house you lived in, but by the scope of the grounds. I suppose such great space impacts on a New Yorker more than anyone else. The living room was enormous, too, scattered with individual islands of furniture, sweeping far down to an indoor pool at the other end. Perhaps the dimness of the lighting added to the impression of cathedral size and discretion.

The man on the gate had phoned up my name, so you were waiting at the door. Immediately you looked at Eva and Eva looked at you, that instantaneous measurement that only women can instinctively

227

perform. Smiling, you reached to take Eva's hand as you murmured, "I am so pleased you could come, Eva."

"I'll bet you are," Eva said dryly.

Being a male, I felt myself tense warily, prepared for female combat. But I had misunderstood the situation, for you both laughed simultaneously. If either of you had intended combat, this meeting, in this situation, would not have taken place. No; the war would be conducted on another level, outside the sexual arena.

Turning to me, you took both my hands warmly into yours. "Dear Russell," you said. "It's been a very long time."

"Yes," I said uncomfortably. "Too long."

You were wearing a long yellow thing that covered you completely; not knowing the rules, I had half expected to find you naked. It was made of some very delicate fabric, though with a rough, nubby look; the lights behind you, dim though they were, showed you naked under it. Eva was looking at your nakedness, too; then at me with a curious light showing in her eyes. She was astonished—though she would never have admitted the thought—that I had enjoyed the love of a woman so perfect in her beauty.

"You can do very much as you please," you were telling us. "If you think you'll be uncomfortable without your clothes, keep them on ... as long as you want to. There's nothing organized, no rituals or ceremonies, no initiations. Unlike some, this is a very loose group. That's the way Paul and I like it."

You turned with us to survey the scattered groupings. "It isn't a kinky group—actually, they're very straight. Though they may play a few kinky games

.., but most, regardless of the byways, are aiming toward the same old brand of good old-fashioned hetero. The stimulants provided by the management are liquor and pills ... in that respect, we try to discourage independent catering." You were gazing as we gazed, as though you were studying them for the first time. Perhaps you were seeing them through our eyes. "We were into the S-M thing briefly. You should be happy that Paul tired of all that very quickly and ditched the entire group." You shivered delicately. "I never did like the whips, and all that leather. I *hated* being tied up into strange positions."

"Then why did you do it?" Eva said quietly.

You glanced at Eva. "This is Paul Ruach's show," you said briefly. "It's his way of unwinding. Come on. Let me introduce you to Paul."

I had been endeavoring to keep my eyes resolutely averted from what I could see of the activity. Eva, however, was curiously intent. You led us by a couple so engrossed in good old-fashioned hetero, as you had termed it, that they might have been on a desert island. Being ignored, we could ignore them.

Then I got my first shock of the evening. Paul was lying naked in a pile of pillows, a girl in each of his arms. Extraordinarily pretty girls, with good legs and large breasts; they were caressing his hairy chest with their fluttering hands, nuzzling at his ears with nibbling mouths. He seemed half asleep under their devoted ministrations.

Another girl sprawled naked between his legs, licking at his tool with a fluttering, coiling tongue, working with an intent concentration that was not rewarded, for his manhood hung flaccidly. Sensing our presence, she turned her head to look up, smiling pro-

vocatively, holding the penis warm against her cheek
with one hand.

You glanced at me, at Eva, and remarked casually,
with no attempt to keep the girl from hearing: "She's
hoping for a screen test. I don't think she's going to
make it, though. Paul is bored with her." The candidate looked crushed, ready to weep; sullenly, she got
up and walked away.

I looked at Eva. Eva looked at me. There was a curious expression in her eyes. I couldn't help it—a laugh
jarred out of me.

Eva laughed with me, shaking her head. "Russell,
maybe we should have stayed in simple little old New
York," she said in a low voice, leaning against me.

"It goes on there, too," I murmured. "Don't kid
yourself."

Leaning over Paul, you caught his big toe, shook
his foot to get his attention. "Paul. Here's Russell."

Paul stirred reluctantly. I think he had been half
asleep. Taking his arms from around the two girls, he
stood up and held out his hand, saying. "Wonderful,
Russ. I'm glad you could come around to our little
shindig." He turned to Eva. "So this is your wife. Eva,
isn't it? Yes. Eva."

It was a new experience to shake hands with a naked man. I don't suppose Eva had ever been kissed by
one, either—at least, in a social situation. Paul performed the ritual gallantly and discreetly on one
turned cheek. Stepping back, he made an expansive
gesture. "The place is yours. Do with it what you
will." At your side now, posed as the genial host, he
put an arm around your waist.

I gazed at him, at you within the circle of his arm.
His vast, shapeless body was remarkable in its hairy

nakedness. But the impression of strength, not of uncontrolled fat, dwelled in his muscles. His sexual equipment was extraordinary; the penis was quite normal, but the scrotum hung like a bull's balls, a thick-skinned bag weighted at the bottom by two great stones. Thinking of that enormous apparatus banging against your bottom, I looked up to meet your eyes. Knowing my involuntary thought, you smiled faintly, turning your eyes away.

We stood together as conventional as a cocktail party, chatting. Paul was telling Eva of his great hopes for my picture, saying he didn't often depend on stage people to make the film but this time he was confident he had made the right choice. Eva, smiling, nodded in pleased agreement. Down at the far end, near the swimming pool, someone screamed, somebody else laughed.

Paul glanced toward you. "Better check on that. I hope to God some of those S-M people haven't got in tonight. I'm sick of all that stupid stuff." He turned graciously to Eva. "Me, I'm going to buy this little lady a drink." He gazed at her shrewdly. "I think she could use one."

He led Eva away, waddling in vast nakedness at her side. You were preparing to leave. I said urgently, "Leslie . . ."

Your hand moved to rest on my arm. "Later, darling. We have other new people tonight, besides you two, so I have to look after them for a bit. Not to mention finding out who's screaming, and why." Your hand squeezed my arm, your eyes suddenly glowing. "Later. I promise. Get yourself a drink now, look about, satisfy your curiosity. I'll get back to you when . . ." Your voice deepened with a thrilling timbre. "When the time is right for . . . us."

You were gone then, an anxious hostess. I stood uncertainly alone. Against the near wall was a bar. Gratefully I went to it, as toward an oasis, found the sour mash, and poured a hefty shot. On the bar was a punch bowl filled with an astonishing assortment of pills. I ignored them; I had already decided to risk nothing but liquor.

A very tall girl paused beside me. "I *love* to undress people," she said.

She was still dressed, too. I said, "Sorry. Not ready to be naked yet." She shrugged and passed on.

Standing with my drink, feeling very much out of place, I wished that you had remained with me. I wondered what Eva was up to; maybe Paul was making her far more welcome than with a drink. Thinking of that enormous hang of balls, I sighed even as I laughed at myself. Good God, she had come solely because I had wanted her to.

Seeing an empty chair against a wall, I went over and sat down, feeling somehow more secure than on my feet. Directly in front of me a couple on a couch were curled into each other in such a fantastic tangle of flesh it was hard to credit the possibility. As I watched, they remained unmoving for so long I began to wonder if they, like Paul, had fallen asleep. But then, observing their expressions of rapt bliss, I decided they must be practising a technique of contemplative, rather than physical, sex. I had read of something like that.

A blond head pushed itself up between my legs, startling me so that my drink sloshed wetly over my hand. I gazed in astonishment into a tiny, smiling face.

Her naked body, perfect in its miniature voluptuousness, had crept slyly underneath me as my attention was focused on the encoiled couple.

"Hello," she said, her small hands busy with my fly. "You're Mr. Walford, aren't you?"

So bemused by her sudden appearance, I did nothing to forestall her intent, but only admitted my identity. She found my organ, rubbed her cheek lovingly against it, her face tilted so she could continue smiling at me. It seemed to be the favorite pose of the week. "Is there a part in your picture for me?" she asked. "I'm Happy Mann."

"I'm using mostly the New York cast."

A tiny frown, delightful but unmistakable, showed on her face. "Oh, that's a *terrible* mistake, Mr. Walford. The New York people won't work out in the picture. You'll find that out." She stopped talking, put out her tongue, teased it delicately around the flange of the glans. Involuntarily, the old devil perked up. She chuckled lightly, voluptuously, extraordinarily pleased with herself.

"Just a small part," she said coaxingly. "A few lines maybe, one scene." Her face became serious. "But no skin. Mama says I can't do skin until the Big Picture." She stared up at me ingenuously. "I'm going to be the next Sex Goddess."

"I'm sorry," I said.

"Oh well," she said fatalistically. "I tried, anyway."

With a sudden greedy movement she ducked her head. Extraordinarily adept and inventive, her mouth was a marvel of delights as it sucked and pressed and slipped, her tongue an erotic imp dancing on my nerve ends, so that I slipped down into the seat, thrustign my penis against her mouth. So quickly at the edge of orgasm, I couldn't help myself. But, knowing her art, she drew away at the last possible moment to look inquiringly into my face.

"I forgot to ask first," she said. "Do you want to shoot off?"

Feeling myself totally unreal, I gazed down into her lovely face. "I want to make love, so I guess I'd better save it."

She drew away slightly, the delectable frown showing again. "Oh, you can't fuck me, Mr. Walford. Mama says I can't fuck *anybody* until I'm eighteen."

Seeing her more intently, I realized with a shock that I had been deceived by the dim lights, the careful makeup. I had not read her in age, but simply as indeterminately beautiful. She was scarcely more than a child; there was immaturity in her face, even in the mouth that had lately been so warmly loving.

"How old are you, Happy?" I asked.

"Sixteen. Just barely." She sighed. "It looks like forever to eighteen, Mr. Walford. Simply *forever*."

I should have been thunderstruck by the shattering realization of the situation. Here I was, staidly sitting with a drink in one hand, allowing a lovely child to toy with my rampant manhood. Somehow, in this atmosphere, I could accept it, even enjoy it. I liked the girl. She was so open and honest and affectionate. Even innocent, though how innocence could know the arts her mouth had practiced upon my flesh I did not know.

Her small hand stroked. "I'll be careful, Mr. Walford, I'll save it for you." She kissed its head tenderly. "But let me play with it a while. I *like* your taste. It's so nice." She made a grimace. "Some of these *old*

234

men, they get pretty rank, let me tell you." She ducked her blond head again without waiting for spoken consent.

Sprawled in the chair, sipping occasionally at my drink, I let her have her ways; and delightful ways they were, too. No woman's mouth had ever been so good on me; her lips warm and loving, her tongue subtle and delicate and astonishingly inventive. Absolutely precise in her perceptions, every time I began to march toward orgasm she would ease off and begin chatting in her bright, happy manner.

At last, sighing, she leaned back against my leg. "I'd better stop now. I don't want to ruin your date." She glanced up at me curiously. "Who are you going to fuck?"

"Mrs. Ruach," I said.

Happy clapped her hands. "Oh, you're so lucky. She doesn't do it with many people—she's always so busy making sure everybody else is happy." She gazed rapturously, so pleased for me that I had to laugh. "And she is lovely, isn't she?"

"Yes," I said. "She is lovely."

Happy glanced carefully about the room, then cut her eyes slyly at me, assessing my friendliness. "Mr. Walford . . ." Her voice came hesitantly. "How are you about . . . grass?"

"It's all right, I suppose," I said cautiously. "I don't know much about it."

She stood up suddenly between my legs. "Come on. I'm dying for a smoke, and they don't like that sort of thing here, they try to discourage it." She made a face. "Pills and liquor, liquor and pills, that's all these old people know."

Taking my hand, she led me through a small door

into a large room shelved high to the ceiling with books. Urging me into a big chair that smelled of leather, she said, "I'll get you another drink," and disappeared.

When she returned—she had correctly poured sour mash, I noted—I could see in this better light that she was not quite naked. A white leather triangle, laced tight to her body, covered her crotch. Her buttocks were bare, except for the two leather strings that looped up to her waist, tying down the pubic shield. Her lovely breasts, full on her small figure, were bare.

Happy saw me studying her costume. "That's Mama's idea. If somebody tries to grab my cherry, it'll give me time to yell before he can get it in me."

"Is Mama here?"

"Sure," she said. She giggled. "Mama *loves* to come to Paul's. She gets lots of good loving here. Mama *loves* to fuck." She sat down in my lap with a voluptuous wriggle of her ass. "Now," she said contentedly. "Let's smoke."

She opened a small silver purse and took out a roach, found a small silver lighter. Taking a deep drag, she held it as she offered me a puff. Obediently I drew in the harsh, acrid smoke, but I didn't hold it. I never liked marijuana all that much anyway; besides, I meant to be careful tonight. It would be so easy to go overboard in this permissive atmosphere.

Comfortable in my lap, the child sat leaning against my chest and smoked the roach down to the last drag, talking in that friendly, intimate, open manner of hers. First she wanted to know if I liked her "boobies." She had never been just sure about them, she thought they were a little too large. Didn't I think they were too big, too, or was I a tit man? I assured her that they were just right, though I had always counted myself a leg man. Her legs were fine, too, for that matter.

It was remarkable how much time and attention Happy could give to these matters. She was apparently content to spend the evening with me; after the roach was finished, she remained cuddled in my lap.

"I like you, Mr. Walford," she confided. "I wish you could give me just a very small part in your picture." She wriggled her sweet ass in my lap. "I'd do you every day, right there on the set. I'd *like* to do you every day for a while. You have such a *sweet* taste. I do need experience in straight acting, Mama says. All the experience I can get until the Big Break."

"I'm sorry, Happy," I said. "It would be nice to have you around. You are a very nice girl."

I had pleased her. She kissed me on the mouth. "I like you too, Mr. Walford, so many of these men out here . . ." Her face came into decision. "I can't fuck you, of course, but you can have my ass. Would you like to have my ass?"

"Happy!" I said.

She began pouting. "I'm very clean. Mama always gives me a high colonic . . ." She giggled, squirming in my lap. "I just love a high colonic, don't you?"

"I've never had one," I said.

She wriggled again. "I get so *hot*, Mr. Walford, a girl's got to have *something* . . . Listen, just let me have it for a minute, I promise I won't take Mrs. Ruach's load, I'll just use it for a minute. . . ."

Unreality time again. I wondered if the marijuana had affected me more than I had realized. For I sat still, let her take out my penis. I felt her sit down on it in a slow, voluptuous easing of her weight. It went easily into her; her anus was open and warm, her buttocks seemed to spread softly in the taking. I had never done this thing with a woman, and only once with a man—the gay choreographer on my musical flop who was coming apart at the seams at the most critical juncture of the pre-Broadway tour. He knew the show was bad, his friend had bailed out for New York, he was leaving, too, but he'd stay if he could just once in his life take a real man instead of another homosexual, or rough trade. I had not found it a thrilling experience—but then, I never did when I had to use sex in aid of a production.

This was, I had to admit, nice. Very nice. Slipping down in the seat, I clasped her tiny hips with my hands underneath the white leather triangle and began to frig herself with a twirling, expert motion. The sensation of her immediate orgasm echoed distantly in her anus in tiny ripples. I was strung out in her, so warm, so easy, no need for an orgasm of my own. But then, raising her ass, she began suddenly an effort to fetch me off. With both hands on her hips, I pressed her close, then thrust her away.

Whirling on me, suddenly angry, she said, "What's the matter? You got some sort of hang-up about shooting off?"

"Happy," I said reproachfully. "You promised."

She flounced away across the room. She stayed a minute, two minutes; then she came back. "I'm sorry, Mr. Walford," she said abjectly. "I just get so damned *hot*."

"That's all right," I said. "I understand. You'll be eighteen before you know it."

Coming to me, she laid herself full length against my body and wept. The small cry finished, she proceeded to make herself comfortable again. I wanted to get away now, I wanted to look for you. But I couldn't leave her.

The door into the living room banged open suddenly, a harsh voice saying, "What the hell's going on in here? Happy? My God, Happy, he hasn't . . ."

Happy rose hastily, saying, "It's all right, Mama. It's perfectly all right!" With a defiant toss of her head, she sat down again in my lap.

I looked at the big woman, so anxious and harried. She was naked, but she was a mother. She had a broad, plain face and broad hips; a great mat of pubic hair padded her crotch. Her breasts were large but drooping. For an anxious moment she regarded me suspiciously.

"You don't know what a mother goes through," she said. "I was just fixing to lie down, he was a very promising fellow, when I looked around and my little girl was *gone*." She put her hand on her heart. "They all know she's cherry, they want to rob it, though I've warned them all she can't do it until she's eighteen." She sighed gustily. "What a mother goes through for the sake of her child's career." She snuffed at the air suddenly. "Now I know, you naughty girl. You sneaked in here to smoke some of that nasty stuff, didn't you?"

Happy pouted. "It was just a roach, Mama. Hardly more than two good puffs."

Mama, though listening to her, was studying me. "You're Mr. Walford, aren't you? Somebody told me you were here tonight. Get up off the man's lap, darling, I want to talk to him."

Happy reluctantly rose again. Mama took the

closest chair, leaning forward. "You like the child, don't you, Mr. Walford?"

"Yes," I said. "She's a very nice girl, Mrs. Mann."

"Have you got a part for her?" she said urgently. "Nothing big, just a line or two, maybe a scene. Straight stuff, no skin or anything like that."

"I'm sorry," I said. "I plan to use the New York cast."

She drew back. "You'll find that a mistake, Mr. Walford. They can give you a stage performance, sure. But they can't give you a *film* performance."

"Well, that's the way I plan to go," I said.

"Child, get your mother a drink . . . and two of those red pills." Happy started out the door. "Don't hurry, baby. I want to tell Mr. Walford all about you."

Happy safely out of hearing, Mrs. Mann leaned toward me once more. "Isn't she something, though?" she said fondly.

The lines of her face were hard, intent. "The minute I saw that little blond head on the pillow beside me, Mr. Walford—she was born with a full head of hair, exactly the color it is today, she's never had a drop of bleach on her head—I knew what I had to do." She straightened her back. "I had a nice husband, Mr. Walford, back there in Kansas City, and two fine boys. I'm a registered nurse. I was head OR nurse at the time. But knowing I owed little Happy her chance, the day she was old enough I left my husband, I left the two boys, and brought her out here." She nodded firmly. "That was two years ago. Since then I've just been working and waiting and biding my time. She's nearly ripe now, nearly ready, and I'm ready, too. All this time—though I still have to work, I take private cases—I've made myself acquainted with all the right people. They know Happy, they love her, this whole town knows she's meant to be the next Sex Goddess."

I stirred in my chair. "I'm sure she has talent, Mrs. Mann. She is truly a lovely child."

"And I've got my ace in the hole," Mrs. Mann said intently. "That cherry of hers. She thinks it's just that I won't let her do it until she's eighteen." She glanced cautiously toward the door. "But it's more than that. A lot more. That cherry is going to make it for her, Mr. Walford. It's going to get her the Big Picture and the million dollars in Publicity."

Bombarded with such intensity, I was becoming uncomfortable.

"I've already talked to the man, he can do it with a snap of his finger. He likes virgins, he doesn't get many out here, but when he does . . . ! I'm saving Happy for him, it's going to be her Big Break. . . ." She sighed. "But God, Mr. Walford, how I sweat. One little mistake, one fellow shoving it in there, a delivery boy maybe, somebody with more balls than sense—and it's *gone*. And right now that fellow, he's all hung up on this boy, so I've got to wait until he wants a girl. But then . . . *then*, Mr. Walford, my dream will come true, that vision I had the first time I saw that cute little blond head on the pillow beside me."

I stood up. "I hope it'll all work out. I'm sure it will."

She rose, also. "It will, Mr. Walford, it will. She's a biddable child, and everybody just loves her. They all know she'll be the next Sex Goddess of the Silver Screen." She regarded me anxiously. "Did she do you,

Mr. Walford? They tell me she does a fellow real nice."

"Yes," I said uncomfortably. "Extraordinary. Now I have to . . ."

She was staring toward the door, her motherly instincts alert. "Now where has she got to? I'd better go see . . ."

The door opened and Happy came in, carefully carrying a drink. She gave it to Mama, handed over two red pills. Mama mouthed the pills, gulped at the drink. Happy regarded me.

"It's been nice meeting you, Mr. Walford." she said politely. "You are a very nice man."

I looked at her, so tiny, so perfect, so utterly young. Except for her eyes. "Happy," I said, "have you actually been in front of a camera yet?"

"No," she said. "Like I told you, I need experience, all the experience I can get. But no skin, Mama says, not until . . ."

"If I can find something for you," I said carefully. "It won't be much. But maybe something . . ."

She held herself poised on the brink; Mama was tense, too, as Happy asked, "Will it have lines?"

"If it happens at all, it will have lines," I said. "One line. Maybe two."

"Oh, Mr. Walford!" Running against me, she hugged me violently. "I *knew* you were a nice man. I knew it the minute I tasted you. I *knew* it."

"Mr. Walford." Mama's voice was troubled. "I hope you haven't got the idea . . ."

"It's the last thing from my mind," I assured her. "You can be on the set every minute of the time. It's just that . . . I like the girl. I can't do much for her. But maybe I can do that."

Leaving them together, I went out into the living room, seeking you. The tempo had picked up; there was more noise, more kissing, more naked flesh. You were far down the length of the room. Before I could move to your side, Eva put in an appearance.

She was naked. "Have you had her yet?" she asked.

"No," I said.

"What are you waiting for?" she said with a hint of asperity. "Waiting on me?"

I saw that she was drunk. "I hope you've stayed away from the pills," I said.

She giggled suddenly. "Just whiskey. That's all I need, love, whiskey." She gazed about, searching vaguely. "There she is. Go get her, Russell. Sic 'em."

I was strangely reluctant. "Eva . . ."

Eva leaned against me, holding onto my arm. Her voice came quietly. "You've still got your clothes on. You want me to do it first, don't you? All right. I'll do it. Next time you see me, I'll be fucked. I promise you, Russell." She laughed, putting her head back; she was so lovely and so good, and so drunk. "I shall go a-scouting, love, for the biggest cock in the room. When I find it . . . when I find it, I'll think of Carlos, darling, I won't think of you at all."

She turned, wavering, straightened carefully, and went away. I looked after her. But I came after you.

I had just reached your side when a scream split the air. We both whirled to look for the disturbance; it was a thin, scrawny girl. She screamed again, and kept on screaming, the sound going into a subtly disturbing rhythm.

"Come on," you said. "Help me."

Your hands captured her, began rubbing her body as you told me hastily to do the same. Others were gathering around, their hands reaching for her, patting and stroking. The girl quit screaming, but she stood with her eyes tightly closed, trembling violently. Hands were touching every part of her body, front and back, soothing hands, rubbing, rubbing, rubbing; in another moment, your arms strong about her waist, you laid her down on her back. We kneeled with her, our multiple hands soothing the frantic girl.

She became quiet, and quieter, lying with her eyes closed, submissive to the hands and then beginning to enjoy their touching; she was smiling now, her body moved luxuriously as the hands reached her more intimately. One man was stroking both breasts in a steady, intricate rhythm; a very fat woman had put a hand into the bony crotch with its scant hair. Gradually, as the girl concentrated more and more on the finger in her vagina, the others quit one by one, sitting back on their heels to watch. Eyes still closed, she was pumping against the finger, her breathing quickening to the rhythm.

I looked at you. Returning the look, you made a grimacing smile and murmured, "Group therapy. Would you call it group therapy?"

"Let me have her now," the fat woman said in a deep voice. She was very strong; she lifted the thin girl in one effortless rise and began to walk away, holding her cradled in her massive arms.

The girl opened her eyes. "Good God," she said. "Why do I always get the dykes?" With a single movement, she escaped from the woman's arms and walked angrily away.

You laughed, shakily at first, then heartily, and I laughed with you. You were still wearing the yellow thing. I was still dressed. But suddenly we were close, very close, though our only physical contact was your hand on my arm.

"Come on," I said. "Now."

You gazed at me yearningly. But you said, "Not yet, Russell. I want it to be . . . right." You were again the busy hostess. "Paul hasn't found anyone to amuse him. He's being so choosy tonight I'm afraid . . ." You quit talking, came to me again. "Will you wait, Russell? So we won't be distracted, have to hurry it. . . ."

"Yes," I said. "I'll wait."

"Explore. Amuse yourself. I'll come to you when I can." You turned away and turned back, saying in a soft rush of words. "I love you. Oh God yes, Russell, I do love you."

Somehow, my love, I was content to wait. I did amuse myself; I wandered through the huge room, fresh drink in hand, taking in the scene in vignettes as though they were camera shots for a porn movie. In the remoteness of my clothed body I could gaze without repulsion, hear without astonishment the fragments of conversation.

"It's just like the combination to a lock," one man told another. "Put one hand under her right knee, holding it very firmly. Put the other hand on the nape of her neck and slide it down, very slowly, so firmly you can feel her backbone all the way. At the base of the spine, press the bony, hollow place you'll find there. Then brace yourself—she'll climb you with a screaming orgasm."

The other man asked suspiciously, "How do you know?"

"How do I know? God God, man, I've been married to her for fifteen years."

Things seemed to get kinkier down toward the end where the pool glittered with underwater light. Perhaps the more Californian one was, the nearer one kept to the swimming pool. I paused for a full minute to regard a human sandwich I wouldn't have believed possible of achievement. I never did figure out how they managed that particular combination, keeping each participant happy at the same time. But they were happy. Oh yes.

"But if we pay her asking price, that puts us right over budget. Her agent still thinks it's ten years ago. So we might as well shelve it. Nobody else can do it, I sat right up in bed one night knowing I had to have her." Two men, fully clothed, heads leaned together over a small table.

"I can get her for you, Sam. Fifty, Sam, would you believe fifty?"

"If you can get her for me at that price, I'll screw your mother-in-law. God's promise."

"Only thing is, you've got to leave her some pride. You'll have to announce her full price."

"I'll announce double her price if that's all it takes. Publicity releases are cheap."

"Let's don't get extravagant. And, Sam . . . ten big ones for me."

"I love you like a brother, send your mother-in-law over tonight if you want. But how can you do it? Just whisper that to me, how can you do it?"

"I hold the mortgage on that big house she won't think about selling."

At the shallow end of the pool, a mob of naked people shouted obscenities at a girl standing, head bowed, in the middle of the circle. Their hard voices beat at her like fists; you could see the bruises it made in her mind to listen to the words. When she began to cry, they swarmed her, lifting her in many arms and holding her cradled while one man, waist-deep in water, balled her, then another, and finally a third, all very quickly and definitively because her vagina was devouring them, using them up, casting them out. When they had finished she was happy and laughing. She tagged another girl in a flurry of chasing and the circle formed viciously, hurling the truths that would bruise her into voluptuous submission. Truth and consequences, I thought. Vicious truth and happy consequence. *God*. People.

"Fuck me for ten dollars?"

"I'm no whore, you big stud, you can fuck me for nothing."

"I won't fuck you if you won't let me pay you."

"All right, pay me, give me the ten."

"I'll give you a hundred, the more I have to pay for it the better I like it."

"Give me a thousand, then, stud, and enjoy the balling of your life."

Beyond the pool, a black man, legs braced apart, stood surrounded by five girls. At first I couldn't make out what they were doing to him; curiously I drew closer. Assiduously, meticulously, they were rubbing his body with oil, their warm hands melting it glistening into the black skin. He stood like a statue, head up, sturdy legs apart; the chest was broad and muscled, the washboarded belly sloping into the groin. His good tool stood erect out of the tightly curled pubic hair, black head naked, glistening with oil. He was beautiful like a statue is beautiful, the skin a glossy ebon, his muscles firm, young. But his face— so much older than the body, with deep lines and a flat, ugly nose. The heavy-lipped mouth showed splotches of lighter color. His shaved head was massive, bullet shaped, the neck sloping strongly into the shoulders.

"What you looking at, white boy? Don't you like what you see?" His eyes, the whites discolored and muddy, had found me. His voice was harsh, strong, so thick with gutturals I wasn't sure, at the first moment, that I had understood his words.

"To me, buddy, black is beautiful," I said starting to turn away. But I stopped, because he took a step toward me.

"Don't call me Black, white boy. I'm a canebrake nigger, that's what I am." He looked carefully, one by one, at the five girls. They had stopped rubbing the oil into his skin, but their hands were still on him. "I been a canebrake nigger all my life, and I'll be a canebrake nigger till the day I die."

"All right," I said carefully. "You're a canebrake nigger."

His white teeth showed suddenly as he laughed. "I do like me a white boy who knows where to put his foot. Now you just watch. I aim to show you a thing you ain't never seen in yo' life."

Abandoning the pose, he instructed two of the girls to drag over a lounge chair. Hastening under his bidding, they piled the chair with yellow and red pillows, with thick cushions hairy with synthetic fur. Lying down, he shifted pillows to his satisfaction, then looked at me.

"Now watch this, white boy. And let yo' eyeballs bulge." He returned to the girls. "All right now, who's gonna take the first shot at the big prize? Who's gonna be the first to lay her pretty little white cunt on the line?" His long arm shot out. "You, baby! You!"

It must have been a known and anticipated performance for I was no longer alone in watching; people, drifting up behind me, had clotted into an intent group. A collective sigh breathed out as the chosen girl walked between his lifted legs, took his instrument delicately in hand, slanting it snugly into her. She went up on him as he lay with his head back, pumping him suddenly with a desperate frenzy. But the frenzy was in her, not in him. His eyes closed, his face serene, he lay utterly at ease beneath the frantic whipping of her loins. Stopping as suddenly as she had started, she clenched herself, trying to hold it at bay. But she couldn't, her legs were trembling, she made a savage cry and writhed helplessly into the orgasm, letting it sweep through her until, finished, she collapsed into the enfolding embrace of his legs.

Without opening his eyes, he reached down and lifted her away. "One little white pussy done shot its wad and ain't even woke old Noah up. Who's next for the big prize, sweet babies? Step right up and take your best shot."

His guttural voice chanted the words like a carnival pitch. Two girls wanted to be next, they fought briefly until one yielded to the other. She didn't have a chance, she was into orgasm before the glistening black organ was all the way home. She wept with frustration as he lifted her away.

The third. He lay beneath her a very long time, for she came to him slowly, beginning slowly, grinding her hips against his loins in intense determination. But even when, eventually, she quickened, and quickened again, he lay serene, eyes closed, his gleaming, oiled body seemingly at utter ease. Yet the black tool was up and in there; once he stirred, just once, and behind me a gasp sounded. There were bets being made, in hurried, whispered challenges; but then she didn't care any more, she laughed, she let it go, she came, and then again and quickly again, surrendering her all. When she backed away, of her own volition without waiting for him to lift her contemptuously from his flesh, she shaped an unbelieving hand on the penis still in full erection, shaking her head and shrugging her shoulders. Then, gallant in defeat, she bowed to the watching audience.

It was the fourth one now, a small girl with red hair and voluptuous mouth. She went up on him, taking him deep and holding him deep, without movement. His eyes opened, looked at her briefly, closed again. She smiled, she worked, she held again, and again the eyes opened. There was a tension in his body now, she knew it, she could feel it in her flesh, and she smiled almost dreamily as she squirmed on the impaling rod. He began to come, he was moving now, his arms reaching to clasp her close. They came into stride, the two bodies, black and white, rocking together, and you wouldn't believe a man could stay in orgasm for so long a time. At the end they collapsed together, his big hands stroking lovingly on her back.

The man beside me was paying off, shaking his head, saying, "I've seen him do seven and eight, and one time nine. He must be tired tonight. That's the only explanation."

"That last girl was good. Really good. When he opened his eyes that first time to look at her, I knew she had him."

The black man sat up, holding the red-haired girl

close under one arm. He spoke almost shamefacedly to the remaining candidate. "Sorry, sweet baby. You missed your shot tonight. But come back again. I had my secret eye on you all the time." Laughing then, he stood up and said gutturally, loudly, "*Re*-ward time, folks. This fucking little sister gonna get a song wrote and sung just about her. Somebody fetch me my box."

One of the losers brought a big-bodied guitar. Sitting down again, cherishing the shape of the instrument against his naked belly, he strummed a rich and intricate fingering. With a calypso beat in his voice, suddenly as rich and pure as the tone of the guitar, he wove a musical tale about Miss Princess Pussy, fit for a king, that had rather whip old Noah than sit on a golden throne. The small girl sat close against him, quiet with satiation and triumph, receiving with gracious restraint the musical tribute. The song finished, the canebrake nigger put aside the guitar and lifted her in his arms, laying his bullet head against her belly.

"Sweet baby, that song gonna go in my next album if I've got one word to say about it." Putting her down, he took up the guitar and walked away.

Drifting in his wake, I looked again for you and saw Paul Ruach instead. Maybe he was amused now; he had the fat woman, who had earlier lost the scrawny screaming girl, sprawled on a sturdy, very wide, sofa. Their two great bodies, piled together in an incredible heap of human flesh, looked grotesque. Massively she rolled under him as his hips thudded a steady, remorseless beat, slow but unvarying, as though he had started long ago and could keep the rhythm the night long. The woman was moaning in a monotonous tone keyed to the slow thud of his meat against her meat. His attention concentrated so deeply into her roiling flesh, when I paused beside the sofa he remained unaware of my presence.

I went on, quickened for you. But before I found you Eva came to me, followed by a man. He had to follow; she was leading him by the penis.

"How about this one?" she said triumphantly. "Have you ever seen the like, Russell?"

She was very drunk; but not too drunk to find what she had declared herself for. "Have fun," I said, and passed on.

Making a fresh drink, I gulped half of it. I could not avoid seeing Eva leading her trophy into a quiet corner. Well, I told myself ruefully, she wouldn't have thought of it without your encouragement. I hoped, very suddenly and very truthfully, that the stranger's tool would be a huge experience, nudging out of her flesh the lingering memory of failure with Carlos. And whatever failure she felt with me. She deserved every enormous inch of it.

You came to me then, so suddenly it was an utter surprise. You seemed so tired, so harried, that I wanted to hold you, comfort you. This was a new thing also; I couldn't remember ever surprising fatigue and concern in you.

"It ought to be now," I said quietly.

"Yes," you said. But, abstractedly, you were gazing about. "Have you seen Paul?"

"Right over there on the sofa," I said, pointing. "It's a sight to behold."

You went to look. I watched as you stood over the twin mountain of flesh, the male and the female. When you returned to my side you had changed;

there was a gayness in you, an immediate readiness for love.

"Let's hurry, Russell," you said in a throaty, urgent voice. "It's been so damn long."

Putting my hand against your back, I could feel the warmth of your flesh through the thin fabric. "Yes. Too many years."

You laughed shortly. "Years? I'm just talking about tonight, I can't even think about the years."

I put my other hand on you then, to know again the shape of your loins. The flimsy covering fabric might as well not have existed. You lifted against my touch, shaping your mount into the cupping grasp, and I could hear your breathing. Your head turned, searching. "There's a place. The pile of pillows in the corner." But, keeping my hand tight against you, I said, "No. Not here."

You looked at me, your eyes harried with doubt and hunger. "What do you mean, not here?"

I was watching your face. "I won't make love where anyone can see us. We have to be private, Leslie."

"We can't do it that way!" you cried. "Don't you understand? It's not fair, Russell, to Paul or Eva, to anybody." You were almost weeping with frustration. "You promised, Russell. You promised!"

"Private," I said, with deliberate ruthlessness letting the stubbornness show in my voice. My finger finding the slit, I pressed it strongly, slowly, upward, then downward, feeling the unwilled response of your loins. "Or would you rather just forget about the whole thing?"

You glanced raggedly toward the sofa where Paul lay pumping the slow movement of his rod into the

fat woman. You stared about the room with such a
grave, sudden fright at the prospect of private intimacy, as though it were the major sin of your society,
that I ached with sympathy for your dilemma. But
your agony of guilty indecision did not move me to
relent.

"All right," you whispered, your voice shaky.
"Wait for me. In the library."

I did not take my hand away. "You'll come? You
promise?"

Your voice had reached the edge of hysteria. "I
have to, don't I?"

Taking my hand away, I let you go. Deliberately, I
supplied myself with a new drink before I opened the
door into the library. I was feeling triumphant.

It was dark in here now, only one pool of light.
Someone said, "Do you play chess?"

A gentle, cultured voice; but it was Noah sitting
black in the pool of light, his large hands shifting the
pieces deftly into the opening positions.

"Yes, but not very well," I said, approaching.

He was clothed, wearing a white shirt, a neat tie, a
conservative pinstriped suit that was tailored flawless-
ly to the powerful shoulders.

Glancing up at me, he smiled slightly. "Surprised,
Mr. Walford?" His voice showed a British accent,
with a rich undertone of exotic eloquence. It was an
instrument, as the guitar was an instrument in his talented hands. He chuckled. "Thought you had me
pegged! I do take some delight in surprising people
who think they have me pegged into their square
hole." He dropped suddenly into the gutturals I had
heard before. "That canebrake nigger jazz, man, it
just makes them white cunts so hot they can't hardly

stand themselves. They just got to unwrap it and hand it over like a Christmas gif'."

Suddenly liking the man, I sank down into the chair across the game table. "I'd just like to know how you do it."

He gave me his cultured tone again, deep in his chest. "I'll tell you a little secret, Mr. Walford. When I first came out to the coast, I wasted more pussy than any ten men could find a use for. As long as it was a black girl, I could hang in there—as good as the next man, and maybe better." He sighed. It was a sound of self-amusement more than anything else. "But a white woman . . . and there were plenty of white women, I assure you of that. They liked old Noah, I was young and strong and black and it made them feel down-right evil to take my black cock into their pretty little white cunts. But . . . I suppose I had my hang-ups, too. I'd lose it the minute I touched them, couldn't help myself, just sprayed it all over their disgusted little bodies."

He spread his broad-palmed hands. "I came to know a holy man, all the way from India to spread his word, and one day I found the courage to tell him about my problem. He listened very carefully, he went into meditation, and then he said he could help me. Or, at least, help me help myself."

Noah's teeth gleamed as he laughed. "It took a while. First, I had to learn how to control my breathing . . . then my heartbeat. Only then could I begin to learn how to control my black-man's cock." His laughter this time was so hearty, so joyous, that I had to laugh with him. "It's yoga, Mr. Walford. I just lay there and practice my yoga while those sweet little girls make their wanton way with my flesh. It's not

that I don't feel it; I read every stroke and twist off
their inventive little asses. But only when it is *right*,
when I perceive with the inward eye a blossom of
sweet beauty in that woman's body, do I allow myself
to participate, a Man to match their Woman."

"Good God," I said. "I never heard such an incredible thing. But I saw it, didn't I?"

"Yes, and if you come around often, you'll see it
again. Why, I'm nearly as famous for that little show
as I am for my music. I couldn't refuse the performance if I wanted to." Sitting relaxed in the chair,
he gazed upon me. "I do wish you'd play me a game
of chess, Mr. Walford."

I stood up. "I have a feeling you'd mate in about
ten moves."

He chuckled. "Let's do it this way, then, You've
got white, so—pawn to king four."

I glanced toward the door. You had not come, so I
sat down again and made the move he had called for
me. Noah made his move and named the white response. I understood, then, that he was playing a game
from memory, move by move. I began to get interested, studying the board as the pattern of play unfolded.

You came into the library just as the end game started. You didn't interrupt, only paused behind me,
putting one hand on my shoulder, to stand watching.
Realizing that you were easy in yourself again, I returned my attention to the game.

When white's checkmate came, Noah studied the
board, shaking his head. "That Fischer," he said. "He
is something, isn't he?" He looked up at you, rose,
said, "Hello, Mrs. Ruach."

"Hello, Noah," you said.

He glanced at me, a sudden light of understanding

in his eyes. Deliberately he yawned, revealing twin ranks of very white teeth. With an air of surprise, he glanced at his watch. "Would you believe it's my bedtime?" he said. "There ought to be a bed empty somewhere in this house." Stooping to pick up his guitar, he said politely, "Good night." We both said, "Good night, Noah," and he went away.

I turned to you. "He is some man," I said.

"Noah?" you said. "Yes. Do you like him?"

"Yes. Is he staying here?"

You laughed. "Noah sleeps wherever he is when it comes bedtime—and it's the same hour every night, no matter what he's doing. He simply finds the nearest bed, climbs between the sheets, and goes peacefully to sleep."

We were easy with each other, we had time in us, ample time for all our lives, and longer. Coming to me, you had shut out everything on the other side of the library door.

"You'd think a man like that—he must be enormously talented, I just heard one song, and a made-up one at that, but he is very good—would have a place of his own." I shook my head. "It's a shame he has to live like that."

Your amusement sounded, easy and rich. "You apparently don't keep up with the music world, Russell. Noah's had a dozen gold albums. He earns more money than he knows what to do with. That's just the way he likes to live."

"Surely he keeps a place to hang his clothes, if nothing else," I protested.

"He hangs his clothes in his agent's office. Noah refuses to own anything, even a place to sleep." You looked at me. "Did you catch his performance?"

"Remarkable," I said.

"I wonder how he does it. I've watched a dozen times, but I've never figured it out."

"He told me. Yoga."

"Yoga?" You laughed unbelievingly. Then, changing suddenly, you took my hand, saying, "Come on, Russell. Let's practice *our* yoga."

I was not reluctant; the time had come at last. You led me through another doorway into a corridor. The house here was very deep, very quiet. We entered into a luxurious bedroom, the decor in shades of rich yellow, the lights low and flattering. The large space was dominated by a canopy bed elevated on a dais, the canopy yellow also, even the spread that covered the king-sized expanse of mattress.

"This is your room," I said.

"It's where you wanted to have it, wasn't it?"

"Yes."

With a mysteriously feminine movement, you emerged almost magically from the long garment, the golden fabric flowing down to puddle at your feet. I gazed awestricken, as though I had never seen your lovely body. It had ripened in the time you had been a stranger to me; the curves were richer, the slants of light against your shadowing flesh so beautiful that suddenly my mouth was dry.

Your voice was a low throb. "I want to see you naked."

Clumsily, too hastily, I got undressed. So anticipatory of old delights in your newly ripened flesh, I showed you my best erection, throbbing with the need to taste your flesh. Your eyes clinging to it, the tip of your tongue curved delicately against your upper lip, your legs began to give way.

You stopped the movement. "No. I'm tired of all that oral bit. That's all anybody seems to do any more—go down on, or be gone down on. I want it in me."

Moving resolutely, you stepped up in one lithe motion onto the dais. With a sweep of both arms you turned back the spread. Placed ready on the rich yellow sheets, you lifted your arms, saying, "Come here, Russell. Make love to me."

Stepping up on the dais, I put my body into the warm cradle of your flesh. Your mouth was fresh and sweet; we kissed for a long time, not passionately but lovingly, your arms tight around my head. Slowly, without the clamor of lust, we began to merge out of love into passion; the tempo of our breathing quickened, your palms clasping my naked shoulders were damp with sweat. When I moved, making the signal, your body opened entirely, taking the deep thrust with a slow upward thrust of your own. It was like entering a tunnel of molten fire as you held me deeply, long enough to kiss again, before we began.

You had ripened in this, too. You knew the lush treasures of your body; with no effort at all you established the rhythm and fitted me into it. You understood your skill at lovemaking, as your arts of beauty; you had come a very long way, over a very long period of time, to learn the marvelously effective strokes and turns and movements you were demonstrating within the simple act.

It *was* simple. You kept us on the straight and narrow path to ecstasy, touching only with our mouths, only with tool in pocket, blending with the lengths of our bodies into one seamless touching. Your great skill had become an unconscious rhythm, so adept at speeding me up, then slowing me down, there was no danger of a premature ejaculation. I would come, I knew with enormous confidence, exactly when you were ready for me to come; and you would respond in perfect timing.

I must render limpidly clear this experience you gave me, my love. Captured, completely caught up, I was utterly ravished by the intricate sensations of the greatest fucking I had ever experienced. So helplessly enthralled, so passionately trapped, so eager to respond totally to your subtle cues; at the same time, there was a part of me that realized it as art rather than nature; art deliberately designed and created as a painting or a drama is created. Even your tiny cries, used to spur yourself on from one level to the next, revealed their ritual quality. You were like a great jockey pacing himself to a precise timing of the furlong markers, so astonishingly sensitive to your steed that you could make me also great in lovemaking as you gathered and gathered, and gathered again, the incredible orgasm that would surge us both across the line in a photo finish.

Yes, my darling. I rode with you in your mighty lust, I reveled in it, I abandoned to it my entire being; but deep within me I knew it was not me that inspired you but simply the concentrated perfection of skill and rhythm and sensitivity that had earned you, in capturing the great Paul Ruach, an equal partnership in his powerful life.

It was as miraculous, in its own way, as Noah's performance with the girls. And my manhood, once your first and only, meant exactly as much, and no more, to your expert body as those white-girl vaginas had meant to his yoga-penis.

YOU

I will tell you true, Leslie, my love. If the other thing had not happened, I would not have come back to you after this experience.

But it did happen. With an ultimate series of tiny, ritual cries, you had hoicked yourself to the last plateau and were posting triumphantly into the home stretch, me snug under the saddle and going with you.

You stopped. Yes. Utterly, abruptly, like a switched-off robot. Holding yourself absolutely still, you gazed bewildered into my face, as though you had come awake in the arms of a stranger. In a small, questioning voice, you said, "Russell?"

"Yes, Leslie," I said. "It's me."

Your eyes were suddenly wet with tears. Your body, emerging from a deeply held tension I had not realized existed in your flesh until it had eased, settled under me, spreading, opening. I was suddenly drowning in you, steeped in your loving juices, and though I was not moving and you were not moving the seed of my loins was spurting into the deep homeplace of my soul. As my penis pumped so strongly, your vagina softened yet more, quivering; you were accepting the outgush of semen, receiving it utterly as utter love, and you did not need an orgasm, there was in you no striving for your own fulfillment because you were already fulfilled by the realization of you-and-me.

When it was done, you wrapped both arms around my head, holding me close, and you began to cry in earnest. But no bitter tears this time; happy tears, in a wet, warm flood.

We lay so for a long time—except that time did not exist, space did not exist, there was in the entire universe only me and only you, the boy and the girl we had been in the beginning, and it was a revealed miracle that they still dwelled within our elder selves.

We had got there, we had broken through; it was accomplished now, our souls utterly wedded along with our bodies. You wanted to cling to this tender moment, so you clung to me; but I knew that, time having started again out of its stop, Paul still existed for you and Eva for me. You came with me to the door of your bedroom, begging in a low, tremulous voice that I not take myself away. It was the hardest thing I have ever done to make myself go on at this right time for going.

I found my way to the big living room, still now, almost empty of people. Two or three energetic bodies were splashing in the pool, and in one corner a couple made love wearily, insatiably. I saw lovely little Happy Mann, her head leaned against Mama's thigh, sound asleep, while Mama, vastly naked still, talked to a man who nodded obediently to her urgent message. I was looking for Eva, but I didn't see her. I spied Paul, on the sofa where he had been at our departure, sitting with eyes closed and a glass of champagne carefully balanced in his hand. A very beautiful black-haired girl leaned against his knee; his other hand was on her head, scratching slowly, voluptuously, in her thick hair while she craned her neck, pushing her scalp against the massaging fingers.

At the sound of my steps, Paul's eyes opened. "Well," he said. "Russ."

"Have you seen Eva?"

"Over yonder somewhere." He waved vaguely, chuckled. "I think she measured every man here tonight. I didn't live up to her specifications, sorry to say."

YOU

I found Eva asleep in a corner, curled against a great pillow. A man snored beside her, his head thrown back in exhaustion; his equipment, slack though it was, looked adequate to fill her bill. Eva came drunkenly awake, fighting against my hand on her shoulder. She found her clothes—she had tucked them tidily away near the front door—and came obediently to the car, sound asleep again before I had driven past the gatehouse.

It was not necessary to contemplate in retrospect our new experience of each other. It was simply *there* in me, as I knew it was there in you. Nor did Eva and I discuss the group-sex scene we had both plunged into; me because of you, Eva because of me. I had expected her to be anxious to tell all about it, but she only complained vigorously about her terrible hangover. Nor was there about her an air of silent reproach, or personal guilt; she remained simply the Eva she had been day before yesterday, and last week, and last year.

I was very busy. The start of principal photography loomed threateningly near. Time had suddenly become Paul Ruach's money, in an excruciatingly direct sense, so that, though my path was made smooth in every possible way, I found myself putting in eighteen- and twenty-hour days. Having caught some of your own wonderful serenity, it didn't bother me in the least that a week, then two weeks, went by without a word from you. I knew you were *there*, you see as you knew *I* was there; when the time came, we would be together again.

Working at home, I took the call myself. You only said, "Party tonight, Russell." I said, "Yes. I'll come." Your voice so low and thrilling with the words, I could picture you completely as you sat holding the phone to your ear.

I went to find Eva. "Party tonight," I told her.

She glanced at me almost indifferently. "We're going, of course?"

"Is it all right with you?"

She shrugged. "Maybe I won't have to get drunk this time. It would be nice if I didn't have to get drunk, wouldn't it?"

"Yes." My eyes were still on her. I said, "Do you mind at all, Eva? Tell the truth, now."

"It wouldn't make much difference if I did mind, would it?" Seeing my eyes watching her, she smiled. "Russell, if you think I have the slightest intention of putting myself in competition with a girl you fucked when you were seventeen years old . . . especially a woman like Leslie. She's so lovely, I can't find it in me to blame you." She made a wry and weary face, laughing along with it. "No, Russell, I truly don't mind. I'll just have to conduct my famous survey for the biggest cock around, and content myself with that not-very-small comfort."

"I never knew you had this thing about size, Eva."

"Funny thing, I didn't know it myself. It was such a deliciously *crammed* feeling, Russell, even if I was drunk. I don't want to be drunk tonight."

"Eva," I said. "You are . . . a marvelous woman."

"You're pretty marvelous yourself." She grinned evilly. "Except you ain't so well hung, buddy. Nice enough. But not big enough."

I had to laugh. "Good hunting."

"You won't have to hunt, will you? She's *there*."

"Yes," I said. "She's there."

Deliberately I made our arrival later than the first

time. I meant to allow time for you to get the party running smoothly; I knew, the moment we saw each other, we wouldn't be able to think of anything else. When you met us at the door, there could have been no doubt that we were keyed to each other. It must have been painfully obvious to Paul and to Eva; you were looking years younger tonight, glowing with happiness as you unself-consciously took my hand in yours, simply holding it as we kissed and spoke in greeting. Paul carried it off urbanely, pecking Eva on the cheek and remarking drolly, "Lady, I sure wish I could qualify for your Pecker Derby."

Eva, chuckling, glanced down at Paul's nakedness. "If your tool matched your balls, Paul, I'd be running like a rabbit."

Shaking with laughter, he put his arm around her, saying, "Get your clothes off, nice lady. I've been scouting for you, and I've got three candidates lined up. Eyesight alone, you understand, there's nothing queer about old Paul. You'll have to do the official measuring yourself."

They went away, leaving us alone. You were wearing a garment exactly like the other, except that it was a subtle, rich green. Still holding my hand, I could feel the damp sweating of your palm.

"Can we disappear now?" I asked.

You looked wistful. "I have to circulate a while yet. Once I get with you, I'll forget all about my job as hostess. I'll just . . ." Troubled, you stopped, began again. "Russell. We should stay out here, like everybody else."

"Do you want to do it that way?"

"No," you said tensely. "No!" Your hand squeezed mine, a signal of surrender to ourselves. "Watch the door into the library. When you see me leave the room, come to me." Your mouth, your eyes, changed. "Quickly."

"Very quickly," I said. "Go on now. The sooner you go, the sooner we can be alone."

I went to the bar, fixed a drink, drank deeply as I surveyed the long room. The tall girl, floating by, made her little speech about liking to undress people. The party, I saw, was well advanced. To kill the time, I drifted casually the length of the room, observing the varied activity. Strangely enough, the scene was not disturbingly unreal this time, but seemed quite thinkable. So quickly can the human animal adapt himself, I thought, as I found myself becoming analytical, as though I were a visiting sociologist. I decided, on the strength of observation thus far, that the social value of the group orgy was to permit the females to act aggressively, the males to become passive. It seemed to be the underlying pattern; men waited for the women to come to them, while the women, in a ferocity of competition, seemed greedy for rampant male flesh. Like Eva, I thought. Never in her life has Eva had the opportunity to measure rods, and something in her must have always wanted to do it.

I paused for a moment beside a group that seemed to be greatly involved with food—cans of whipped cream, strawberries, ice cream in various flavors, chocolate puddings. They were extraordinarily inventive in their eating habits. The epitome of the oral society, I thought, remembering how you had said you were getting so tired of going down on, or being gone down on.

Beyond the swimming pool, Noah was practicing his yoga. I was informed it was the sixth candidate.

YOU

My informant volunteered that, personally, he had bet on seven, putting a thousand on the line, but with Noah you could never tell. I didn't stay for the climax; my view of the library door had been blocked by a swirl of bodies dancing a maypole dance around a huge plaster phallus held aloft by a nude black girl. Passing near, I was bemused by the observation that the girls were wearing dildoes strapped to their naked loins. I watched as one of them, a big girl but shapely, grabbed one of the men and broke out of the dance, pushing him down on his stomach and climbing rampantly astride. It was difficult to tell who was getting the most pleasure out of the perverse event ... maybe me, simply by watching and making my impersonal judgments.

My attention was distracted by the abrupt materialization of Happy Mann under my elbow, saying, "Hello, Mr. Walford," as she leaned warmly against me.

"How do you always manage to sneak up on me?" I said.

She giggled. "I'm a fairy, didn't you know that?" She turned the giggle into a laugh. "Not that kind. I mean ..."

"I know what you mean," I said. "Don't ever explain yourself, Happy. Just be." She was wearing her white leather triangle, strapped tightly over her sacred loins.

Her small hand slid down the slope of my hip, searching for the zipper. "Want me to do you, Mr. Walford?" she inquired, her eyes glinting up toward me in mischief and merriment.

"Not tonight."

So quick and clever, her hand was already clasped

about my naked root. She turned it loose, pouting. "You want to save it all for that Mrs. Ruach."

"That's exactly what I want to do."

"But I *liked* the taste of you."

"I've got the part you asked for, Happy," I said.

She stood very still. "Please don't lie to me, Mr. Walford. I read the play. There's nothing in it for me."

"The role I have in mind was cut out of the stage production because it was only the one scene, and we decided the tiny nuance it gave the second act wasn't worth the expense of another cast member. She couldn't even understudy; the type was too different." I smiled at the still little girl. "There's good reason to put it back—it's a very nice little accent for the character development of the son. She's his friend, you see, and she comes to take him away, just before the second-act curtain, instead of him just walking out of his own volition."

She breathed again. "A scene?"

"Yes. A handful of lines. You'll have to establish the character very quickly. It's all there in the first two lines, but they must be exactly right." I was watching her face. "You *can* act, can't you? Or don't you know?"

She changed. Not only her face, her entire body; she was suddenly small and prim and very young. With a tiny whimper, she said, "*But I'm not that kind of girl, Robert. Please don't think I'm that kind of girl.*" She came out of it, grinning. "How's that?"

"Fine," I said. "But this girl . . ."

A man, from behind her, put his hand on Happy's naked shoulder. "Happy. You promised," he said reproachfully.

"Please, Mr. Davidoff, I'm busy now."

He took away his friendly hand. "All right. But I understood you to be a person who always keeps her promises."

She looked back toward me. "Will you wait until I
. . . ?"

I glanced at the library door. "Yes. But not for long."

"I won't be a minute."

Taking Mr. Davidoff's hand, she led him to a chair against the wall. Crouching between his knees, she thrust her blond head into his crotch. She did not hurry the task, but gave him the full benefit of her artfulness. When she returned, I looked at the bruised softness of her lips.

"This girl," she said. "You were going to tell me all about her."

"It's right for you," I said. "Not sexy, you understand, nothing obvious, but the audience must know why she came; he hasn't been to her for so long that she knows it's *too* long. So she marches right into the midst of his family and takes him away."

It was breathtaking to see how this voluptuous, decadent child had already become the character I had described. Taking a few steps away, Happy came back, moving with a defiant and warm and brave stance to her body. She paused, she looked at the boy's mother. Then she looked at the boy. "Line," she said. "Give me the line."

"*Harry*," I said. "*The furnace quit working last night. Nobody can make it work but you.*" I made it a monotone recital, giving her no clues.

"*Harry*," she said. Her voice throbbed on the name, held it. "*The furnace quit working last night.*" A lift

269

of the chin, a glance at the mother. "*Nobody can make it work ... but you.*"

"Why haven't you acted in a picture yet?" I asked her.

"They keep giving me screen tests." Her eyes were shadowed, old. "That's all they want, to keep on testing me. I've had seven tests now and every one of them was good, they all said so, they all loved me." She gestured toward Mr. Davidoff—the old man sat sprawled where she had left him. "I've got another one tomorrow now."

"In about two weeks you've got a part," I said. I smiled at her. "Just go to work, girl. You don't have to scheme for the Big Break. You can make it on talent alone."

"Oh, Mr. Walford, you're the nicest man!" She was glowing. "You sure you don't want me to ..."

"No," I said. "Really, Happy."

"Oh, I know, that Mrs. Ruach." Brightening, she stood on tiptoe to put her mouth against my ear. "Split a joint with me?"

"I'm sorry," I said, lifting my glass. "I'm not even drinking much." I looked around. "Where's Mama tonight, anyway? Don't you want to tell her your news?"

"Oh, she's over there somewhere, screwing like crazy," Happy said indifferently, gesturing with wide uncertainty. "I'll tell her later." She giggled. "Of course, if you want to talk to her, all I have to do is holler *Mama!* and she'll be here in a split second."

"I don't have to talk to her. Just tell her to call the Ruach offices tomorrow morning."

"I do it sometimes just to make her jump," Happy confided. "She *worries* so about me."

I gazed at the lovely little thing. I had no trouble now recognizing how young she was—her happy, childlike nature came through in spite of the makeup, the near nakedness, the old eyes that did not belong in her face.

"She shouldn't worry," I said. "You're going to be all right."

We parted. Getting restless, I opened the library door in case I had missed seeing you slip away. The room was empty. I circulated again; there were vignettes, conversations, astonishing combinations of flesh with flesh that did not astonish me any more.

The same two men were huddled over the same table, both fully dressed.

"Your mother-in-law was something else, it was a pleasure, nothing but a pure pleasure. But don't you know when a man's making a joke?"

"I knew, Sam, I knew. To me it was a joke. But when I told her, such a good joke, she didn't think it was a joke."

"A pleasure. But she keeps coming back, she hasn't laughed at the joke yet. You know that I am a very busy man."

Two men strolling by in the opposite direction, both middle-aged, both paunchily naked. "She measured my cock, too. I told her, baby, it's not how much, but how. She just laughed and went away. It's enough to make a fellow ashamed of himself."

I saw you coming, you held out your hand, pressed mine, and let it go; you were hurrying toward a commotion at the pool. The scrawny little screamer again, strung out for mass comforting. I stood watching as you led the group therapy, thinking, They all bring their peculiar hang-ups. All this intricate dance of ritual, this meshing and mingling and separating of bodies, is only to achieve a sort of crude matching of diverse hang-ups. If they're lucky they can be, for just a moment in time, happy and fulfilled. Or think they are, which is the same thing. But it's sad. It is actually very sad.

I went to stand at the bar with a fresh drink in hand. The thinking went on: So why am I here? And then: And you, lovely Leslie. Are we simply matching our hang-ups, too? Is that all there is to life?

But there was the memory of our island, so long ago. We had made your elaborately beautiful bed an island once, I told myself, so tonight we could make it an island again. If that's a hang-up, so let it be. If one thinks he's happy, I guess he is happy. If one thinks he is fulfilled . . .

My eyes had been drifting unseeingly. Suddenly they focused, picking out Eva, on the couch where Paul had laid the fat dyke. Eva was covered by a long-limbed man; even as I watched, he started again and I saw her head go back, her mouth open in a soundless scream of pleasure.

And Paul—sitting nearby in a straight chair, his massive thighs spilling over the sides, he watched Eva's action with a girl clinging to each arm, their naked breasts pressed against his flesh. As I drew closer—I wanted to see it clearly, and know how I felt about Eva and her search for the master tool—I saw the other girl under him, hanging to him by the mouth like a limpet, her hands cuddling his great bag of balls.

Circling the couch, I looked down into Eva's face. She must have sensed my presence, for she opened her eyes. Her mouth was so sad and loving that I ached for her. But her body, even as she looked at me, remained with the great organ inside; with a sudden surge she caught at consummation, taking the rangy man along with her.

Paul made a sound. I looked at him. He was getting it, too; his hands holding the girl's head vised, he had half risen to pump spewing semen into her mouth. She moaned and gagged, but, utterly ruthless, he was jamming it down her throat. His eyes on Eva, on Eva's lover, he was taking her by proxy.

The rangy man fell away. Even finished, his penis was enormous; it seemed to unravel out of her as he withdrew. Eva lay collapsed, a slack fulfillment showing in the wet, bruised lips of her vagina. I reached down to take her hand. Her eyes were closed again, but when I touched her she looked at me.

"Everything all right, Eva?"

"Everything's lovely," she said. "Just lovely."

Paul's heavy voice reached out. "Got one more for you, little lady. The biggest of the lot." Swiveling his thick neck, he inquired peevishly. "Now where did that guy get to?" He nudged the girl between his legs, lying with her head cradled on her arms. "Go get him—that fellow yonder. Tell him it's his turn."

I told myself I would go away now. But Eva clung to my hand even as her eyes sought the new candidate, dwelling on the enormous club that burgeoned out of his body. Ready though he was, he was hesitant, so Eva, taking her hand from mine, half sat up and pulled him down on her sprawled body. She sighed as the great organ bulged into her, then whimpered, divided between hurt and pleasure.

Paul, catching one of the spare girls by the arm,

dragged her between his knees so suddenly she fell on her bare rump. "Come on," he said. "Get to work."

I must have sensed your signal; I glanced up to see you standing in the library door. I looked at Eva; I looked at Paul; I left them, coming directly to you. Before I had reached the door, you had passed through; but you were waiting, your arms took me as I closed it behind me.

You clung, your whole body trembling. "It's our time now." Your breath was panting under the rapid words. "The party's in full swing. Paul's been managing Eva's Pecker Derby all evening. It's the most delightful diversion he's found in a long time." So close against me, your flesh was wedded to my flesh though we were still dressed. "So there's time, our time, all the time we need, love, all the time in the world."

We went together, hurrying, holding hands. In your bedroom there was a jarring note; Noah, lying flat on his back between the sheets, snoring lightly. Glaring at him, you punched at his shoulder with both hands. But when he rolled over, coming reluctantly awake, your voice was gentle.

"Noah. You can sleep in any bed in the house but this one."

He yawned, sitting up to look from one to the other. "Sorry, people," he said. "Let me get myself out of here."

He got naked out of bed, picked up his clothes folded neatly on a chair, and went away. You were in the bed before he was out of the room. Then you were up again, saying, "I want clean sheets. Sheets no one has touched but me and you."

I watched as, working frantically but efficiently,

you stripped the bed and brought folded sheets from a bathroom closet. Pale green sheets this time, to match your garment. I was undressed before you had finished; you turned your body into my nakedness, lifting the gown as you did so, and with a subtle shifting of angles took me standing. A tug of your body weight brought us down on the bed, and there was no need to conquer you again; that great surrender, the last time, of your new self still reigned in your flesh. I kissed you and probed you as I had once done on the most seaward island, and you answered in the same mode, so sweet and virginal and, God, so hot and loving and needful.

We emerged out of the first urgency into sheer happiness. We were gay with each other, romping in the big bed as we coupled. You laughed and teased, we murmured outrageous puns in the midst of loving talk, we shook with shared laughter at the utter liberation of our bodies, our minds, our spirits. Even when we rested, my head cuddled in your arms as you stroked with tender hands, you did not surrender to that deep female sadness you had always known at such times, but remained within the happiness, keeping it wrapped around us like a warm garment. For the first and last time in our lives, I do believe, we were truly happy; there were no shadows hovering over us, we had both the innocence and the true love of the beginning and the great, intimate wisdom and art and love of the last. Again we dwelled not in time nor in space, but only in our great timeless love.

It seemed forever, ever burgeoning and ever new. But there was, there had to be, an ending. I remember in complete detail how we were when the ending began to happen. My rod was snugged deeply, unmoving, for you were milking it with that warm, loving stroke you had spontaneously learned so long ago on our faraway island. Nothing, I thought, could have separated us. But one thing did. Paul Ruach's voice.

"So this is where you've hidden yourselves."

I felt you congeal about my ardent flesh. You had given me that cold and bloodless flesh once before, the time we had met in my hotel room in Piercetown. As then, it chilled me to the bone. I looked into your face; it was tight with fear, almost ugly, and I had never seen you ugly. You were lying in my arms, looking at your husband over my naked shoulder, and there was a deadness in your eyes.

It was necessary to stand up and face him, but I could not move. You pushed at me with both hands. I got to my feet and turned to Paul. He was not looking at me yet; he was still looking at you.

"Hidden. Secret. In your own private bed." He was not angry. The menace of his heavy, assured tone went so far beyond anger that it was unbelievably frightening. The cold, deliberate speech shuddered into you, your flesh quivering as each slow separate word cut into your mind.

Paul transferred his gaze to me. "Russ. I didn't care if you wanted Leslie. I knew you would fuck her; she told me so." The words were thudding at me. "You're a good man. I was pleased she'd have a good man." He spread his hands. "But like this? Like this, Russ? Hiding yourselves, making your fucking something special and apart from all the other fucking that's going on in my house? Russ, I wish I didn't have to know it."

"Paul . . ." you said. Your voice was very small, very fragile.

"You have done it, Leslie. You have done it, Russ. But—you won't do it again." His toadlike hand shaping itself strongly against my shoulder, he pushed me toward the bed. "You'll have to do it now with me watching. It's the only way to take the taste of what you've already done out of my mind."

The shove sprawled me onto the bed. Flinching away as though it would sear my flesh to touch you, I again got to my feet and faced Paul.

"I won't do it, Paul," I said.

He did not sneer. He simply looked at me as though he could not believe that I existed.

"You won't?" he said. "You can't, Russ, that's what you mean. As long as I'm standing here, that lovely woman couldn't raise your cock no matter how hard she tried. True, Russ? True." He stopped talking. Still it was not anger, not contempt, but something so far beyond it was totally complete, totally real, as mere anger, real contempt, could not have been.

"You can do it secretly, though. You can tempt my wife from her social duties, persuade her to hide herself from me and from my guests just so she'll get fucked by you." His voice took on a patently false plaintiveness. "Because you've got the need to rob this old man, Russ. That's the only way it can be for you. Take this old man's young wife, seduce her in secret, so the old man will never know."

"Paul," you said again. So small. So fragile.

His eyes turning, he regarded you for a still moment. "Stretch your legs," he said. "Open it up."

You stretched your legs, opening your privacy to the sight of our eyes. No pink flesh showed; it was cold, cold. But, obediently, it was revealed.

"Russ, maybe you can't do it," Paul said. "But you can watch me. You *will* watch me."

"Paul," you said, small fragile. You were gazing directly upward at the overhead canopy. You still held yourself open. "Please. No."

"No?" Paul Ruach said. "You can't say no to me, my dear Leslie. Nobody says no to Paul Ruach."

His penis, limp between his legs until now, jerked its head so violently that the bag of balls swayed like a pendulum. I could not stop my eyes from watching the erection coming into his flesh as though by an act of sheer will. Turning your head, you looked despairingly at his increasingly rampant manhood.

"Please." But this time you did not say no.

He didn't answer you, but spoke to me. "You watched your wife getting laid, Russ, just a little while ago. Now you can watch Leslie getting hers. I will show you how she is with a man who knows her like I know her." His eyes were watchful on my face. "There might even be a surprise or two in store for you."

"Mr. Ruach," I said, "I'm leaving. Now."

Putting his hand on his organ, he squeezed so hard the moist, red head bulged beyond his fist. "No. You will stay, Russ. You will watch."

So enormous was his authority, I could not move. Your face ugly and old, you lay open, ready, obedient. Your eyes glued to his erection, your heels moved to dig into the mattress, arching your golden mount ready for his godlike descent into your flesh.

Heavily, awkward in the heaviness, he heaved himself onto the bed. On his knees between your legs, he gazed beyond anger and hate and contempt into your ugly face, in an invocation of raw power so brutal that I knew you would obey every whim and need, draining him with art and expertise, making him believe he was great in your flesh. Your whole life had been a lesson for these moments in which you were the pliant and loving wife of Paul Ruach.

I knew also that I would watch him perform the act of mastery; I would see you taken as I had seen Eva, I would know you in the throes of response to his rampant maleness. I wondered if, afterward, you would cherish his head in your arms. Somehow, I understood that he had never allowed that female moment of sad fulfillment.

As he tilted the rigid instrument over you, a drop of moisture fell from the eye. The flesh of your thigh quivered where it struck, and clung gleaming subtly like a miniscule gem. He was near, and nearer; the bull bag of balls was already resting its weight on your thighs. He was not guiding his tool with his hand; he expected you to reach for it, take it, with an accurate upthrust of your vagina.

I should have killed him as he braced his powerful weight over your fragile flesh. But, in telling me why I had needed to take you in privacy, he had robbed me of initiative; I could do nothing but watch as he took you forever away from me. That, I knew, was his intent—and he would succeed. Only by becoming new people, Paul Ruach people, would we be able ever again, after this, to endure each other's lusting flesh.

I did nothing, my great love. But you did. Placing one hand flat palmed against his hairy chest, with that mere touch you held him away.

"Paul. You can't do this," you told him.

Your voice was no longer tiny, as ready to shatter

as a fragile seashell. Nor was it angry and strong. It was, simply, your normal tone.

You were gazing into his eyes; he was gazing into yours. Suddenly I was no longer present. The duel was between Leslie Dollar and Paul Ruach. His manhood. Your womanhood. His will. Your will.

"Can't?" he said. "Now you're telling me can't, Leslie?"

"Yes, Paul." Your voice so normal, instructive, even friendly. "Because you won't like it, Paul. It won't be any good."

"Can't?" Paul Ruach said, his mind clinging to the operative word.

He saw it then, as I saw it; your body receding out of the obedient arch of passionate greeting, closing utterly against him. Against Paul Ruach.

He could have wedged his tool into your receptacle; you would not have resisted him physically. But ... once, I had tasted that profound frigidity. Paul Ruach had never experienced it. But he knew it, for he knew you. He might as well surge his orgasm into the flesh of a dead woman.

Even as he gazed into your eyes, holding you yet by the great authority of the man he had made of himself, his penis, flagging from its ultimate of erection, began to wrinkle in on itself.

He looked down at his fading manhood. Moving ponderously, he hauled himself off the bed. He was not looking at either of us.

"All right," he said. "You said can't, and you've made it stick. But I know what I can do."

Going to your dressing table, his thick hand took up a pair of manicure scissors, the small instrument flashing light as his thumb and finger fitted themselves into the finger holes too small for their size.

"I've thought about it more than once," he said. "Now I will do it."

Moving heavily, he went to the door, opening it and passing through, out of sight. I took a deep breath, sat down on the bed, and put my hand on your hip. "Leslie," I said. "I'm sorry."

Your head turned toward me, your hand found my hand. "I'm sorry too, Russell. But we couldn't have done it any other way, could we?" Suddenly your body went rigid, your face changing with a sudden in-flash of thought. In violent movement, you flung yourself out of the bed.

"Oh no," you cried. "Not that!"

Swooping for your garment crumpled on the rug, you were halfway to the door before I could move, screaming at me, "Get your clothes on. Hurry!" Then you were gone.

I didn't know what you knew. But it was no time for indecision. Snatching on my pants without underwear, I scrambled into my shirt and shoes and, leaving them unbuttoned and unlaced, ran after you.

You had caught up with Paul in the library. Holding his thick arm with both hands, you were saying, "No, Paul, please, no, anything but that. Please, Paul, please, I beg you!"

Paul, keeping a steady pressure against your frantic grip, was trying to open the door with the hand that still held the small scissors. But you would not yield, fighting him physically as your words battered against his determination like stones thrown against a fortress.

"Paul, please, please. Be kind, Paul, you can be so

kind when you want to be. Be kind now. For my sake, Paul. Please."

Ceasing to resist your importunity, Paul let his arms fall to his sides. "I tried," he said. "You wouldn't let me be kind. So I shall now do as I wish."

Going close against him, you cupped both hands under his balls, lifting the weight. "Come back to the bedroom, Paul," you said. "You can take me, and Russell will watch." You turned your eyes toward me for a brief second. "You will, won't you, Russell? Promise Paul that you will watch." You went back to him. "Then Russell will take me, while you watch."

He was standing stone cold still, and your voice tore on a frantic edge. "Bring one of your girls, Paul, and we'll go all night, we'll do it all, it'll be so wonderful." Holding the bag of balls still cupped in one hand, with the other you sought his penis. He did not attempt to deny your tantalization of desire. But there was no response.

"One of your nice girls," you said. Your tone dropped to a coaxing whisper. "Remember the time the albino girl and I made love to each other for you? I never did it again, I told you I didn't like it. But we'll do it all tonight, anything you like. Just name it, and it'll be done."

Falling silent, you waited for it to move in him. I still did not understand, but I waited also, knowing I would fulfill my share of your promises, simply because you needed so desperately for that to be the thing that Paul Ruach would let happen.

"Too late, Leslie," Paul said, his voice heavy, assured, absolutely fatal. "You told me *no*, Leslie. You told me *can't*."

One step broke your hold on him. He opened the

door. I waited for you to scream, to weep, to go after him. But, having failed to engage him, there was in you no greater effort.

You looked at me, your eyes tragic. "I tried, Russell. You'll always remember that I tried, won't you?"

I came to your side, but you did not know that I touched you. Moving into the doorway, we watched Paul Ruach approaching his mission with a determined, waddling stride. I stayed by your side as you followed slowly into the crowded room. But only when it began did I understand what you had grasped immediately.

Happy Mann came toward Paul almost as though she had been summoned. She was smiling at him, as she smiled at everyone, when he put one hand against her belly. She stopped. She saw the scissors in his hand but somehow she did not believe the scissors, so it was as though she understood her role in the drama, and accepted it.

Paul, inserting a thick finger under the white leather triangle, pulled it away from her body enough to get one blade of the scissors underneath. With slow, gripping motions he began cutting. The leather was tough, the scissors were small for the task. But his hand was strong, his will was persistent. Happy Mann made no resistance, simply watching with a puzzled expression on her face. The triangle of leather, ragged edged where he had cut through it, came free, and he flung it away. Gazing at Happy's blond pubic hair, his penis jerked into a sudden, full rise.

Happy knew now. Her mouth opened, a small, round O. But no sound came out until, dropping the scissors, he lifted her tiny, voluptuous body in both arms and began walking toward the wide couch. She began to scream, "Mama! Mama!" as he laid her down and, with both hands, opened her squirming thighs.

Mama came like a naked thunderbolt of outrage, beating at Paul's back with both fists. He was trying to fight her off, but she would not be defeated. The child was huddled on the couch now, turned against the sheltering backrest to conceal and defend the naked vulnerability of her crotch.

Paul, getting heavily to his feet, pushed Mama away. His dominant voice thudded, stopping her in her tracks. "You'll have your damned exploitation film, Mrs. Mann. Just let me take the girl's cherry."

Mrs. Mann halted suddenly. Hair down in her face, still hunched in battle posture, she glared uncomprehendingly at Paul Ruach. Paul stood before her, penis rampant, heavy balls hanging, seemingly unaware of the crowd gathering for what it sensed as the main event of the evening. Your hand gripped into mine, you pulled me with you as you squirmed through the massing audience until our progress was blocked by the couch. A hand caught at my other arm; it was Eva. Dressed again, she must have finished her Pecker Derby for the evening.

Mrs. Mann, bewildered, pushed her hair back out of her face. "What did you say, Mr. Ruach?"

Paul's voice, confident and assured, trod on the heels of her words. "You can have your picture, million-dollar publicity budget and all. I can make it happen for her just as well as the next fellow. I'll even put her under personal contract."

Mrs. Mann looked at Happy huddled on the couch, her naked body, her stricken face, turned into the sheltering backrest. She had dreamed it, planned it, talked about it. But she could not believe it. She came back to Paul.

"You mean it, Mr. Ruach? You really mean it?"

"Mrs. Mann. Don't do it," you said in a clear, penetrating voice.

Paul didn't turn. He was watching the woman. Mrs. Mann looked at Happy again. Her voice came slowly. "I've got witnesses, you know. Plenty of witnesses."

"Come down to the office tomorrow, Mrs. Mann. We'll talk about concept, start thinking about the scriptwriter, get the project rolling. Tomorrow."

Mama, going to Happy, knelt beside her. Hands on Happy's shoulders, she turned her. Happy gazed into her face for a pent second. Then she screamed, "Mama! Please, Mama! Don't let him!"

Mama, holding her shaking body, said intensely, "You heard Mr. Ruach, darling. The Big Picture. He'll make you America's Sex Goddess."

Happy, clawing into her lap, buried her face against her mother's naked breast. Her body curled in on itself in utter revulsion, she was shaking, crying, pleading, for Paul was coming near now, his toadlike hands reaching.

I saw the scene in one complete seeing: the watching eyes, the encircled faces, the sexual tension crackling like electricity. Their breathing was one collective sigh as their jaded senses devoured the tiny girl named Happy Mann as she lay with Mama embracing her upper body, her naked hips writhing to escape the onslaught. Her mouth open, babbling words without meaning, she was fighting the assault with every outraged atom of her innocent being.

Then Happy Mann broke my heart—she quit fighting. Her small, perfect body going slack, she gazed with wide eyes at Paul Ruach, not seeing his face at all but only the instrument of her destruction, understanding at last that it was her fate to be violated by that one particular man. Because Mama had consented, and so she must also consent.

I could not stop Paul Ruach. You could not stop Paul Ruach. And nobody else wanted to; the avid crowd only yearned to watch him in the exercise of his power. Happy, turning her eyes away, looked for the last time into her mother's face; her mouth framed one last soundless scream of protest. Then she lay quiescent, in absolute surrender, as Paul's hands once again parted her legs. This time, they stayed that way.

Paul gloated over her blond mount. Utter silence ruled, and he was completely in command: of the girl, of the mother, of the watchers. He wanted her, now he would have her, and he would be revenged on Leslie Dollar. Slowly thrusting, he moved in on her; the bulging red head of his tool touched her mount. Involuntarily, her whole body shrank away. He drew back, waiting for acquiescence to return, sure of the conquest, determined to enjoy to the full each phase of the violation.

I would have watched it; I could not have moved. But you moved. You turned, not to me but to Eva, and said, "Take me out of here."

"Yes," Eva said.

The three of us went away, pushing abruptly through the crowd, letting it close between us and the scene. Our way was clear to the front door, for the living room was empty except for the crowded space around the couch. I opened the door, stepping back to let you and Eva pass through. At that instant, Happy screamed, the terrible sound ululating through

the great empty room. You looked at me, your face
white. Your eyes were so terrible I could not endure
them.

It was not, as I had hoped, simply the one great
scream of penetration. She kept on making a sound,
lower now, in a tone that raised the hackles on my
neck, a continuous, despairing whimper that rose and
fell with the beat of the great man's weapon inside
her fragile body. We could hear it all the way to the
car, until I got the motor started.

Not a word was spoken until we were safely inside
our apartment. You waited in the living room while
Eva brought one of her nightgowns, followed obediently as she led you to the guest bedroom. Because I
did not know what else to do, I went into our bedroom to take off my pants and shirt and shoes, realizing I had left the rest of my clothes. I put on pajamas
and sat down on the bed. Eva came in. She did not
look at me, but went to the closet, found another
nightgown, and threw it across a chair. I watched her
undress, put on the nightgown. She got into bed on
the other side and propped herself up on pillows.

We were silent for a long minute; we were both
remembering. Then Eva said, almost tentatively.
"What a terrible thing."

"I liked that little girl," I said. I shuddered. "I'll
never be able to forget it, Eva. Never."

Her eyes were gentle. "A sweet child."

"Lovely," I said. "Yes. And talented." I stirred.
"She'll go on, Eva. She'll make it, she's got that kind
of toughness. But, Eva, the most terrible thing is, it
won't mean anything to her. Because she lost Mama
tonight."

"How could Mama let it happen?" Eva said almost

in awe. "Actually holding that child in her arms while
Paul Ruach . . ."

"She told me, once," I said heavily, as though we
were speaking of someone who had died. "How,
when she first saw that little blond head on the pillow
beside her, she had a vision of the future. She left her
husband, her two sons, to bring Happy within range
of opportunity." I sighed. "They always, both of
them, spoke those words in large capitals . . . the Big
Break, Sex Goddess. So I guess anything to realize the
dream."

"But what a terrible, tacky dream," Eva said. "People. Good God, Russell, can you believe people?"

I tried to smile. "About half the time."

"Did you believe me tonight? With all those great
cocks?"

I looked into Eva's face. "I'd believe you, Eva,
whatever you did."

She brooded. "Paul Ruach used me, too . . . he
turned my lust for a huge pecker into a personal en-
tertainment."

"I know," I said. "I saw."

She was watching my face. "And you . . ." She
stirred. "You can go to her, Russell. You don't have
to stay with me."

"She won't want to see me," I said. "I caused it,
you know. Happy, I mean. We caused it, me and
Leslie."

"Don't tell me. I don't want to know," Eva said in a
rush of denial. She let a small silence gather between
us. Her voice came firmly when she spoke. "Go on.
She's waiting for you."

"Eva, I can't walk from your bed to her bed. I just
can't do that."

Her voice was brisk. "You don't have to worry about me." Twisting to one side, she took the telephone and began dialing a long number. It would have to be long distance, direct dial. In the still room I could hear the faint ringing, then the query of a voice.

"Carlos?" Eva said. "Oh, I'm glad I caught you, Carlos. It's Eva." Her voice rose impatiently. "Eva!" She listened. "Wait a minute. I'm flying in on American tomorrow. I don't know which flight yet, the earliest possible. Just meet them all until you see me." She paused, listened, her voice was warmly amused. "But I *know* now, Carlos, that it's only nine inches. Your honor will not be at stake." She listened to the rapid pour of words. I watched her face. She had tucked away the phone number long ago, she had never forgotten it, as she had never forgotten his major asset. "Yes," she said. "God yes, right there, the closest motel you can find." She laughed softly. "Have the key in your hand, Carlos. Show me the key right away."

She hung up the phone. She looked at me defiantly. "Go on," she said. "You can go to her now."

"Eva," I said. "I love you."

"Sure, I know. Now get the hell out of my bedroom."

Still I hesitated. She was already dialing again, speaking rapidly about flights to New York. She hung up, settled herself in the bed.

"Turn out the light as you leave. I've got an early flight to catch in the morning."

I could leave her then, knowing she had made it the thing to do. I found you in bed, sitting up, like Eva, with a pillow behind your back. The bedside lamp, shaded though it was, showed your face shattered, your eyes burning holes in your skull.

I sat on the edge of the bed. "We'll go away tomorrow," I said gently. "We'll never have to see this place again."

Your voice was lifeless. "You can't leave. The picture. Have you forgot about the picture?"

"I'll be off the picture as soon as Paul gets to the office in the morning."

You stirred against the pillows. "You don't know Paul Ruach. He'll hold you to the contract. He wants that picture, and he'll insist on it."

"The way he hates me now?"

"Paul will hate you only if you fail to deliver a good film."

"And you?" I said.

You shrugged slightly. "Don't you understand? Paul doesn't waste himself with hating. He simply wiped me out, that's all. He looked for the best way to wipe me out, and he found it."

"The poor little girl," I said.

"Yes. Poor little girl. Paul Ruach will fulfill every iota of her lifelong dream. And he'll never touch her again. Paul does have his own peculiar sense of honor, believe it or not."

"But Paul Ruach didn't do it," I said. "We did. You and I." I paused, watching your face, hoping it would shift back toward me. "So we must go away together, Leslie. We can't let love escape us, too, when it's all we've got left."

You looked at me, a long and measuring look. You had not looked at me in quite that inscrutable way before.

"You did a terrible thing to me, Russell. You

290

wouldn't let what I've worked so hard to become be enough for us."

"I had to have my innocent love again. It was still in you, as alive and real as the year you were sixteen. I knew it was there, so I reached for it. Is that such a terrible thing?"

"I didn't want it. I wanted you to be satisfied with the woman I am, shaped out of the life that I've had to live."

I put my hand on your thigh under the covers. "I want the girl. But I want the woman, too. I want it all, Leslie. We can have it, it's all there, just as it's always been." I was leaning toward you. "Don't you realize the truth about us yet? Everybody else does— poor old Bill knew it all that long time ago. Eva knows it, and Frank, back there in Piercetown. Paul knows it too, certainly. They only had to see us together to know what we've used up most of our lives finding out."

Your face changed under the impact of the words, you came back toward me a tiny distance from your tragic remoteness. But not enough yet. Not enough.

"I can't think about it, Russell. I can't *feel* about it, I'm numb clear through. All I can do is remember Paul violating that terrified little girl just to revenge himself on me—and on you." You shuddered. "You'll have to let me go away by myself, Russell, give me a chance to get those terrible pictures out of my mind." You pulled yourself up. "You can't go now, anyway. There's the film to be made. If it's successful, another film after that, and another, and by that time you won't want to leave. It's your work, Russell. You can't abandon your work."

"It doesn't count. Not the way that you count."

"Russell," you said. "No. Don't put that burden on me, too."

I waited a minute. Your hand rested lightly against my chest, holding me away. As you had held off Paul Ruach when you had decided to sacrifice your earned position.

"Will you promise me, then?"

"I can't make any promises. Least of all to myself, because I don't *know*. I can't believe, in this minute, that I ever will know."

"But if you . . . when you do. Will you come to me?"

"Yes," you said. "But don't count on it, Russell, don't keep waiting for me. Go on with your life, go on with your work. Go on with yourself."

I understood, precisely as you understood, with a weariness in my bones, a sadness in my heart, that when one has done the best one can, there remains only a stopping. All over again, for the third time, we had arrived again at the place for stopping.

I stood up. "Good night, Leslie. My love."

"Good night, Russell. Good-bye."

I took two steps away from the bed. You said, "Kiss me, Russell? Just one kiss, for old times' sake?"

I returned to you, I put my mouth on your cold mouth. Your lips did not come warm. I had not expected it, for the ice ran clear through your body and your heart into your soul. I made the room into darkness from the doorway as I left.

. . . That is it, my dear, deep love, my girl with the golden cunt; the ultimate ending out of all our endings. But you were right about Paul Ruach. He insisted that I fulfill the contract between us; but, holding precisely to his word, I did not see him until the answer print was ready for viewing. I suppose Paul always lived up to his bargains as he saw them, a stern virtue self-imposed in a culture of shortcuts and expedient betrayals. I didn't get to be the first director of Happy Mann, either, for she was suddenly busy with Paul Ruach's successful campaign to fulfill her dream, and Mama's dream, of becoming the next Sex Goddess of the Silver Screen. So maybe, right there, I have missed my only chance at immortality.

After we had viewed the answer print together, Paul granted me the right of final cut, and the next day I was summoned to his office, where he offered me a five-picture deal, three of which I could choose myself. I believe he was surprised when I turned it down, and kept on turning down the escalations until he admitted to himself that I would not work for him any more.

When I rose to leave, he said, "Russ. Do you see Leslie at all?"

"No," I said.

"When you do," he said. "Give her my love, will you?" He shook his head. "Russ, she is one hell of a woman. Isn't she one hell of a woman?"

"Yes," I said, and went away from him.

Perhaps that's why I wrote the first letter, my love, simply because Paul Ruach said "when" and not "if." After all, he knew you in ways that I did not.

Maybe I have waited too long. But, wanting you most of all to come to me of your own decision, all that first year I went here and I went there, I did this and I did that; while all the time an alertness in me looked for you behind every opening of a door, every ringing of the phone. Eventually the tiny candle of hope in my soul flickered and began to die. But still the idea of a letter did not arrive. Perhaps it could not until I had anchored myself into a time and a place and started looking for myself instead of for you—or, failing you, someone to take Eva's place.

Even when I came here, starting all over again for the third time, I told myself it was a stopgap sort of thing. It was writing this time, a whole new thing, because I could no longer trust myself to work with people; I saw too clearly their transparent responses to my necessary but equally transparent manipulation of their talents and their personalities. That decision of understanding left me only this solitary vice of writing, a private manipulation; but so quickly it has become absolutely necessary to the Russell Walford I am now.

One day, quite without planning it, I began the first letter ... exactly why, I don't know, for I told myself in front that I would not beg you, in that letter, to come to me. I simply wanted to put it down, write it out, look at it with the cold eye of a working writer, as though you and I were fictional characters created for a book. But we are too incredible to be fictional. . . .

For here I am, at the end, asking you to come. I am asking, am I not? But I shall ask only in this manner:

From where I am, from what I am now, we can have it. We can share an island in innocence and in joy, Leslie. We can share a love. We are ripe now, individually and together; but we are also seventeen and sixteen, we are just meeting, we are beginning all over again.

That is the view from where I am. From what I am. I do not know where you are, or what you have become beyond our last time together. But if these truths are your truth, as they are mine—but only then—then come, my love, and let us love. Let us end together, as we began, with love on an island.

I will wait, now, for my girl with the golden cunt.

CABLEGRAM

ARRIVING BARCELONA MORNING FLIGHT TOMORROW STOP PAINTING CRATED TO FOLLOW STOP HAVE DREAMED ALL MY LIFE OF LIVING ON ISLAND LIKE IBIZA LOVE

LESLIE

ME

Anonymous

The millions of readers who have eagerly anticipated this new book in the world famous series of raw, candid love stories will not be disappointed. Here is all the honesty of *Her*, the power of *Him* and the natural sensuality of *Them*.

Me – where every expectation of lust and love, of dream and desire, will be met, experienced – and surpassed.